Temple Mount

Other novels by Keith Raffel

Dot Dead: A Silicon Valley Mystery

Smasher: A Silicon Valley Thriller

Drop By Drop: A Thriller

A Fine and Dangerous Season: A Novel

Temple Mount

A Novel

Keith Raffel

This is a work of fiction. Names, characters, organizations, places, events, and incidents are either products of the author's imagination or are used fictitiously.

ISBN: 978-0-9885098-8-7

Cover design by John Donaghue

Print layout by eBooks By Barb for booknook.biz

To the 193

"To three possessions thou shouldst look –
a field, a friend, a book."

Hai Gaon (939-1038)

"Know Where You Came From and Know Where You Are Going To."

Akavya ben Mahalalel

Prologue

Jerusalem, 1983

The man wearing army fatigues was bent over at the waist. A paperback Bible poked out of one back pocket and a pistol from the other. Leaning into the circular hole in the cavern wall, he was working two levers back and forth as if controlling a bulldozer's scoop.

He stood up and said in Yiddish, "Now you please come. Please look."

A full-bearded giant of a man in his sixties, wearing a long black coat so caked with dirt it looked like a cowboy's canvas duster, strode across the granite floor. The opening might have been wide enough for some men to crawl into, but not for this one who stood six foot six and weighed in at two-fifty-five. His gut clenched as he stuck his head and shoulders into the narrow passage.

"Do you see it, Rebbe?" called the man in fatigues.

The large man wondered if he was committing sacrilege by using a mirror to look for the sacred object. Only the High Priest was permitted to gaze upon it and then only on *Yom Hakippurim*, the Day of Atonement. Anyone else would be struck dead by the hand of God. Perseus avoided being turned to stone by looking at Medusa's reflection and not her face. What worked in Greek myth would work here, God willing.

"Not yet, Shlomo," he said and returned to jiggling the two levers. He gripped the handles hard when he saw it—something box-shaped, almost entirely covered in pelts. The light was too dim to determine what animal they'd come from, but bright enough for the one exposed corner of the chest to shine a dull gold.

The rebbe pulled back from the hole and stood up in the shadowy, domed chamber carved out of rock. He swayed, thanking God in Hebrew, the holy tongue, for letting him reach this day.

Then he stopped mid-prayer. He heard voices emanating from the passage on the other side of the cavern, the one they'd used to enter it. Voices getting louder. Voices speaking in Arabic.

Chapter 1

Present Day

I hadn't made love to my wife in a year and hadn't had a meaningful conversation with her in two. Veronica and I lived in the same house, slept in the same bed, and loved our daughter with the same intensity. Years of trying for more kids had brought only frustration and doctors' bills. And now Katie had gone off to college at Harvard and left an empty bedroom and empty lives behind her.

At dinner parties and charity events, friends told us they envied our marriage. Veronica and I weren't purposely deceiving them. Like veteran actors in a long-running Broadway production, we played our assigned roles with little conscious effort.

As my fiftieth birthday loomed, I realized the air had leaked out of the balloon of my dreams. Our daughter aside, I was deflated by disappointments and regrets. Oh, by Silicon Valley standards I'd done fine. Enticed by an offer price of six times revenue and a promise that we'd form the core of a new strategic business unit, we'd sold the company I founded to Sibyl Software. When the inevitable economic downturn had come, the Sibyl CEO tossed away the business like a snotty tissue. Since then, I'd watched a start-up company copy our technology and go public last year at a valuation of ten times sales.

Veronica and I lived in a mortgage-free house perched on

top of a hill in the town of Woodside. Thanks to my morning runs and gym workouts, I'd struggled back to within spitting distance of what I'd done in college for a 10K run and a bench press. I spent afternoons ensconced in my home office on a purple paisley armchair, hideous but comfortable, staring out the window at the shimmering waters of San Francisco Bay. Seven months ago, my father, who raised me on his own, had died after silent armies of cancer cells infiltrated his colon, then his spine, and finally his brain. Now I sipped tea and read both classics and bestsellers, while trying to figure out how to play the cards life had dealt me.

Of course, I'd thought about leaving my wife, but leaving her implied I would be going somewhere else. I had nowhere to go.

Chapter 2

It was Monday, mid-afternoon, and I was reading the *Economist*. Or really not reading it, but staring at some random page in the science and technology section while my mind floated like a bottle in the ocean.

"Alex?"

"Huh?" I knocked over the mug of green tea that had been resting on the arm of the chair.

"Ooh. Sorry. I didn't mean to frighten you."

Veronica remained at the door. Some women of forty-four would have shied away from wearing a sleeveless red dress that stopped five inches above the knee. No need for my wife to show such caution. Thrice-weekly appointments with her personal trainer had left her limbs sleek and toned. From twenty-five feet away she still looked twenty-five years old. When I'd married her, my friends had tripped over their tongues with envy. Even now, I wasn't sure they'd ever stopped. How did a nerd like me end up with a beauty like Veronica?

I looked down at the wet spot spreading across the red mahogany planking of the floor and then back up at Veronica in the doorway. "What are you doing home so early?" I asked.

She worked for a private foundation in San Francisco, deciding which causes were most worthy of a flighty real estate magnate's billions. One year the target might be eradicating malaria, the next illiteracy in the Third World. Nothing bite-sized for them.

"I need to talk to you," she said.

"And it can't wait till tonight?"

"No."

"Okay, come in." I got up from the armchair. She could sit there, and I'd move over to the desk.

"No, I'd rather stand. This is your room. I'm never comfortable in here."

We faced off at three paces. "Okay."

"This isn't working."

"By this you mean us?" I asked.

She nodded and then looked down. I waited for her to go on. After twenty seconds she still hadn't. "So we should split up?" I asked.

She raised her head and looked at me. Then she nodded again.

"Okay, so we can split up," I said.

She lowered her gaze.

"That's not enough?" I asked.

She took a deep breath.

Veronica still wasn't looking at me when I said, "Oh, you want a divorce."

She nodded for the third time.

"You must have met someone?"

This time she spoke. "Don't get mad."

"I'm not mad."

"I met him..."

"You don't have to tell me."

She tilted her chin up. "He's not as smart as you. Not as successful. Doesn't look like much either. But he does pay attention to me. He cares that I'm alive."

I stared at the bookshelf over her head. After a few seconds,

I lowered my gaze and shrugged. "You don't have to make excuses. Go. Be happy."

"After twenty-one years, that's it? It's that simple?"

"No. Thanks to California's divorce laws, it won't be simple. But I'm not going to stand in your way."

"What are you going to do?" she asked.

"I don't know."

"Start another company?"

"I don't know."

"Just sit here the rest of your life?"

"Maybe. I don't know."

"We'll have to tell Katie," she said.

"Yes."

"We should do it together," she said.

"Yes."

She took the three steps to where I stood, encircled me with her long arms, and rested her head against my chest. I could feel tears soaking through my shirt front. I patted her hair a few times, then stopped.

Only after she left and I was on my hands and knees cleaning up spilt tea did I wonder whether she'd wanted me to protest, to tell her to stay with me, even to fight for her. I hoped not. I didn't have it in me.

Chapter 3

The phone rang. There I sat in the paisley chair with the same *Economist* open on my lap. I checked my watch. At least two hours had passed since Veronica left, and I couldn't say what I'd read.

I went over to the desk and picked up the receiver.

"Hello."

"Aron Kalman?"

"This is Alex Kalman. You must have the wrong number."

"Are you the grandson of Rabbi Yitzhak Kalman?"

"Who? No."

"This is Rabbi Natan Zweiback."

"Should I know you?"

"No. Who is your father's father?"

I couldn't think of how knowledge of my grandfather's name would enable identity theft. "Isaac Kalman."

"And what happened to him?"

"I don't mean to be rude, Rabbi, but why should I answer these questions? How do I know you are even a rabbi?"

"You are Jewish."

"Well, yes." Technically. My father had not been observant. I hadn't been in a synagogue since I danced the hora and limboed lower at the bar mitzvahs of my friends over thirty years ago.

"Your grandfather is alive."

"No. He died before I was born."

"He did not. Your father was estranged from your grandfather. He left his house after you were born."

"And you are telling me this alleged grandfather is a rabbi?"

"Yes. Our rebbe, in fact."

"Rebbe?"

"A rabbi, but more. Our teacher, our leader."

"And why do you think your rebbe is my grandfather?"

"He is dying. He is asking for you."

"I have obligations here, Rabbi."

"Of course."

"I do not know if I can come on such short notice."

"I understand."

He provided me with an address in Brookline, Massachusetts "just in case."

After hanging up, I leaned back into the paisley chair. No job and soon no wife. I picked up the *Economist* again.

An hour later, I was wishing this Rabbi Zweiback had argued more forcefully in favor of my coming. That would have made it easier to resist. Besides, the trip would give me an excuse to visit Katie.

I booked a red-eye online, packed an overnight bag, scribbled a note to Veronica, emailed Katie, and left for the airport just ninety minutes before the flight was scheduled to take off.

* * *

In my own college days, I used to wait behind a long queue of cars, buses, and limos to take the dark, narrow Sumner Tunnel under the harbor into town. Now my cab, piloted by a turbaned Sikh, could sweep through the well-lit and wide Ted Williams Tunnel and emerge on the Mass Turnpike. Even though it was morning rush hour, we pulled up at 63 Windsor Avenue in the leafy enclave of Brookline only forty-five minutes after my plane touched down. Some hundred feet from the curb, a formidable house of brick and wood squatted behind a screen of trees and shrubs. The pair of dormered windows on the top floor watched me like eyes under hooded brows as I climbed six flagstone steps and walked up a path to the front door.

Before I'd taken my finger off the bell, the front door swung open.

"Mr. Kalman?" I could only see the shadowy outline of a man through the screen door.

"Yes."

The screen opened, and from the dusk a hand was thrust toward me. Squinting, I could see a man of medium stature wearing a yarmulke and a black suit with a white open-necked shirt. Below the jacket I saw the fringes of that undergarment Orthodox men wear. The face that peered back at me was covered by a bushy brown beard.

"Natan Zweiback." Shave off those whiskers and he'd look more a college freshman than a Jewish cleric. This was a whole different species of rabbi from the ones I'd met at the Silicon Valley bar mitzvahs all those years ago.

The handshake was firm. "What a pleasure to meet the grandson of our rebbe. Come in."

If this was some kind of sham, it was an elaborate one: they weren't figuring me for an easy mark.

He led me to a kitchen infused with moisture, warmth, and yeast—as if a Danish bakery had been transported to the tropics. There, a woman of sixty-something tended an elaborate cast iron stove. She had what looked like a do-rag on her head.

"This is Mrs. Seligson," the rabbi said. "She is your grandfather's housekeeper."

I extended my hand.

Without extending hers, she said, "Nice to meet you."

Nonplussed, I dropped my hand.

The rabbi helped her out. "Women here don't touch men other than their husbands."

"I see. Fine. Nice to meet you as well." I'll bet Orthodox women cut way down on colds and flu that way.

"Would you like some tea?" Mrs. Seligson asked.

"Yes, thank you very much."

The rabbi and I sat down on old-fashioned high-back chairs at a substantial table that could have fit a dozen more of us.

"You were able to excuse yourself from your commitments?" the rabbi asked.

"Yes." I looked at him. "You expected me to come?"

"It's *beshert*," he said. "You were meant to come."

"Who meant me to come?"

"The hand of *ha-Shem* brought you here."

"*Ha-Shem*?"

"Yes, the Name. It is what we call the Eternal One."

"You mean God?"

He shook his head as if at a child. "Out of respect, I do not say any of the names of the deity aloud."

"Okay, fine. Now tell me about the man reputed to be my grandfather."

"I will take you into him in a moment. One look at your face is all I needed to know who you are."

I rubbed my knuckles against my chin. Needed a shave. "Okay."

Mrs. Seligson put a steaming mug in front of me. I sipped. The syrupy concoction tasted like equal parts tea, milk, and sugar—a far stretch from the Japanese sencha I favored back in Woodside.

The baby-faced rabbi gave me an indulgent smile.

"The father of Rebbe Kalman was the fourth Bialystoker Rebbe. In 1938 your great-grandfather sent your grandfather to the United States along with nine congregants."

"And his father died in the Holocaust?"

"Praised be *ha-Shem*, no. He died of natural causes the day after Passover ended in 1939. Your grandfather then became the Bialystoker Rebbe."

"You make it sound like a royal dynasty."

"It does not sound American, I know, but it's been a kind of dynasty."

"And my father?"

"He was raised to be his father's heir. I have heard that, even as a teenager, he was a Talmudist able to hold his own with the heads of yeshivas in New York and even Jerusalem."

"What happened?"

"Your grandfather thought your father should go to a great American university. We Jews are minnows in a sea. Your grandfather thought your father should understand the ocean as well as the fish."

"So he went to Harvard and then went his own way?"

"It might be best if your grandfather explained."

Chapter 4

When we entered the living room, I saw a hospital bed surrounded by half a dozen men dressed in the same uniform as Rabbi Zweiback—dark suit, white shirt, and fringed undergarments. They were chanting in melodic undertones. Must be Hebrew.

From the hospital bed floated up a blue-veined hand that twisted twice in a slow-motion wave. The members of the prayer circle stepped back and filed past me. On their way out of the room, each shook my hand and nodded gravely. The last man called me "Reb Kalman."

The bed itself must have been oversized. The emaciated figure in it stretched at least a few inches over six feet from crown to sole. My right hand felt like a little boy's in the enfolding grasp of the man in the bed. The black yarmulke on his head contrasted with the translucent parchment of the skin stretching over his skull. He looked so much like my own father in the months before he died that any doubts of who this man was, of his relation to me, evaporated.

"I am Alex," I said.

He look right at me through dark, almost black, eyes and whispered, "Aron."

A few years before, Veronica and I had sent cotton swabs to a mail order lab for DNA testing. It made for amusing cocktail talk for Veronica to tell friends the biblical Aaron, brother of Moses and the first high priest, was her husband's ancestor. Was I his namesake, too?

"Grandfather?"

"Yes," he squeezed my hand.

"What happened?"

He squeezed again. "Your mother was killed in the car crash."

"Yes, and then?"

"Chaim said there were only two possibilities. Either the God that ruled the universe was a sadistic tyrant or there was no God at all and life was no more than a series of random events. It didn't matter to him which. He left this house with you. He never came back."

I was surprised my grandfather didn't use the euphemism "*ha-Shem*" as Rabbi Zweiback had.

"Chaim was my father?" My grandfather nodded. Dad was known back home as Charles. "And my real name is Aron?"

"That was the name you were given at your *bris*."

A *bris*? A ritual circumcision? For once I didn't mind a memory lapse. "Why do you want to see me now?"

He raised his free hand. "I am ninety-four and about to die. It is time."

"You're not afraid?"

"Of course I am afraid, but that does not matter." He beckoned me closer with the index finger of his free hand. My ear was three inches from his bluish lips. "I have broken a vow to your father."

"A vow?"

"When he left, I promised I would never seek him out. Nor you."

"Why?"

"To provide him comfort. To help him forget."

"You kept your vow to him. He's dead. So it's my decision now whether to see you. Here I am."

"*Hineini*," he said.

"What?"

"It is what Abraham said, what Moses said, when God called them. 'Here I am.' It is a generous thing to say, to say I kept my vow. Do you know what a mitzvah is?"

"Like a bar mitzvah?"

"Yes. It's a good deed we Jews are commanded to perform. Are you ready to undertake a mitzvah?"

"Yes," I said. What else could I say to him? He was dying. Besides, saying you are ready is different than saying you will.

"Over thirty years ago I was with Rabbi Shlomo Goren in Jerusalem."

"Okay."

"He showed me a tunnel under the Temple Mount."

Like anyone who followed international politics, I knew the Temple Mount. Jews believed their first and second temples had been built on it. Atop it now were Muslim holy places. Deciding who controlled the Temple Mount was a huge obstacle to any Middle Eastern peace agreement.

"Yes."

"He took me to a tunnel below the Mount. I saw there the Holy Ark. The Ark of the Covenant."

As far as I knew, the Ark was in the government warehouse where it had been cached at the end of the first Indiana Jones movie.

"What did the Ark look like?" I asked. Was I just humoring a dying old man?

"I didn't look directly at it. I saw its reflection in a mirror at the end of a pole."

"Its reflection?"

"We feared what might happen if we looked directly at it."

"So what did you see in the mirror?"

"A box covered with animal skins. I saw a corner that was gold."

"It turned out not to be the Ark?" I asked.

"It was the Ark."

"Did you bring it up?"

"We saw it, but did not reach it. The Arabs found out we were digging."

"But they did not find out about the Ark?"

"No, we were able to hide the tunnel, but there was still rioting. The Israeli government wanted no trouble. The government closed up the passage we'd used to go under the Mount. Sealed it."

"For fear of more rioting?"

"The Foreign Ministry told us its discovery would end chances for peace."

"So the government asked you to keep what you'd seen secret, and you did?"

"To my regret. No peace came. We should have listened to the ancient sages who told us discovery of the Ark would bring the Day of Redemption closer."

The man on the hospital bed closed his eyes. He took two shallow breaths and then lifted his lids to look at me. I took a step back.

"Rabbi Goren," he said, "was always afraid if the Arabs discovered the Ark first, they would destroy it." He paused and then resumed in a voice, deeper and more vigorous than a moment before. ""Life is a search for *emet*," he said. "I gave up too soon. Now *you* must find it. Will you look?"

This made no sense at all. This man, my grandfather, was scarcely still in this world. Why should he care? And why me? I was no Indiana Jones.

Before I could answer, he closed his eyes. His hold of my hands loosened, and he started breathing evenly.

I looked at my grandfather, then back at Rabbi Zweiback. "Is *emet* Hebrew for meaning?"

"No, for truth," the rabbi told me.

Truth? Maybe the same thing.

"Shall I wait for him to awaken? I have questions."

"While he sleeps, I will show you your parents' old room," the rabbi said. "My colleagues will watch him."

We left behind the men in black coats who continued a low-volume chant. I followed the rabbi up two flights of a dark oak staircase. He then opened the door to a huge room with slanted ceilings. It must have been the two windows on the far wall that I'd imagined were eyes watching me as I walked up to the house. Squeezed between the windows, twin beds stretched toward us from the opposite wall. He gestured to a bureau covered with picture frames.

I picked up the closest one. In a color photo a man stood wrapped in a white garment, almost like a doctor's coat. Even though he wore a heavy beard and was young, oh, so young, I recognized my father. Next to him, resplendent and beautiful in an ivory wedding dress, stood my mother.

"You've never seen this photo?" the rabbi asked.

"No."

"The room is as your father left it."

I picked up another photo in a gleaming sterling frame. Dad stood in what must have been the uniform of the day—a dark suit, white shirt, and homburg—next to my mother, who wore a high-necked dress and a kerchief. Their arms cradled a chubby little infant. Me. Taken just before my mother died.

"Perhaps you would like some time alone here?" Rabbi Zweiback asked.

"Yes, thank you."

I had more questions for my grandfather, lots more. Why would he send a Silicon Valley guy like me on a mission that called for archeological expertise? Why choose me, whose understanding of the universe contained no room for a deity or an afterlife, for a religious quest?

I stood staring at the photo of my parents as questions without answers caromed off the sides of my skull.

* * *

Rabbi Zweiback returned. "You should come downstairs."

Downstairs my grandfather lay, no longer peacefully sleeping. Now each breath was a gasping rattle.

"We should call a doctor, Rabbi," I said.

"He sent them away this morning before you arrived. He said there was no need. He was ready."

"Okay."

"You should take his hands."

And I took them, huge, veined, and limp, into my own.

Rabbi Zweiback and the others formed a circle around my grandfather and me. They chanted prayers while bowing back and forth and watching the figure on the bed fight for oxygen. He would never answer any more of my questions. I was still holding the hands of the Bialystoker Rebbe when he stopped breathing twenty minutes later.

"You're the grandson," Rabbi Zweiback said. "You must say *Baruch ata adonai eloheinu melech ha-olam dayan ha-emet.*"

I repeated the words.

"*Emet* is truth, but what does the whole thing mean?" I asked the rabbi.

"Blessed are you, *ha-Shem*, King of the World, Judge of Truth."

Chapter 5

"So your great-grandfather had six daughters but only one son, and that was your grandfather?"

I was seated in what passed for an armchair in my daughter's bedroom in Kirkland House at Harvard, seven miles from Brookline. I felt like I was riding on the back of a balding sheep—each motion I made on the lumpy cushion loosened another tuft of protruding white wool. Across from me, Katie sat cross-legged on a utilitarian black metal-tube twin bed.

"Right."

She would not be deterred. "And he had only one son, and that was Grandpa, right?"

"Yes."

"So you're the heir in the male line. Does that make you the Bialystoker Rebbe?" She was pulling my chain.

"That would be something, wouldn't it? I know about two words of Hebrew, *shalom* and, thanks to my grandfather, *emet*, which means..."

Katie interrupted, "Truth."

"I'm impressed."

"In my sophomore tutorial, I did some reading on the legend of the Golem."

"Sort of a predecessor of Frankenstein?"

"Right. Made of earth and called to life by Rabbi Loew in

the seventeenth century to protect the Jews of Prague. He wrote *emet* on its forehead. When it was time for the Golem to disappear, the rabbi erased the first letter, which made it read *met* or death."

"You know more than I do about all this." I shrugged. "The only time I ever read the Bible was in a freshman English course and that was the King James Version."

"Which brings us back to royal dynasties."

"The Bialystoker Rebbe—it's not inherited like the British throne. You need to show you can do the job. Bloodlines alone don't do it." I'd done some Googling on the taxi ride to Harvard.

She sighed. "Too bad. Well, I guess I've survived this long without being a princess."

I gave her a skeptical glance.

"Stop it," she said and then went on." She smiled. "But the new rebbe and his family won't get crown jewels or live in Buckingham Palace."

"Well, there *is* a pretty nice house, but it's in Brookline, not London," I said.

"So who's going to inherit it?"

"I think the Rabbi Zweiback I mentioned."

"You said he wasn't much older than I am," Katie said. "Isn't that young? Why him?"

"I gather he's a brilliant student of Talmud. And he does kinda have a claim by blood. He's married to a cousin of ours, a great-great-granddaughter of the rebbe that came over here from Bialystok."

"So you're just going to pick up and go to Israel?"

Her conversation skipped around like a hummingbird with ADD. I was used to it.

"Maybe," I said.

"Why?"

"Why not?"

"I know the 'why not' answer," Katie said. "It originated here. You can do better."

According to Harvard legend, one final exam given by nineteenth century philosophy professor William James had a single question—"Why?" The student who answered, "Why not?" received the only A in the class.

I turned my hands palms up. "My grandfather held on to life until I showed up, and he could ask me to go to Israel."

"Seriously? You might go to Israel to find the Ark of the Covenant? Better watch out for snakes and pack a bullwhip, too."

"I didn't actually promise."

"What do you know about ancient times in the Holy Land?"

"I read *The Source* by, uh..."

"James Michener. That's like saying you're an expert on the Civil War because you read *Gone with the Wind*."

"I thought I might go down to D.C. and see Mitch Samuelson, too."

Mitch was my old college roommate—we'd lived only two entries over from where Katie and I were sitting—who was now a muckety-muck in the State Department.

"You're turning this into a federal case?"

"Nah. I just want some background on the situation in Jerusalem. The rebbe—your great-grandfather—said the Israelis pretty much freaked out when he and the other rabbi said they'd seen the Ark."

"If you weren't listening to the delusions of a dying man."

"If I wasn't listening to the delusions of a dying man," I agreed. He'd seemed pretty sane to me, though.

"If you do end up going, maybe I can help a little, too. You remember I took that class on the ancient Near East last year."

"Yeah."

"Well, I did okay. The professor should remember me. She

was visiting from Hebrew University. I could email her. She should know what's going on in Jerusalem, archeologically speaking."

"That would be great, sweetie." I cupped my hands and blew on my palms as if to warm them. But the room was not cold. "I'll let you know if I go."

"What about Mom? Are you going to take her to Jerusalem?"

"She'll be fine."

She narrowed her eyes and said nothing for close to a minute. She had her mother's bouncy honey-blonde hair, perfect teeth, and high cheekbones. What she got from me were blue eyes—which was fine—and a thin nose a little too long for her face—which was fine with me, too. It made her profile striking, Nefertiti-ish even, but not movie-star beautiful. It was tough enough being a woman in the twenty-first century without that burden.

"You two are breaking up, aren't you?" she asked.

I never could keep anything from her. I nodded.

I don't know what I expected, tears maybe, but Katie stood, threw her arms around my neck, and sat on my lap for the first time in a decade. She started patting my back as if she were the parent.

"Mom will be fine," she said. "It's you I worry about."

"I'll be fine, too."

"No, you haven't been you for two years, since you sold the company."

The play-acting by Veronica and me might fool others, but not her.

"Maybe you should go to Israel, take your mind off things."

"Even if it's a fool's errand?"

"Especially if it is."

She kept patting my back until the door flew open.

"Here I am." Into the room stepped a modern-day Golem—

or at least a headless horseman. Whoever or whatever it was had his belt unbuckled and was holding up an unzipped pair of jeans with his right hand. If he did in fact have a head, it was covered by a purple T-shirt that was defying the efforts of his left hand to pull it off.

Katie spoke up. "Um, Elliott."

He yanked the T-shirt off.

The now-shirtless young man froze with his right foot three inches above the ground as he saw Katie on my lap.

With faultless manners and commendable sangfroid, Katie said, "Dad, this is Elliott Dubbin."

The just-introduced Mr. Dubbin started to reach for my right hand but retreated when he realized that good manners would mean a pair of trousers around the ankles.

His hands were fumbling with his belt and then his fly. He took a couple of steps back while trying to reverse the steps that had brought the T-shirt over his head, but he had knotted it up pretty good.

"Wait, Elliott." Katie stood up and reached over to the contorted fellow. With a Broadway dresser's economy of motion, she had his shirt back in place in seconds. He continued to work on getting his jeans buttoned. Katie showed commendable discretion in not helping with that task.

I followed my daughter into a standing position. "Nice to meet you, Elliott. Take your time."

I never questioned Katie about her social life. She'd tell me what she wanted to, when she wanted to. My own father used to say if you don't want to know the answer, don't ask the question. Now, without asking any questions, I knew the answer. It didn't really seem fair that my twenty-year-old daughter was having regular sex while I was not. Come to think of it, her mother must be, too.

"I'm glad to meet you, sir." Young Mr. Dubbin had a firm handshake. "I beg your pardon."

I shook his hand. No sense giving the poor chump a bad time. Not yet anyway.

Chapter 6

Elliott turned out to be a pretty good guy—if I could overlook his lust for my only child.

After checking into a comfortably old-fashioned room at the Faculty Club—alumni could join—I returned to Kirkland House to rescue my daughter and her beau from the monotony of a college dining hall meal. We cabbed it from the Square to Oleanna's, a trendy restaurant that Katie, an inveterate foodie, was anxious to try. Over turbot cooked in a claypot with peppers and herbs, I learned that Elliott hailed from Greenwich, majored in history, started at right wing on the lacrosse team, and served as vice president of the campus Hillel. That went some way toward explaining Katie's unexpected knowledge of Hebrew words and Jewish monsters. When the waiter rendered the bill, I saw why the couple hadn't been to the restaurant on their own.

The next day Elliott insisted on coming with us to the funeral of my grandfather. It was just as well to have a guide to customs that I did not know—my genetic inheritance didn't seem to help. He explained that a traditional Jewish burial happened within a day or two of death, the sooner the better. I think he was worried, too, about what we might be caught up in. He told Katie and me that a friend had been to a service for another Hasidic leader in Brooklyn. It had been marked by contention between the supporters of two feuding sons: each had claimed to be his father's rightful successor. When fist fights broke out, police had been called in.

Elliott also served as my haberdasher. I was dressed in a navy pinstriped suit he'd loaned me. A little long in the sleeves and small across the shoulders, it still fit well enough to be worn. A dark pin-dotted tie and knitted blue yarmulke, both also borrowed from Elliott, completed the outfit.

Within a few blocks of the synagogue, traffic congealed. Once we abandoned our cab and set out on foot, we discovered why—crowd control. The police were manning barricades two blocks from the building.

"Down there. That's the street where my grandfather lived." I pointed to the right as an officer waved us and another hundred mourners across the intersection with Windsor Avenue.

"It has to be within walking distance of the synagogue," Katie said into my ear. "Orthodox Jews don't drive on the Sabbath."

Parked across the street from the synagogue itself were three white vans, two from local television stations and one from CNN. Amidst the hubbub, I saw a man pointing his video camera at a slim, elegant woman illuminated by TV lights. "And from Brookline," she was saying in the crisp voice of her profession, "this is Hank Phillippi Ryan for Seven News."

Hank? I turned my head to stare at her, wondering at the incongruity of this cowboy handle being attached to a chic reporter. Katie pulled me forward by the sleeve.

Once within twenty feet of the entrance, we were sucked inside like particles into a black hole. Five minutes later Elliott and I found ourselves standing shoulder to shoulder in the back of the long, narrow, high-ceilinged hall of the synagogue. Set fifteen feet up in the white plaster walls were honey-colored wood facades with slats. Katie was behind one of them with the other women. I hadn't been too crazy about being separated—it seemed so sexist—but we had no choice. A man had glowered when I'd kissed Katie on the cheek as she headed up the stairs.

Most of the congregation wore the black-suit uniforms that marked them as followers of the Bialystoker Rebbe. Some of these men were yelling in conversation with their companions, others stood with their eyes shut, and a good quarter of them were wailing in grief. I guessed there were two thousand in a room intended for half that many, and that was without counting the women upstairs. My head throbbed.

Near the front of the hall a lanky man, obviously a civilian like me despite the yarmulkes we both wore, turned around. The state's junior senator. He was talking to an African-American man next to him.

Elliott followed my gaze. "The governor," he called into my ear.

Finally, Rabbi Zweiback stood up on the *bimah* and, like a conductor ending a Beethoven symphony, swept his hands downward.

It was as if a volume switch had been clicked to off. The Niagara of noise froze.

The silence held for the ten seconds until he began. "*Libi chalal bekirbi.* My heart is experiencing a void."

I wondered if the senator or the governor understood more of the service, largely in Yiddish and Hebrew, than I did.

* * *

Two hours later Elliott and I were again standing shoulder to shoulder, now at the cemetery. Amidst an unremitting drizzle, maybe five hundred people had shown up to pay their last respects. The box was pine and the graveside service straightforward. Katie, her head shrouded in a kerchief, stood on the other side of the grave with the female mourners. Elliott kept up a whispered commentary.

When Rabbi Zweiback finished, cemetery workers lowered the casket as the pulley ropes squealed in protest. The rabbi then pulled a spade out of the mound of dirt by the graveside and strode over to me, holding out the shovel.

"You go first," he said.

I scooped up a shovelful of brown earth and tossed it into the maw of the grave. The clods thudding against the raw wood provided stark testimony to the finality of death. The rabbi took the shovel and covered another third of the coffin. Then we stood side by side, watching others take turns filling the grave.

The rabbi insisted we accompany him back to the house. The hospital bed was already gone, and the living room and every other room of the house were chock-full of mourners. Rabbi Zweiback introduced his wife Tziporah—was she my second cousin once removed? She took it upon herself to keep me, Katie, and Elliott fed.

"Where did all the food come from?" I asked her.

"People brought it," she said.

"Who coordinated it all?" A caterer would have needed a staff of twenty.

"People know what to do."

As great as the meal had been the night before, I found the plates of old country Jewish food to be even better. My genes probably had special receptors, and from now on my favorite dish in the world would be *kreplach*, crunchy little raviolis stuffed with meat.

It was hard to leave. One by one, each of the people in the house came up to offer their condolences. I didn't always understand the words—Yiddish vied with English in terms of popularity—but the intent was always clear. It didn't make a lot of sense that I was viewed as the chief mourner for a man I hadn't known before yesterday. But I went with the flow. I shook hands with the men who expressed concern and bowed a little toward the teary-eyed women.

Rabbi Zweiback, the new Bialystoker Rebbe, walked us down the walkway.

"Why are you the successor?" I asked him.

"The rebbe chose me."

"That simple?"

"Still with the dynasties? You're looking for another War of the Roses? The rebbe made sure there wasn't one. A month ago he called in each of the synagogue elders one by one and told them."

"I'll bet he could be pretty convincing," I said.

"Any regrets? If things had been different, you could..."

"Be a rebbe? No, thanks. I'm not much for a job that requires you to wear a suit every day."

The rabbi's smile formed a white-toothed gash in the midst of his bushy beard.

"So instead, the rebbe is sending you on a quest?" he asked.

A quest. I hadn't thought of it that way. "He did ask me to go."

"And are you going?"

"Maybe."

"As Rabbi Yochanan says in the Talmud, 'Go and see which way you should follow.'"

* * *

I gave Katie a hug before going through the security line at Logan. She held me out at arm's length.

Katie said, "Well, I'm not sure what will come of it, but at least you'll be busy. And keeping your mind off Mom. You all set in D.C.?"

I showed her a message on the screen of my iPhone: "See you Monday at 5 PM, State HQ, Foggy Bottom, Mitch."

"Good," she said and handed me a scrap of paper folded over a couple of times and asked me to place it in the Western Wall if I went to Jerusalem.

"Is this like a birthday wish?" I asked. "Do you have to keep it a secret?"

"No. It's a prayer that both you and Mom find happiness."

Chapter 7

It had been fifteen years since I'd visited Mitch at the main State Department building. While I'd seen him a dozen times since then, our reunions had all been overseas. He'd worked his way through postings of increasing seniority in Ghana, Belize, and Lebanon before being named ambassador to the United Arab Emirates. We'd kept in touch between visits first through old-fashioned snail mail and phone calls and, more recently, by email with an occasional video chat. A few months ago he'd returned to D.C. to take over the Middle East for the Department's Policy Planning Staff.

Fifteen years ago, all I had to do was give a guy at a desk my name and Mitch would come down to meet me. A five-minute process. Things had changed. I filled out forms, showed my driver's license, and went through a security line in which I was searched, sniffed, and x-rayed. Progress.

Mitch was waiting for me after I'd run the gauntlet of human, canine, and electronic security.

"Alex."

I wouldn't have guessed a hug was appropriate in front of the bank of carved elevator doors in the State Department lobby. But Mitch knew the protocol better and threw his arms around me.

"You look good, kid," he said. His birthday was one day

before mine and that had made me "kid" since freshman year. Not only had our ages been almost identical, we'd been the same size, a shade over six feet and one seventy-five. He had no paunch, but his brown hair was thinning a little in front—then again, so was mine. I'd even met his wife Sarah before he had. After our one and only date, he'd asked me if I was going to ask her out again. When I said I liked her but had no romantic interest, he'd given her a call. Now they had two grown sons.

"Where are your specs?" I asked. Sarah used to joke that the only way she could tell us apart was that Mitch wore glasses.

"Lasik surgery last year."

"What's up with your leg?"

"You can tell? Sciatica. No big deal."

I bet it hurt like the dickens, but said nothing more. On the elevator up to his office, we began to catch up. Twenty minutes later, sitting in comfortable red leather club chairs, he asked, "So what's this about a trip to Jerusalem?"

I told him what my grandfather had told me.

"You, a scion of a rabbinical dynasty? I didn't even know you were Jewish till that time you came to church with me. And you only told me when it was time for communion."

"You were looking for company. All I usually did on Sunday mornings was sleep till the Lowell House bells woke me up. Why not go?"

"But taking communion would have been going a little far?"

"A little."

Mitch pulled out an official-looking folder festooned with red and blue ribbons and waved it in my face.

"Here's what our consulate in East Jerusalem could come up with on short notice. In 1983 the Muslim authorities who controlled the Temple Mount felt underground vibrations. What did they find when they investigated? Rabbi Shlomo

Goren, the country's head rabbi, jackhammering merrily away in a tunnel about fifty feet under the surface."

"He started digging a hole on the Temple Mount and no one noticed?"

"No, no. They branched out from a tunnel running under the Western Wall. Still, can you imagine? Every night this rabbi in his sixties sneaked down with this other rabbi named Getz and dug. Like Steve McQueen in *The Great Escape* or something."

"My grandfather told me Goren took him down there and showed him the Ark."

"He saw it?"

"From a distance."

Mitch held both his hands up, palms out like a traffic cop stopping traffic. "You ever been to Israel?"

"No."

"Well, it's a crazy place." Mitch stood up and started pacing. "It was reconstituted as a Jewish country almost two thousand years after the Romans thought they'd finished it off. Could the Ark of the Covenant show up again after three thousand? Almost like the Dead Sea Scrolls. Pretty unlikely, sure, but in that place not impossible."

"My grandfather also said there was rioting, and the Israeli authorities sealed off the tunnel they'd dug."

"Yeah, I know. It was the prudent thing to do."

"Prudent? You're lecturing me about prudence?"

"Not the TR business again? Won't that ever go away?"

I'd had to fetch Mitch from the campus police station after he was found seated at Teddy Roosevelt's desk in the Widener Library stacks at four in the morning. He'd picked the lock on the security door. Come to think about it, if that's the wildest thing he'd done, he *was* pretty prudent.

"Nope, never."

Mitch sat back down. "You know there were rumors that

the Arabs did a little exploring under the Mount, too. To see what Goren and company were looking for."

"But I thought you said the Israelis sealed up the tunnel."

"The Arabs could come down from the surface of the Temple Mount."

"But they didn't find anything?"

"Not that we know of. Anyway, I'm not sure they wanted to. Arafat used to claim there was no proof that Solomon's Temple ever existed, that it was a Zionist fantasy."

"Well, wouldn't the Israelis want to prove them wrong? Wouldn't that help make their claim to Jerusalem even stronger?"

"That's the point. Arafat would have instigated rioting. You saw what happened with the second Intifada—Sharon goes for a walk up on the Mount and next thing you know eight-year-old Arab boys in Hebron are throwing stones at soldiers. And what about the Orthodox in Israel? If the Ark was really there, they would have wanted to kick the Muslims off the Mount and built a third Temple on it. They would have rioted, too."

"So you have the ultra-Orthodox and Arabs both rioting. What a mess."

"It gets worse. Evangelical Christians in this country believe the Jewish Temple must be rebuilt before the end of days can come."

"I guess it would have been a God-awful mess, excuse the expression."

Mitch waved the folder again. "There's more. The Muslim world thinks that the Mount was Mohammad's launch site for a visit to heaven. That's a big deal to the Saudi king who takes pretty damn seriously his role as the protector of Muslim holy places. Y'know, there were even rumors that it was Saudis who caught Goren in the act and made sure the Israeli authorities were notified."

"What would the Saudis have been doing there?"

"They subsidize the *Waqf*, the authority that runs the top of the Temple Mount. The Israeli government wouldn't care who told them. They didn't want rioting and moved to squelch any chance of a war over an Ark that in their minds didn't exist."

"So that's why they stopped Goren and Getz?"

"Yup. Just like your grandfather said. The Israelis blocked off the tunnel branch with six feet of concrete. But you know what? That main tunnel is open to tourists. You can walk right past where the spur was dug out."

"So, what if the Ark is really there?" I asked.

"We're with the Israelis on this one. Let sleeping dogs lie."

"And forget about the dying wish of an old man?"

"Yes. Using Teddy Roosevelt's desk got me in trouble, but no world war resulted."

Mitch might have been the one the police took in, but I was the one who caught holy shit. Sarah, his girlfriend at the time, kept saying, "You know he gets these cockamamie ideas—writing about the Rough Riders at Teddy Roosevelt's own desk. It was up to you to stop him. How could you let him be so irresponsible?" She shivered with fury and then delivered a right cross to my solar plexus that would have done Mike Tyson proud.

Mitch brought me back to the here and now as he said, "Let sleeping dogs lie."

"I hear you."

"But you're going to Israel anyway?"

"Maybe. Probably not."

He stood up again. "Good call. Listen, Sarah's made dinner. You really don't have any choice. It's a command performance."

We headed down to the garage, Mitch dragging his right leg behind him.

"This is me," he said, stopping behind a Ford Escape. I guess if you worked for the government you needed to drive

American. The hybrid sticker would show anyone who cared that he was a *conscientious* despoiler of the atmosphere.

He jingled the keys a few times in his hand. “I told you I have this sciatica acting up on my right leg. Driving is a bitch. Could you take the wheel?”

“No problem-o.”

He tossed me the keys.

“You know it’s a heckuva lot easier getting out of this place than getting in,” I said. Mitch waved at the security guard as we left the State Department garage and exited on to Independence Avenue.

“Turn left here,” Mitch said.

I almost crashed the car looking at the eerily lit Lincoln Memorial and then swung over to the Arlington Memorial Bridge across the Potomac and into Virginia.

Turning on the brights when we left the George Washington Parkway, I followed Mitch’s lefts and rights through Cherry-dale. Maybe like Theseus of Greek mythology, I should have been unrolling a ball of thread to find my way out of the labyrinth of gloomy tree-lined streets.

“This is us. Turn right here.”

I pulled to a stop at the end of the driveway and clicked off the headlights. A frigid gust slapped my face as Mitch swung open the passenger door. A split second later came the crackling of breaking glass. In the faint illumination of the door light, I saw a hole surrounded by a spider web of cracks appear on the windshield.

What the fuck?

Mitch had one leg, his bad one, on the concrete of the driveway. He turned to look at me, to make sure I was okay, I guess. It took me a second or two to reach over and yank him back into the SUV. I felt him jerk. He fell back onto the seat with his head on my right thigh. I whirled my own head around. I saw nothing behind us except for the serried gray trunks of elms.

Sarah was running toward the car, her mouth in an "O," her voice ululating like a police car siren.

My left hand found the door handle. I swung the door open. I screamed, "Get back in the house, Sarah. Call 911. Get an ambulance. Get the police."

She slowed and stopped.

"Do it."

She turned around and then accelerated back into the house. I heard the clickety-clack of her heels on cobblestones.

I looked down at Mitch.

"You okay?" I asked.

"Damn leg hurts."

His leg? I saw a red stain spreading over his shoulder like ink on a blotter. He smiled up at me and then closed his eyes. I ripped off my tie and pressed the silk against the wound.

Chapter 8

Once Mitch had graduated from morphine to codeine and could form coherent sentences, he thanked me for saving his life. He'd almost died from loss of blood, and some white-coated resident had told him my attempt to stanch the wound had made the difference. His gratitude was embarrassing. By contrast, Sarah was the epitome of hospitality, but I could tell she blamed me for the shooting: I came to visit, Mitch was shot. Rationality had nothing to do with it. Sarah saw me as a bad luck talisman and a reminder of tragedy scarcely evaded. If it had been up to me, I would have stuck around longer to entertain Mitch and help Sarah, what with their sons back at home and all. But she wanted me to get out of Dodge.

Maybe in the aftermath of seeing him almost die, my brain wasn't operating rationally either. How could it make sense out of what had happened? A grandfather had appeared from nowhere to ask me to play Indiana Jones. Five days later person or persons unknown had almost killed my oldest friend. I wasn't ready to go back home where there was only a company that no longer existed and a wife who didn't want me. I couldn't hang around Boston to be with Katie—she quite clearly had her own life. Sarah wanted me gone from D.C.

I know it was a non sequitur, that there was no real logic to it, as Katie and Mitch had pointed out. Maybe it was just cussedness. Maybe it was to say "screw you" to the sniper. Maybe it was just to do something, anything, rather than sit staring out over San Francisco Bay from a paisley armchair. As for Mitch's concerns, I'd be careful, just scout around. I'd never been to Israel and why not now? For the first time since I'd sold my company to Sibyl, I was going to swim against the current, not be carried by it.

I tapped into my iPhone and made the reservation.

* * *

As the plane winged over Greenland, my mind hovered over the foggy border between wakefulness and slumber. The leather business class seat of the El Al flight was tilted back and the cabin lights were turned off.

I'd stopped by Mitch and Sarah's before heading to the airport. "I didn't want to pitch for the Yankees anyway," Mitch said to me as I said goodbye. When I climbed into the Hertz rental for the drive to the airport, I gave a quick wave to the uniformed State Department security officer in the gray Ford in front of the house.

US Airways shuttled me to LaGuardia and a van deposited me at JFK for the midnight flight to Ben Gurion. Standard airport security was kindergarten compared to the Ph.D. course run by El Al. I'd gone through five checkpoints and was queued up in a sixth to get my carry-on searched and x-rayed, when a petite blonde with a clipboard stopped beside me.

"What is the purpose of your visit?"

"Never been to Israel. It's time to look around."

Looking at my face rather than her clipboard, she went through a litany of half a dozen more questions. Then she asked, "What's your Hebrew name?"

"Aron," I said.

She lifted the tape and motioned for me to come through.

As though I were Ali Baba and had mouthed the incantation that opened the magic door.

"I don't need to get my bag x-rayed?" I asked.

"No."

I raised an eyebrow.

"You can skip the other lines," she said with a smile, her left hand upraised and her right beckoning. "You are one of us."

I hesitated for a second, wondering what club I was joining by walking under the tape.

Now I sat motionless in the giant aluminum cigar hurtling to the Holy Land. It had taken Moses and the Israelites forty years to travel the 150 miles from the Nile to the Jordan. It would take me ten hours to go fifty times further. I must have looked more awake than I felt because a stewardess asked if I needed anything. I shook my head and shut my eyes. On an American airline the men and women who gave the spiel about what to do in case of a water landing, who served food and drinks, and who sold duty free, were deemed "flight attendants," not stewardesses. But El Al was a blast from the past. Leggy, dark, almond-eyed young women modeled blue uniforms and scarves that were a throwback to those worn on Pan Am and TWA during the Golden Age of Jet Travel. Back in those more sexist days, a flight attendant was not a surly waiter in the sky, but a glamorous globetrotter in high-fashion finery.

Groggy even after landing, I made it through immigration and then to a taxi stand. The driver's English was fluent, but he was a little more suspicious than the pixie who'd lifted the tape for me at JFK. He demanded I show him I had enough shekels to pay for the ride to Jerusalem.

That little contretemps brought me back to the land of the aware and awake. Five miles from the airport on the Tel Aviv highway, past the suburban sprawl, we were driving on a modern four-lane highway through sand-colored hills dotted with scrub and shimmering in the late afternoon sun. King David had probably enjoyed the same vista on the way back to his capital from a summer stay on the shore.

Ahead I spotted a pile of twisted metal that jarred in the austere biblical landscape.

"Why don't they clean that up?" I asked the driver.

"Those are tanks from the War of Independence."

"And they've been left here since 1948?"

"We didn't have a real army back then, just a bunch of kids and refugees. Jordan had the Arab Legion."

"They had British officers, didn't they?" I asked.

"Oh, yes. My grandfather was here. If they hadn't got past the Jordanians, Jerusalem would have fallen."

"The tanks are left so you remember?"

"Remembering is what we Jews do best."

Chapter 9

The window of my room in the Sheraton Plaza faced due east. The rising sun's rays ricocheted off the gold of the Dome of the Rock on the Temple Mount.

I powered up my iPhone and ran my eye over the inbox. Bingo! A response to the email I'd sent to Katie's archeology professor before taking off from JFK. I looked down at my watch. 8:20. I had forty minutes to shower, shave, and get to a café in the Old City.

I was striding across the lobby at 8:40.

"Excuse me," I said to the burly, mustached, gold-button-uniformed clerk.

He continued to stare into space.

I decided to put a substantial subset of my Hebrew vocabulary to use. "*Shalom*," I said. Nothing. "*Shalom*?" I banged the desk with the flat of my hand.

Returning from wherever he'd been, the clerk said, "Yes, sir?" Evidently, my Hebrew greeting hadn't fooled him into thinking I was Israeli.

"How do I get to the Square Cup Café?" I asked.

"You can grab a taxi in front. Should take around thirty minutes."

"Isn't it only a mile—uh, less than two kilometers?"

"Yes, that's right."

"I'd make faster time walking, then?"

He shook his head as if the idea of an American walking were a new one. "Turn left on your way out of the hotel on to Gershon Agron, follow it to the right when you come to the pedestrian walkway, through Jaffa Gate, and then walk through the Cardo—that's the covered area. It will be right there in Hurva Square." He pointed on a map.

The cars on King George, outside the hotel, had substituted honking for moving. Maybe the clerk's half-hour estimate for a cab ride had been optimistic. Walking down the sidewalks of the Holy City, I might have thought I was still in some northeastern American metropolis if not for the trilingual street signs that displayed English as well as the block letters of Hebrew and the flowing cursive of Arabic.

I turned a corner, and there before me were the pockmarked walls that bounded the Old City. Were those scars from the Israeli reconquest of the city in the 1967 War? Or were they, like those hillside tanks, vestiges of the 1948 War of Independence? Or from the British General Allenby's conquest of the city from the Turks in 1917? Or from something more ancient still?

I walked through the Jaffa Gate only to confront a blank wall of matching khaki stones in front of me. I followed the crowd to the right through a narrow passage. This twist would keep soldiers and their vehicles, whether tanks or chariots, from going straight through into the Old City even after forcing the gate.

I moved from the broad artery of David Street into the twisting, cobblestoned alleyways that formed the capillaries of the Old City. A couple of turns and I came upon two wrought iron tables with tattered green umbrellas bearing ads that reminded patrons of the refreshment contained in each bottle of Orangina. At one table sat a fifty-ish couple, the man with a Nikon suspended from his neck and the woman leafing through a copy of *Shopping in Jerusalem*. At the other table sat a tanned woman in a long-sleeved blue Oxford-cloth blouse and a mid-calf canvas skirt. Curly wisps of red hair escaped from both the front and back of a kerchief. Israeli she might have been but her face would not have looked out of place in a Silicon Valley synagogue. Same gene pool, I guess, even if different nationalities. She sipped from a tiny espresso cup while perusing a Hebrew newspaper.

"Professor Golan?"

"Ah, Mr. Kalman?" She stood up.

She was the same five-foot-seven or so as Veronica, but was built differently—she was broad shouldered and fit, not personal-trainer-led-workout buff and lean. I hadn't extended my hand—I'd learned my lesson back in Brookline—but she extended hers. Her grasp was firm.

"Ah, so you are the father of the brilliant Katie Kalman?" she asked with no accent.

"What a wonderful way to be greeted."

"Please sit down, Mr. Kalman.

"Alex, please." Her deep green eyes did not move from my face as I descended into the seat.

Emerging from a dark doorway, the proprietor took my order for tea.

"I only hope I can convince your daughter to follow a career in archeology," the professor said.

"Really?"

"Her paper on ritualism during the reign of Akhenaton.... Well, I encouraged her to submit it to the *Cambridge Archaeological Journal*. It's going to be in the October issue. I'm on leave this year, but I have told her there would be a place for her at Hebrew U. for a Ph.D. after she graduates."

"She told me she'd done okay in your course," I said.

"*Okay*? Do you know what you have with her?" She leaned across the table. "I have taught ten years here at Hebrew

University and a semester at Harvard and a year at the Oriental Institute in Chicago. I have never come across a more brilliant student. You should be proud."

"And you think I'm not?"

Any looming confrontation over Katie's academic potential was interrupted by the waiter slapping a crackled mug filled with a mossy-colored liquid in front of me. The professor sat back. I gave a conciliatory smile and took a sip.

"I guess that's not your cup of tea," the professor said. She did know her idiomatic English.

"Oh sure, it's fine." I took a healthy gulp of a lukewarm minty beverage, different from, but just as repulsive as, the tea I'd been served in Brookline. She smiled. "Wait," I said. "I'm trying to keep a poker face here."

"Your smile afterwards is pretty convincing," she allowed.

"But?"

"You flinch a bit before each sip."

I brought the mug up to my lips and swallowed.

"Ah, better," she said. "Now what can I do for you? In her email Katie said you were interested in the *Kotel*."

I hadn't had much time for research, but the guidebook in the hotel room told me that the *Kotel* was Hebrew for the Western Wall, Judaism's holiest site, the place I was supposed to slip Katie's prayer.

"Yes, my grandfather told me I should be sure to see it."

"Have you ever been to the *Kotel*?"

"No."

She stood up and dropped fifteen shekels, a few dollars, in coins onto the table. "Then let's go."

"I'll pay."

"Next time, Mr. Kalman," she said from over her shoulder.

By the time I stood up, she was twenty feet ahead of me. I trotted after her. An Olympic walker would have worked up a sweat keeping up with Professor Golan. The narrow alleys were filling with camera-bedecked and Nike-shod tourists. A daughter of Moses, the professor assumed the sea of people would part for her and so it did.

"You said you were on leave from the university? What are you doing, then?" I asked once I'd caught up.

"I'm working for the government's Department of Antiquities."

"Doing what?"

"Managing the digging under the *Kotel*."

My Katie had sent me to the right person.

Chapter 10

Finally past the barriers into the *Kotel* plaza and in front of the Wall itself, I fished the folded paper Katie had given me out of my pocket. I hadn't read it, but, holding it close, I could see faint imprints of the Hebrew characters that had leaked through to the other side. Maybe Elliott had helped her. Still, my guess was that any God would understand English, too. Finding a place to stick it would not be easy. Little strips of white filled the spaces between the stones of the wall like mortar.

I crouched and managed to find an inch-long crevice not already occupied by entreaties to the Almighty. I rubbed a couple of knuckles raw squeezing in Katie's message. Did Katie and all these others figure that the *Kotel* was a FedEx box where God made regular pickups?

On the way up, my *kippah*—the skullcap bought for the shekel equivalent of three dollars at Professor Golan's behest—slipped off. As I reached down, I peeked to my right for a hint on how to behave. There, a black-clad teenager with wispy whiskers bowed up-and-down and side-to-side like a meth-addled hipster as he read aloud from the small leather-bound book in his hand.

Maybe the boy inspired me. Whether God existed or not, what could it hurt to say a prayer? Maybe I should say something about Katie's future or ask for success in finding the Ark.

I stood there staring at the stones, but the words didn't come. Face it, I didn't have a clue how to pray. Was it a missing gene? Had I inherited my father's rejection of religion? Did Dad have doubts when growing up? Or had going to a secular college eroded his beliefs? Or had everything changed in an instant with the car crash? I wondered if Dad had rejected God's existence or if he'd been afraid of God's power. Was the only way to maintain faith in this world by living apart from it? I could pose the questions; I only wished Dad were still around to answer them.

Oh yeah, got to get back to the professor. I looked around again. For the holiest spot of the world's first monotheistic religion, the progenitor of both Christianity and Islam, the site wasn't much. A mixed stream of Orthodox in black and tourists in mufti approached and retreated from the exposed hundred-foot section of sand-colored stones. Over to the right, separated by a wooden barrier, stood a group of women. I saw one of them pull something from under her jacket. She started unrolling a miniature scroll.

I was walking back to the metal gate where Professor Golan waited. I saw a volcano of anger erupt behind her. A group of ten teenagers, their faces contorted under black hats, were jostling and pushing at the metal gates between the plaza and the *Kotel*.

The professor grabbed my arm.

"Let's get out of here," she said.

Two youths, who'd been running toward the others, stopped ten feet from us, shouting in accented English, "Go back to Germany where the death camps await you!"

They must have thought the professor had been one of the women with the scroll. But she said nothing. Her hand still closed just above my wrist, she started to walk around them.

One of the boys cocked his arm. I jerked the professor out of the way. On Mitch's driveway, I hadn't moved fast enough.

This time I did. A plastic bag filled with a muddy material sailed within two inches of her head. I followed its trajectory until it spattered on the cobblestones in a brown splash.

I shook my arm free and took four steps to grab the lapels of the boy's coat. He couldn't have been much taller than five-one or heavier than one-ten. I lifted him up. He opened his mouth and sprayed spittle over my face. He tried again, but nothing came. So he switched from saliva to invective. He was screaming in Yiddish. His breath smelled of onions as I hoisted him.

A hand alighted on my shoulder. I whirled to confront the other boy, but it was the professor. The leg of the boy I was holding slammed against her hip.

"Let him go," she said. "This is not your fight."

"It is."

"No."

"He threw a bag of shit at you," I said.

"Wait to fight another day. The police will handle this. They're used to it."

I let him go.

* * *

The professor and I were back at the Square Cup, the café we'd left an hour before. I was drinking the same foul minty tea. This time, though, my heart was thumping against my ribcage. I'd been jogging to keep up with the speed-walking professor.

"So what was that all about?" I asked.

"The woman smuggled in a Torah."

"Smuggled?"

"Yes. Our Supreme Court has said women cannot read Torah at the Wall."

"That's outrageous."

"The court said it would foment rioting by the *haredim* who do not believe women should read from the Torah. As you saw, the justices were correct."

"So in the 1950s the American Supreme Court should have ruled in favor of segregated schools because mixing the races would lead to rioting?"

The professor shrugged. "Before the ruling, disturbances were frequent. Now, much less so."

"So the most prejudiced and narrow-minded segments in society get to decide what's acceptable?"

"I'm observant myself and think women should be allowed to read from the Torah. I just don't think this kind of confrontation helps us get to our goal."

"Equality for women isn't worth fighting for?"

"Here in Jerusalem, if your heart beats like crazy with each injustice committed in the name of religion, you will die of cardiac arrest like this." Her fingers snapped with the crack of a branch in a storm. "One must pick one's battles."

"And what battles do you choose to fight?"

"To dig under the Wall."

"And that's a battle because the Muslims object to you tunneling under the Mount?"

"Another injustice. The tunnel isn't new. It was dug by our ancestors two thousand years ago, six centuries before the Muslim conquest. The tunnel goes under houses, not the Mount. When there are protests over our digging, well, then I must admit, Mr. Kalman, my heart *does* beat faster."

"May I see the tunnel?"

"It is open every day for tourists, but if you meet me at the entrance tomorrow morning at nine, I'd be glad to show you around myself."

"Thank you, Professor."

I stood and grasped her long-fingered, hard, calloused hand. Her nails were short and broken as though she eschewed pick and shovel in her digging. She saw where I was looking and let go.

I pulled my wallet out and dropped a ten shekel note on the table.

When I looked back up, she was ten paces down the alley. She didn't turn around, but I heard her call, "Yes, this time you can pay, Mr. Kalman."

Chapter 11

"Alex?"

"What time is it?" I said into my iPhone.

"It's a little early to be asleep, isn't it?" my wife asked.

I looked out the window at the black vaulted dome of the sky over the Holy City. Then I looked down at the glowing hands of my watch—6:20. I hadn't changed it from Pacific Time. Local time—4:20.

"I'm in Jerusalem."

"Your note said you were going to Boston. Then Katie told me you'd left to go to D.C."

"Yeah. I *was* there, and then I flew in here."

"What are you doing in Israel? Doesn't matter. What does matter is that I spoke to Katie. She knows we're splitting up. I thought we agreed to tell her together."

I didn't think I'd quite made a promise, but Veronica was mad. I bet she'd cut Katie off before she could tell her mother where I was. Ah, well. I was not going to fight. I was going to follow the professor's advice and pick my battles. "I didn't tell her. She told me."

"What do you mean?"

"She guessed."

"You mean she knew we weren't getting along?"

"Apparently."

"Oh, God. I wonder if we've blown it? I wonder if she'll ever be able to have a loving relationship."

"Every gene Katie got from us has mutated. She'll do everything better than we did."

"I love her so much."

Was there an implication I did not? I took two deep breaths. *Stay calm.*

"She'll be fine," I said. "I'm sorry. I should have told you she guessed."

"I was blindsided."

"I'm sorry."

"You should have told me."

"Yes, I should have."

"You know how close she and I are."

"Yes, I do."

"When will you be back? My attorney says we should meet."

She'd already hired a lawyer?

"Okay. I'll let you know as soon as I know. Then we'll sit down with lawyers."

"Let me know."

"I will. Veronica?"

"Yes."

"Don't worry about Katie. You did a great job raising that girl."

"I'm going to fly out and see her soon. Good night."

"Good night," I said in return, but I was too late. She'd already hung up.

I pulled another overstuffed hotel pillow across the king-sized bed and put it beneath the one my head rested on. I laced my fingers behind my neck and looked up at the ceiling.

After half an hour, I knew sleep was not coming back. The five hours before Veronica had called would have to do. I went over to my suitcase and pulled out a pair of Nikes. I hadn't run since I'd left home. Time to get back to it.

In the lobby were a few tourists awaiting the first airport bus. A doorman held the door open.

"Think they'll be able to win another series?" he asked me.

"I beg your pardon?"

"The Giants," he said, pointing to my head.

"The San Francisco Giants?" I asked. Then I understood. "Oh, my hat." I was wearing a baseball cap with the intertwined capital "S" and "F" of my hometown team.

"I'm from San Mateo. Made *aliyah* last year," he said. "My name is Bruce."

"*Aliyah*?"

"Oh, you're not Jewish. It means going up, and it's the word for emigrating to Israel."

"Alex," I said, and we shook. "I don't know about the hitting past Posey," I told him.

"Ain't that the truth. I watch games sometimes on the Internet. Have a nice run."

A dusting of hoar-frost lay across the hotel driveway. Breathing the cold night air deep into my lungs was as good as a double espresso.

In the olden days, Veronica and I used to run together almost every morning. A few years ago—no wait, it was fifteen years ago—we'd finished the Boston Marathon in twenty-five minutes over three hours. Even though I jogged most mornings, I was not ready for another marathon, but I was breathing more easily than expected.

This was the way to see the city. To glide like a specter through deserted byways. A sign told me I was running down Haran Street. The streets didn't run straight, but why should they? They'd been laid out thousands of years ago by the great builder-kings of the city—David, Solomon, Herod. To accommodate the automobile age, ancient paths for carts and livestock had been paved over.

I couldn't blame Veronica for wondering what in the hell I was doing here. She usually accused me of being hyper-rational, of not following my gut, of requiring data before making a decision. What could I say now? That I was on a mission from a grandfather who, like a vampire on one of the TV shows she watched, had risen from the grave for a day?

Jerusalem was a city built on hills. Just as when I ran in San Francisco, I breathed hard when climbing and coasted on the way down. Looking up from my feet padding on the pavement, I recognized the lighted Knesset building, seat of the Israeli parliament, from news photos. In twenty minutes I had not seen another pedestrian. A car whizzed by and caught me in a pair of yellowish cones of light. I turned my head and saw a pair of fellow runners in hooded sweatshirts about two hundred yards behind me. My first thought was to slow down so I could jog along with them. But who knew if they spoke English? And, besides, I didn't really know Jerusalem. Can you imagine waiting in Central Park for two guys in sweats to catch up to you in the pre-dawn gloaming? I picked up my pace a little and then turned onto a street whose sign revealed it to be K'far Bar'am. After a few more minutes of twists and turns, I stopped for a moment and heard the slap-slapping of shoes on pavement coming from behind me still. What the hell? Were they following me? Muggers in the Holy City? A quick glance over my shoulder showed two men, both bearded and big, one wearing dark glasses. I started sprinting. A final turn in the labyrinth brought me to the wide pedestrian mall of Ben Yehuda Street. Its souvenir shops, jewelry stores, and restaurants were all shuttered.

From an alleyway a dark shadow emerged and swung a stick like a baseball bat against the top of my left arm. My howl was cut off by a strong forearm across my windpipe. I grabbed the phantom's arm with my right hand. Not enough leverage. Struggling cut off more of my air supply. He was calling back to the two runners. Through the descending black curtain, I heard voices calling in Arabic. Amidst the distant unintelligible words, did I hear "Kalman"? Delirium perhaps, but it spurred a last wild kick upward and behind me.

"Oof." A lucky bulls-eye right in the balls. The mugger's arm loosened its lock around my neck. I breathed in the glorious oxygen of the Holy City, made a quick pirouette, and felt a satisfying crunch as my right fist landed against his smooth-shaven jaw, and he fell to his knees.

I didn't stick around to wait for the guy's colleagues to join us. From the end of Ben Yehuda, I ran down King George Street where headlights and streetlamps cut through the darkness, but a quick look back told me my pursuers were not runners. I was pulling away.

Two hundred more paces, and the feeling started coming back into my left arm. I started pumping it in rhythm with my other one, but daggers seemed to stab it with each stride. At least it wasn't broken. Six or seven minutes later, in front of the hotel's revolving front door, I put my hands on my knees and gulped down the chill air.

My head began to spin.

Strong fingers wrapped themselves around my biceps. I started to struggle but was just hoisted up.

"Whoa." A few inches from my face was Bruce the Doorman. With his open-mouthed smile came the smell of Dubble Bubble chewing gum. "You okay, sir?"

"Yeah. Thanks."

He let go of my arm. I teetered for a moment, and his hand clamped back on.

"Sir, you didn't have to run like you're being chased by a stampede," he said.

"You sure?" I asked.

"What do you mean?"

After I explained, Bruce insisted on calling the police, but they found nothing except for a bloody eyetooth near the alley.

On the elevator up to my room, I asked myself how much sense it made for me to be here in Jerusalem running for my life. Objectively, not much. But what was the alternative? Sitting in a stupor, barely alive, on my paisley chair back in Woodside?

Chapter 12

It was as if we were walking through the passageway of a huge dungeon. Blocks of stones arced a dozen feet over our heads, and what looked like prison bars separated us from the excavations on either side. The archeologists might have passed for members of a chain gang if their picks and shovels had been full size. Oh, and if they hadn't shouted out "*Shalom*" to the professor as we passed by.

She kept up a steady patter, playing guide.

"There is the biggest stone in the *Kotel.*"

"This is still the Wall?" I asked. The stone she pointed to must have been fifty feet long and ten feet high.

"What's in the plaza is a very small piece of it. Most of it is down here."

"And how much does that stone weigh?"

"Over five hundred tons."

"Wow."

The professor slowed, and she tilted her head toward six women in headscarves, bowing and praying in a niche hewn out of the rock. "See that?"

"Sure."

She stopped once out of earshot of the praying women. "You complained about how women were treated at the *Kotel.*"

"Yes."

"Why is the *Kotel* so special?"

I'd done my reading in the guidebook the Sheraton provided. "Because it's the last remaining wall of the Second Temple.

"Very good." Her head bobbed up and down. "But wrong."

"How so?"

"The *Kotel* was never part of the Temple. It's a retaining wall built by King Herod in the time of Jesus."

"Okay then. It's a big deal because it's as close as you can get to where the Holy of Holies was." That was the little room in the Temple where the Ark was stored.

"Very good. But wrong again. Where those women are praying is the closest point."

I laughed. "So that's why, when you pick your fights, you don't fight about women at the *Kotel*. If they pray here, you win."

"You could say that."

She started moving again, arms swinging as though doing work on a speed bag.

We had moved only fifty feet or so when I called out, "Wait."

She turned and came back to me.

"What is that?" I pointed at a circle of gray some six feet in diameter amidst the yellowish stones. "They had concrete two thousand years ago?"

"I mentioned we were only excavating outside the perimeter of the Temple Mount?"

"Yeah, I remember."

"Behind that concrete is a passage that leads under the Mount."

"How far..."

She interrupted. "Wait till we get to my office."

We walked in silence another hundred feet. She unlocked a barred door with Hebrew letters on it.

"What does it say?" I asked.

"*Sakana*. That's the word for danger, but it's not really that dangerous."

We went in, and the door clanged shut behind us. My rational mind told me we could leave the same way we'd entered, but I shivered anyway. We padded along a narrow metal catwalk fifteen feet above randomly strewn boulders. I understood the warning on the door now. In the far corner stood a battered gray desk and two chairs that might have brought a dollar each on eBay.

"Nice office."

"I move my desk around to be close to where we're excavating. Please sit down."

I did and leaned across the desk toward her. "That tunnel blocked by concrete is where Rabbi Goren and Rabbi Getz were digging?"

She retreated, balancing on the two back legs of her chair. "You surprise me, Mr. Kalman. You know almost nothing about the *Kotel*, but you have heard of the rabbis' excavation?"

"What can you tell me?"

"They were convinced the Ark was hidden directly under the Holy of Holies. Can you imagine, the country's head rabbi sneaking down here at night and trying to find it?"

"If it's there, why not?"

"Because it's not there. The last time the Bible mentions the Holy Ark is before the Babylonians destroyed the First Temple twenty-six hundred years ago. If the Jews had hidden it, the Babylonians destroyed it."

"It couldn't have been hidden then?"

"If it were, why wouldn't the Israelites have put it back in the Holy of Holies when they built the Second Temple sixty years later?"

"Good question."

"When Pompey…" she looked up at me.

"The Roman general?"

"Right. Well, he entered the Holy of Holies in the Year 63 before the Common Era. He said he didn't understand why there was such a to-do about an empty room."

"So you say the Ark was lost when the First Temple was destroyed and was never in the Second Temple."

"Yes. That's what I say. I have a feeling a 'but' is coming from you, though."

"But my grandfather was down there with Rabbi Goren and says he saw it."

"Do you know what a *bubbe meise* is, Mr. Kalman?"

"No."

"That's Yiddish for an old wives' tale. Some rabbis and scholars claim the Ark is down there, but it's just a *bubbe meise*."

"My grandfather told me he saw it," I repeated.

"Wait." The two front legs of her chair banged against the catwalk as she leaned toward me, the emerald of her eyes gleaming. "Your name is Kalman. What was your grandfather's first name?"

"Isaac."

"Like Yitzhak?"

"Yeah."

"Holy shit. Your grandfather was the Bialystoker Rebbe?"

Chapter 13

"Yes. You've heard of him?"

"Heard of him? Anyone who has been to a yeshiva in Israel or the States has heard of the Bialystoker Rebbe."

"And why is that?"

"He was really your grandfather?"

"Yes."

"Then I am sorry. May you and your family be comforted among the mourners of Zion and Jerusalem. When did you last see him?"

"A week ago Tuesday."

"The day he died."

"Yes. And why does everyone know of my grandfather?"

"Because he was the greatest teacher since, um, since, um, since I don't know. He followed *Halachah*, Jewish law, but did not believe the Torah was only for men. When he taught, he made you think. A single question from him was worth a year studying with another teacher. He saw each human life as a divine gift."

"A gift to be repaid?"

"Then it would not be a gift. Each of us must decide whether to give a gift in return. That is where free will comes in. But come—you are testing me. You know all this."

"No. My father and grandfather were estranged."

"What a shame. Now I understand where your daughter gets her brains and her affinity for *Eretz Yisrael.*" The professor started drumming her short nails against the desk. "So tell me, what did the Bialystoker Rebbe find inside the Ark?"

"He said he saw the Ark through a narrow tunnel but couldn't reach it."

"He looked directly at the Ark?"

"He used a mirror to see its reflection."

"Huh, that makes sense. And what did he see?"

"A box covered with animal skins except for one corner."

"And that corner was beaten gold?"

"Beaten? He didn't say. But yes, gold."

"How large was it?"

"He didn't tell me that either."

"He didn't say much, did he?"

"He wasn't well."

"He held out till he told you that he saw the Ark?"

"Perhaps."

"But the rebbe did say it was the Holy Ark? He was certain?"

"Yes."

"And so tell me again why you are here."

"He asked me to seek *emet*, to get to the Ark."

"That could be dangerous."

"So I understand."

"And how do you expect to get to the Ark?"

Shrugging, I said, "I'm sort of winging things here."

Chapter 14

"Ugh."

The point of the pick bit into the limestone.

I swung again.

"Ugh."

The vibrations on the surface had given away the covert excavation of Rabbis Goren and Getz. That's why the professor had me using my own muscles instead of a compressor-powered jackhammer. But the jackhammer didn't get tired, its back didn't scream as the bit dug deeper.

Another swing. A trickle of dirt started flowing from the hole. It had taken me two hours to make it through the first limestone block. I put the pick down and leaned on it. I grunted again. My hands were sore, but then again, if not for the work gloves the professor had provided, they would be hamburger. I reached down and took a swig from a PVC bottle of apple-flavored water.

What I needed was more positive reinforcement. I started swinging again, widening the hole. Five minutes later I was standing in loose dirt up to my ankles.

"You'd better stop."

I dropped the pick. "Shit."

"Sorry," the professor said. "I didn't mean to scare you. I thought you'd heard me coming."

"I wasn't scared, just startled." What a stupid thing to say.

The planes of the professor's face were accentuated by the lights and shadows cast by her flashlight. "Okay then, startled."

I reached down for the pick.

She raised the light and peered in the hole. "That's good work. There's always employment in Israel for a manual laborer."

"I dug foundations for apartment buildings in Foster City, in California, when I was sixteen. A summer of shoveling made college look awfully good."

I'd started digging after the guards left at six. Until then I'd hidden out, along with two backpacks of provisions and tools, in a nook in the chamber where the professor had her office.

"We don't know how much dirt is backed up against this wall," she said.

"It's a retaining wall?"

"Maybe. You open it wider, and you could be washed over in a landslide."

I looked down at the sharp, rocky outcroppings fifteen feet below the wooden walkway I stood on.

"I'll be careful."

"Let's push the dirt off the boards."

I swapped the pick for a square-ended spade and started scraping the dirt off the catwalk. It cascaded down to the rocks below.

"No one will notice there's extra dirt down there?"

"No one comes in here regularly besides me. That's why I picked it for my office. In a couple dozen meters you should meet up with the tunnel that the Rabbis Goren and Getz dug."

"How long will that take?"

"You're making faster progress than I expected. Maybe a week."

"I only hope my back and arms last that long."

"Take your time, then. If by a miracle the Ark is there, it's been there two thousand six hundred years. It'll wait."

I stuck the spade in the hole and shoveled out some dirt. I cast it over the side of our platform. The clods hitting the rocks and boards below sounded familiar.

"Okay. You can leave any time after nine-thirty." She pointed at a backpack on her desk. "There are blankets there in case you want to sleep. I brought some energy bars, too."

She herself had no trouble coming or going past the guards at the entrance to the tunnel. Not only was she the boss, she was a professor. Eccentricity and late nights were expected. But for me to get out, I would have to fall in with the tourists in the morning.

"Thank you."

When the professor got to the door to the hollowed-out room, she turned. "When you need to go, piss right over the edge."

I appreciated the practical bent of the professor's mind, but before I could answer, the door slammed behind her. Before the echo stopped, I was swinging the pick again.

It was therapy. I didn't think about what I was going to do with my life or my pending divorce. I didn't even worry whether the Ark would be there after these nights of labor. No thoughts could be heard over the shrieking of ligaments and muscles. After a dozen swings of the pick and the dozen grunts that accompanied them, I, or rather the automaton I'd become, just shoveled out the dirt and cast it over the side.

Then I remembered what the dirt hitting below reminded me of. Burying my grandfather.

* * *

The next morning when I walked out the end of the tunnel, the professor was waiting for me.

"Again tonight?" I asked.

"No. It's the Sabbath. No work on Shabbat."

"Okay."

"Come to my place. We'll have dinner."

"No, I don't want to trouble you."

"Providing hospitality to a guest is a mitzvah. Besides," she said, running her eyes from my feet to face, "you look like you can use a day of rest."

Chapter 15

When I was in my early twenties, I'd spent six months living at Lake Tahoe playing blackjack with my friend Mark. We'd done well, making a couple thousand a week counting cards. We weren't kicked out. I guess it was too little for Harrah's to care. Anyway, we played from around eleven at night till six in the morning. I'd been suited for a night owl's schedule then and still was. With a Do Not Disturb sign dangling from the outside doorknob, I'd slept in my room at the Sheraton from ten in the morning until eight. At nine I was sitting in the professor's flat, the second floor of a big house on Masaryk Street.

"Why do they call this neighborhood the German Colony?" I asked her.

"Because this is where the Germans congregated in Jerusalem in the days of the Ottoman Empire."

"Not too many left? Ooh." I grimaced.

"You okay?"

"Fine." If not for the pain that shot up my back with each twist or step, I might have counted my night of tunneling as a dream.

"Anyway, the Germans have been replaced by Americans and other foreigners."

"Why Masaryk Street? Masaryk was Czech, not German."

"If not for the Czechs selling us arms in 1948, Israel might have lost the War of Independence."

"Ah. Now let me ask an unrelated question. Why are you really helping me?"

"I'm an archeologist. Finding the truth of what happened here in Jerusalem in the thousand years before the Common Era, well, that's my job."

"That's what you said before. Is that all?"

"The rebbe sent you..."

"Were you really a follower of his?"

"More a great admirer. And then you are the father of my favorite student. Do you know the story of Joseph and his brothers?"

"Sure. Generally. Joseph was his father's favorite. His brothers were envious and sold him into slavery in Egypt. He became the pharaoh's chief advisor. They all met again when the brothers came to Egypt during a famine." Who hadn't seen *Joseph and the Amazing Technicolor Dreamcoat*?

"Okay, but here's my point. When his brothers begged for forgiveness, Joseph told them it wasn't their fault. He understood it had all been part of God's plan. If he had not been sold into slavery, he would not have been in Egypt to sell them the grain they needed to survive."

"You're saying my being here is part of some kind of divine plan?"

"Who knows?" She shrugged. "Monday I'll get you made an official part of the archeological team. If you can email me a passport-type photo, I'll get you an ID card. It will help you enter and exit from the tunnel."

"But then if they find me digging, you'll be blamed," I said. "You would be interrogated."

"I'll deny you knew anything. Wait—will they torture me?"

"Be serious."

"Okay. No promises of what I'll say under torture, but otherwise vehement denials."

Laughing, she said, "Come, I've got some cooking to do."

In the kitchen she handed me a beer bottle. Amidst the Hebrew characters on the label, I could read "Dancing Camel" in English. A first sip. Not bad. I took a long quaff. Not bad at all.

"Can I help?" I asked.

"You've done enough work today. Sit down."

I hoisted myself onto a barstool at her wood-topped kitchen island and watched the professor glide around her kitchen. Maybe DNA directed what I did, maybe my fate was determined by the way my father brought me up, maybe my grandfather's request could not be refused, or maybe it was God the playwright scripting my role in a divine comedy. Whichever, I didn't much care for the idea that I wasn't making my own decisions. Still, here I sat in Jerusalem, and I'd have a difficult time explaining why, except that the alternative was sitting in my office back in California staring out the window.

Enough philosophizing. I refocused on the professor. She was dressed in a pleated white blouse, a green skirt, and ballet flats.

"Why don't you have your scarf on?" I asked her.

"Because I'm home."

"But not alone."

"What I do here is my business."

"But you keep kosher, don't you?" She had two ovens, two sinks, and two dishwashers so that milk and meat wouldn't mingle.

"Yes." She unwrapped a butcher paper package on the counter to reveal a white-bellied, gray-scaled fish more than two feet long. Laying it on a board, she lopped off its head with a single downward stroke of a carving knife and ran a smaller knife along its spine. Then she unfolded the fish, stuffed it with cloves of garlic, and delivered it via two spatulas to a griddle sizzling with oil.

"And that is?"

"What it's going to be is pan-seared branzino. Sea bass from the Mediterranean."

She reached for her wine glass with her left hand and for the first time I noticed a gold band.

"Where's your husband?" I asked.

She dropped her glass and shards went flying.

I leapt off my stool. "Let me clean this up."

"No, no. My fault. You asked a logical question. You see, I don't wear the ring when I'm at work. Too easy to lose."

"I do see."

In the outside world she wore a scarf, but at home her hair sprang free. At home she wore a ring, but in the tunnels her fourth finger remained bare. She moved her legs into a wider stance and crossed her arms over her chest. The glare of the overhead lights ricocheted off the green of her eyes. If El Al put a picture of her standing like that on a poster, its planes would touch down at Ben Gurion crammed with lonely middle-aged men.

"No, I don't think you do. My husband is dead."

"Oh, God. I really put my foot in it, didn't I? Sometimes I talk, talk before I think."

"No, it's okay. It's been a long time." She uncrossed her arms.

"I'm sorry."

"He was in the army. He was killed in Lebanon." She held her hands palms up.

"That must have been tough." I stood there useless and inadequate.

After a few moments, she took pity on me and restarted the conversation. "Yeah, we met while I was at Hebrew U. for my junior year abroad."

"Abroad? Uh, I don't understand. You're not Israeli?"

She freed a hand and used it to whisk a tendril of hair off her forehead. "Of course I am. But I wasn't born here, if that's what you mean. After I met Ophir, well, I stayed."

"Oh. I did think you were born here."

"I don't have a Hebrew accent when I speak English, do I?"

"You don't. It's the inflection, the rhythm of your sentences that sounds Israeli."

"No wonder. I've been here for more than twenty years. But dig deep enough and Becky Goldschmidt from Boca Raton is still down there."

"Becky Goldschmidt? You changed your name." Brilliant, Sherlock.

"Guilty. When Golda Meir lived in Milwaukee, she was Golda Meyerson. Why shouldn't Becky Goldschmidt become Rivka Golan?"

"You changed *both* of yours," I said.

"Yeah. I went whole hog."

"Is that an appropriate expression for someone who keeps kosher?" I offered a clumsy half-smile.

Laughing—whether at my discomfort or my joke, I didn't know—she said, "Let's light the Shabbat candles."

She took a shawl from a drawer and tented it over her red hair. After lighting two candles, she waved her hands over them, a sorceress casting a spell. Then she brought her right hand up to cover her eyes. I watched her face, scrunched with concentration, as a Hebrew incantation tumbled out of her mouth in a half-whisper.

When she opened her eyes, she blinked several times as if surprised to find herself here in the kitchen of her apartment.

Dinner was delicious, the conversation a little stilted. Stilted, even though—or perhaps because—we did not mention her late husband Ophir again.

On the way out I spotted two framed photos on the middle

shelf of her bookshelf in the living room. They showed same lanky man in uniform, but one looked as though it were taken ten years before the other. In the earlier one he wore a happy smile that contrasted with the deadly serious rifle he had hoisted over his shoulder. In the other he stood on a hill with binoculars in his hands. This time his expression indicated he didn't like what he'd seen.

"Your husband," I said.

"Here," she said, picking up the photo of the man with the binoculars. "This was the last photo taken of him. He was dead five hours later."

"Oh, God. How terrible." Eloquence was called for, but I had none to offer.

She put down that photo and picked up the other one. "This is our son."

"I didn't know you had a son. He looks like his father."

"It's as if my husband still lives. My son is nineteen and in the army, too."

"He wants to stay in?"

"He volunteered."

"I thought everyone went into the army."

"Not if a parent has been killed. He needed special permission."

"That's hard. You must be proud of him, though."

"Of course," she said.

"What is your son's name?"

"Ori."

"Where is he now?"

"By the Gaza Strip."

"How often do you see him?

She smiled. "He pops up every month or so."

"You must worry."

"And don't you worry about Katie?"

"Of course," I said.

"It's a parent's plight."

"What will you do tomorrow?"

"I'll go to my shul. And you?"

"Rest my weary bones."

"Rest is what Shabbat's for."

Our handshake goodbye at her front door seemed awkward.

The imprint on my right hand of warmth and roughness—left behind by long, calloused fingers—had almost faded away by the end of my twenty-minute walk back to the hotel.

Chapter 16

Bruce the Giants Fan spun the Sheraton's revolving doors for me when I returned.

"You sure you want to be out in the dark after what happened yesterday morning?" he asked.

I thanked him again for his help and headed up to my room. It was Shabbat, and the elevator stopped at every floor. That way the Orthodox wouldn't have to push a button and violate the Sabbath by doing what they considered work. For the next five hours, I read a Bible I'd borrowed from the front desk, taking sporadic breaks for toothbrushing. The latter did little to eliminate the garlicky aftertaste of the professor's delicious dinner, but the former served a useful purpose. If I were on a treasure hunt, the Bible was the pirate's map.

The Book of Deuteronomy described the Ark as a simple wooden box where Moses stored the tablets he'd received on Mount Sinai. In the Book of Numbers, the Ark was said to be made of acacia wood and rimmed in gold with the arms of two cherubs stretching over it to form a throne for God.

Just before the time of King David, the Philistines captured the Ark. But after being afflicted by plagues of mice, boils, and hemorrhoids—this was three millennia before the invention of Preparation H—they returned it to the Israelites. David founded the City of Jerusalem, but God, the old stickler, wouldn't let him build the Holy Temple on account of a small matter of murder. You see, David had knocked up the delectable Bathsheba. Her husband was away at war, so there was no passing the pregnancy off as a product of her marriage. What's a king to do? Well, as I read in Second Samuel, this one made damn sure the unlucky spouse was killed in battle. I was surprised. The whole story sounded as though it had been plotted out by an Iron Age precursor of Jackie Collins.

In the end, it was David and Bathsheba's son Solomon who received the divine okay to build the Temple. After the priests installed the Ark in a special room, the Holy of Holies, the Temple filled with a cloud that indicated God's presence. As I made my way through the Prophets and Writings, I reaffirmed what the good professor had told me. In the section of the Book of Ezra that describes the rebuilding of the Temple, there's nary a mention of the Ark. The professor had argued that the Israelites would have put the Ark back in the Holy of Holies of the rebuilt temple if they had recovered it. Sounded reasonable enough. But what bothered me was the complete absence of any mention *at all* of the missing Ark. Shouldn't the ancient scribes have noted its disappearance when the Second Temple was built? Psalm 137 reported the Israelites wept in exile by the shores of Babylon and promised never to forget Jerusalem. Shouldn't they have lamented the disappearance of the Ark? The Ark that contained the tablets given to Moses by God, that allowed them to win battles, that gave the Philistines piles. What was going on? Knowing Jerusalem had been conquered once, could the Israelite powers-that-be have thought it safer to leave the Ark in a hidden vault than to move it back to the showroom upstairs?

* * *

It was exactly 9:57 when I opened one eye to peek at the alarm clock on the nightstand. It was Sunday morning. There'd be no digging until the evening. So I ducked in the shower, pulled on some clothes, and headed over to Ben Yehuda Street. Sunday was not the prescribed day of rest in this country. Boutiques and restaurants were open, and the plaza teemed with people.

"What the hell!"

No, not another attempted mugging. A man sporting a black hat, white shirt, and dark beard had grabbed my left hand. If a pickpocket, he was the world's worst. Then he started to wrap leather thongs around my arm as if taming a wild horse.

"You need to pray," the man said, paying no attention to my profanity.

I tried to shake my hand out of his grasp. I don't like being touched by strangers. Within a few seconds the two of us reached a stalemate. He wanted to wrap more leather around my arm, and I wanted to get the two twists of leather straps off it.

"What are you trying to put on me?" I asked.

"*Ha-Shem*'s words are in the box."

Yup, there was a small black receptacle at the end of the leather straps.

"No, thank you."

"You must. *Ha-Shem* has told us 'You shall bind them upon your hand.'"

"Bind what?"

"The *shema*."

"The what?"

"Ah, you are not Jewish." Not in his mind, anyway.

Two seconds after I'd yanked my hand away, the man began wrapping the leather around another passerby's arm. The woman with him squealed, "Oh look, Normie. He's putting *tefillin* on you. This is so cool." I moved on.

The rumblings of my stomach reminded me that I had eaten only five cardboard-y energy bars since dinner at the professor's thirty-six hours before—it wasn't easy finding a restaurant open in Jerusalem during Shabbat. Here on Ben Yehuda, I picked up the Israeli equivalent of a Big Mac, a pita sandwich of hummus —a smooth chickpea spread—and falafel—another manifestation of chickpeas, this time as deep-fried brown spheres. My gut was close to cast-iron. Growing up when Silicon Valley was covered with orchards—before a forest of tilt-up concrete buildings replaced them—I used to down an entire three-pound bag of dried apricots with no ill effects. My friends writhed on the ground after eating half as much. Here in King David's City, I'd found my gastric kryptonite. The falafel rumbled and rolled, loose cannonballs careening around my midsection.

Exercise seemed like the best remedy, so I kept walking. Stopping at a jewelry store, I practiced my bargaining skills. I headed toward the exit twice before buying Katie a pair of gold-hammered earrings for a third less than they were marked. If I'd spoken Hebrew, I bet I could have had them for less, but I still enjoyed the sport of give-and-take. At a bookstore, I picked up an English-language Bible to replace the one I'd borrowed. I paid list. It seemed a little sacrilegious to haggle over the price of the Holy Book.

Back at the hotel, I soaked away residual soreness in the tub. By the time I finished, I'd digested the falafel and so headed downstairs to the restaurant where I stored up the fuel I'd need for a night on the one-man chain gang. I wolfed down three thousand calories worth of scrambled eggs, smoked fish, pasta, bread, salad, and fruit.

The darkening skies boded sunset as I left the hotel and headed to the Old City. When I entered the tunnel at four-thirty Sunday afternoon, a female guard, Uzi slung over her shoulder, nodded as though she remembered me. As I waited in my niche for seven o'clock, I considered the professor's idea of becoming an honorary archeologist. By seven-ten, even that thought had left my head as I switched to my secret identity as the Human Jackhammer. Maybe my subconscious, affected by the Bible reading, spurred me to swing the pick and wield the shovel just a bit harder and faster. My left arm ached a little extra thanks to its rendezvous with a bat on Ben Yehuda, but not that much more than my right.

As I widened the hole, a glacier of dirt crept forward over my feet. I tossed shovelful after shovelful into the pit below. I don't remember much, but after a few hours, I did piss over the railing onto the dirt below and played a game of seeing how few tosses of the shovel were required to cover the dampened mound.

By four in the morning, I could climb through a hole in the stones and stand up on the other side. I took the compass the professor had provided to determine which way was east and then shoved a spade into the wall of dirt before me.

When I reentered the tunnel late Monday afternoon, I wore a newly purchased *kippah* and carried my Bible. The same guard who'd nodded at me the day before looked right through me this time. I was just one more religious fanatic who wanted to worship as close to the Holy of Holies as possible.

Chapter 17

"You did it," the professor said.

It was Thursday night, the night before the two days off that Shabbat would bring.

"What?"

"Look." She held her Maglite—some things we Americans still make best and that brand of flashlight is one of them—up to a hole about the size of a dinner plate.

I stuck my head up to the hole.

"I smell something unpleasant."

I moved away, and the professor put her narrow nose where mine had just been.

"What are you, a bloodhound?" she asked. "But I do smell a little mustiness."

"It reminds me of when a rat got caught behind the wall at home."

"We're not going to let that stop us, are we?"

I shook my head.

"You've done a great job," she said.

"For an old man."

"A great job."

"Well, you'd said we'd get through tonight," I said. That was why she'd joined me. "I followed instructions."

I'd been the one who swung the pick, and she'd been

carrying the dirt back out of the tunnel. Now, like a dog digging for a bone just below the surface, she was scratching at the hole.

No musty odor was going to stop us. She was driven by curiosity, maybe even professional ambition. I wasn't sure what impelled me, but impelled I was.

"Move away," I told her.

I flailed away at the hard clay until the hole expanded from the diameter of a dinner plate to that of a manhole cover.

"I can make it through," she said.

"Let me widen it a little further."

"I'm okay."

She couldn't wait any longer. I stepped away. "Go ahead," I said. She deserved it.

She glided through the portal, which was a little longer than she was. My turn. I slid on my belly, but I got myself wedged in anyway. The narrow passage seemed to close in. I began to breathe faster.

"Here we go." The professor grabbed my hands.

"Twist on your side," she ordered.

"You were right. We should have widened that hole further," she said once she'd pulled me through.

"It worked out fine." My heart was still pounding at double speed.

I had to hunch over in the tunnel we'd just found, but the professor could stand erect. I stamped my feet to shake out the clods of dirt that had made it down my jeans as the professor pulled me out of the passage.

"Men were shorter twenty-six hundred years ago," the professor said.

"Is the tunnel that old?" I asked.

She shone her light on the wood supports along the sides and across the top.

"No. Well, at least the supports are modern. Getz and Goren must have dug this tunnel. See here."

I came over and leaned over her shoulder.

"Feel," she said.

I ran my hand over one of the supports.

"What am I supposed to feel?" I asked.

"If you'd felt rough axe or chisel marks, the wood could be from ancient times. This is smooth, sawed in a lumber mill."

"Two old rabbis did this?"

"Goren had been the army's head rabbi. He knew where to get help." She paused. "You still smell something?"

"Maybe. I'm not sure anymore."

"Me, I do feel something. It's like a magnet." She dropped to one knee. It was her way to give me permission to stop hunching. I followed her example.

"You're excited?" I asked. Silly question.

"I couldn't wait to get in this tunnel, but now I want to soak in the moment."

"Okay."

In the overlapping coronas cast by our flashlights, I could see her lips moving. Praying. For what?

Then she whispered, "You're different than me. For you it's the goal, not the journey."

"I'm fine. I'll wait till you're ready."

She stood up.

"Let's go."

Chapter 18

The professor strode forward, flash in hand. Hunched over as if ready to ring the bells of Notre Dame, I scuttled after her.

Climbing through the portal had been my first clue. Now, moving down the tunnel, the diagnosis was confirmed. I had come down with a case of claustrophobia. The ceilings pressed down on me, the walls pressed in. My gut clenched and my breaths came in short gasps. As long as I kept moving, I'd be fine. Or so I kept telling myself.

"Oof."

Focused on keeping the acorn of panic from sprouting into a full-grown oak, I'd run right into the professor. Thanks to the downward slope of the tunnel, she needed a few steps to stop.

She turned to face me.

"Sorry," I said.

"It's okay. I can see the tunnel widens just ahead."

She turned and waved the flashlight. The underground artery we'd followed had an aneurysm. Ten steps and I could stand erect, even spread my arms out without touching the walls. I focused on controlling my breathing. Although the air in the tunnel was cool, I wiped my forehead with my sleeve.

"You okay?" she asked. God knows what the professor saw in the reflected light of the flashlight. As for her, in the muddy light she looked like a teenager playing around in a haunted house on Halloween.

"Sure. Fine."

"Right here we're moving from the extension of the Mount built by Herod to the original Mount Moriah of Solomon's time."

"I get it. You said the Western Wall was the outside edge of the extension."

"Right. That's where it ends, but here is where it begins."

She aimed her light at the passage at the other end of the aneurysm.

I walked across the widened area. "This hole was cut through stone," I said.

She used the flashlight in her right hand to look at the compass in her left. "The tunnel heads east-northeast." She was talking in gulps. "In no more than a hundred meters we should be directly under the Holy of Holies." What the narrow passage had done to my heartbeat, proximity to our goal was doing to hers. "You up for this?" she asked.

Was I? "Why not?" I replied.

My grandfather had asked me to do this. Finding the Ark would be like Columbus sighting land or Armstrong taking his giant step onto the moon. But they had fulfilled their destinies in wide open vistas. I could see that the continuation of the passage under the Temple Mount of King Solomon's time narrowed even further. The artery we'd been following was turning into a capillary.

"You know on Passover when we celebrate getting out of Egypt?"

"Sure." Even a pagan Jew like me occasionally scored an invitation to a Seder.

"Well, the Hebrew word for Egypt is *mitzrayim*, which literally means narrow places, places of confinement."

"Interesting metaphor for our situation," I told her. A little too literal for me. "Instead of escaping from *mitzrayim*, we're heading right into them."

The hole in the wall at the other end of the widened area was three feet off the ground. I made a cradle of my hands and boosted her. She in turn extended her arm and helped pull me in.

Ahead of me, she was as stooped as I'd been in the first tunnel. That left me walking bent over at the waist in a caricature of Groucho Marx, missing only mustache, cigar, glasses, and brothers.

After ten steps, my shoulders began brushing the sides of the tunnel. I had to walk turned at the waist.

This was worse than ever. If I keeled over with a heart attack, I couldn't be saved. Ten more paces and I might wedge myself in for all time, and the good professor would be entombed along with me. Part of me, the mental me, was looking down at my physical self. But that was only a third of my mind. Another third was busy panicking and the final third was staring at the outlined figure I was following into the bowels of the earth.

"Shouldn't be more than forty meters," my companion sang out.

The professor plugged the passageway. I could not see past her. "Can you see the end?" I asked.

"No, there's a turn up ahead."

Get a grip on yourself. Take a step. Now another.

Then the shadows flew everywhere as though someone had twisted a black-and-white kaleidoscope. I could see the professor's dark outline starting to founder. I took two quick strides and grabbed the waist of her pants. It was enough to break her fall, but not enough to stop it. She put out her hands. I saw the flashlight rolling in front of her and then heard a crackling like cellophane.

On all fours, like a baby ready to crawl, she said, "You are quick. What sports did you play in school?"

"What difference does that make?" I asked. "You okay?"

"Thanks to you. Well, what sport?"

"Swimming and water polo mostly."

"Good stop. You were goalie?"

"We can discuss my less than stellar athletic career another time. Can you get to the light?"

It shone five feet in front of her. "No problem."

"Just a sec. Let me get my light." The backup was hooked to the back of my belt. "I'm letting go."

I flicked on my smaller and less powerful flash. The professor screamed.

Her knees rested between the pointy hips of a corpse. Her hands rested on either side of a skull with bone showing through tattered cloth and parchment-like skin. The mouth was stretched open in a death grin, long yellow teeth showing through what was left of its lips.

At the end of the three or four seconds it took my brain to make sense of this horror-movie tableau, the professor was still shrieking. I pointed my light away from the corpse, back the way we'd come. That did it. She stopped.

I couldn't see her as more than a dark shape, but I knew her chest was heaving as she found herself inches from a macabre embrace.

About a half minute later, she said, "I'm sorry. I'm usually calmer than that. It was the shock."

"Natural enough."

"I'm sorry to have behaved so unprofessionally. God, I hope I didn't ruin this body. I know I cracked the pelvic bone." She took in gulps of air between words. "What now?"

"Can you get to your flashlight?"

"Yeah. Let me catch my breath."

I waited.

"Let's examine what we have here," she said. "Would you shine your light back this way so I can climb over our friend here without doing any more damage?"

"I'll help you get into a crouch. Reach back with a hand."

I moved between the splayed legs of the body. No anatomy expert, I saw tendons and bones peeking through the material the deceased had worn.

Hoisting the professor up with one hand, I held my light in the other. As if moving through a minefield, she put a foot down between an arm and the ribcage and then another over its head.

"It makes sense there would have been guards on the way to the hiding place of the Ark." She was muttering, forming a theory on the fly. "Sealed in here with no oxygen, well, that could explain why the body is more mummy than skeleton."

I admired the quick transition she made from fright to reason. "And what could have happened to him?" I asked her.

"He could've been killed to keep the location of the Ark secret."

"A little bloodthirsty, isn't it?"

"Different times." She snatched the Maglite and whirled around. "Got it."

"He might have been killed to keep a secret but not twenty-five hundred years ago."

"What do you mean?" she asked, raising the light.

I held up a hand to shield my eyes from her beam. "They didn't wear jeans back then, did they?"

Chapter 19

"What are you talking about?" she said.

"Take the flashlight off my face and aim it at our friend on the ground."

"Oh, sorry." She did what I said. Then she leaned over and took a piece of fabric between her fingers and rubbed. "Denim."

"I don't know what the Israelite helots or serfs or whatever wore back in the time of Nebuchadnezzar..."

"But you wouldn't bet on Levis," she finished.

"My grandfather said he was in the tunnel. I guess he and his chums weren't the only ones, were they?"

"Unless..."

"Unless a bunch of old men, who, by the way were rabbis, were killing to keep their secret?"

"I didn't mean to imply that," she said.

Taking my own light—I was never sure whether to think of it as a giant penlight or miniature flashlight—I started a closer examination of the corpse-mummy.

"He looks Arab," I said. My light shining on his face showed some hairs on his upper lip and a dark complexion.

"His skin probably changed color after death. Even if it didn't, dark skin doesn't tell us much. Egypt, Syria, Yemen, Iraq all kicked their Jews out, and they came here. You can't tell the difference between Jews and Arabs by looking at them."

I tugged at the remnant of the striped shirt. The teeth of the dead man chattered as the fabric pulled free.

"Uh, leave it alone," the professor said. "We shouldn't move it."

"Look," I said, holding the label out for her inspection.

"Oh." She saw it was in Arabic. "It says 'Darwish Tailor Shop, Riyadh.'" The last word had been in English characters as well.

"Wait," I whispered.

"What?"

I pulled up the raggedy shirt a little higher. "Shoot the beam right here," I said pointing toward the right side of his ribcage.

She did as I asked, and there it was again—a metallic gleam. Aiming the beam of light right at it revealed a shattered rib in front and, lodged in another rib bone in back, a dull gray bullet.

"Sharp eyes," she said.

The professor brought her face within an inch or two of the remains.

"Can't tell for certain," she said, "but I'd guess it's from a nine-millimeter semi-automatic."

An expert on firearms as well as antiquities? "Well, no doubt how he died," I said.

"We need to go to the police."

"What will we say?" I asked.

"Let me think."

"How about 'Excuse me, officer. I've been hiding this crazy American in the excavations I'm in charge of and we've opened up a tunnel that the authorities sealed off and...'"

"We still need to go to them."

"No. You'll lose your job."

"That's for me to decide."

"You're right. Let's discuss this later." Israeli bureaucrats would be no different from their American colleagues. I wasn't interested in red tape. I'd spent a week digging like an inmate trying to tunnel out of San Quentin. I don't know how it happened, whether it was splitting with Veronica or falling under the spell of my grandfather, but I was digging for my freedom, too. An escaping convict wouldn't call for a prison guard when thirty yards from the last fence, and I wasn't about to either. "Can we go ahead and take a peek around the corner? You said it was only a few more meters."

She looked down at her watch. "We should head back."

"C'mon, another thirty meters."

She shrugged and then took a deep breath. "Okay."

I knew I was playing dirty. No archeologist who ever lived could resist what might await us. I followed the professor as the tunnel began to loop. If her flashlight had been a magnifying glass, she would have been doing a creditable impersonation of Sherlock Holmes on the trail of Moriarty.

Ten more steps. "Wait." She stopped and shined her beam on a rusty-colored patch of dirt.

I crouched down. "Dried blood?" I asked.

"Looks like this fellow was shot, retreated here, bled, and died," she said.

Eight more paces and she stopped again. She lifted her light slowly. We'd come up against a blank wall. When her light reached halfway up, she stepped forward and rapped against it. "Wooden door," she said.

"If it was put up by the ancient Israelites, it's gotta be pretty old. How solid can it be?"

I brushed by the professor and threw my shoulder against it.

"Evidently, pretty solid," she said.

"Let me try again."

"This is not a good place to break a shoulder." She used her flashlight like a paintbrush, playing the beam up and down the door as if covering it with a fresh coat of Sherwin-Williams. "There." Inside the disk of light appeared a bolt.

I reached across the professor and tried to push it aside.

“You’re not going to be able to move it. It’s locked.”

“Locked? Locked two-and-a-half millennia ago?”

“Yes. You need a key. I’ve seen locks like this from Egypt and Mesopotamia, but never from here. This is a discovery in itself.”

“Terrific, but how do we get to the other side?”

“The lock works like a modern one. The pins of a wooden key push the lock pins out of the holes, then the bolt can be moved and the door opened.”

“We don’t have a key.”

“Shouldn’t be too hard to pick, but not now. We’ve got to go.”

Chapter 20

"What did he say?" I asked the professor.

"He said, 'You're in early.'"

We'd passed one of the professor's co-workers coming into work as we walked through the main tunnel. He'd stopped as though expecting an introduction, but the professor hadn't broken stride. Brusqueness seemed an essential ingredient of the Israeli character. He'd get over it.

Neither of us said anything as we high-tailed it through the Street of the Chain and David Street. I was too busy thinking. What should we do about the dead body? Nothing we did would make any difference to him. If Katie had been abducted, I'd drop anything, do anything, give up anything to get her back. That's the kind of compulsion I—for reasons unknown—felt toward that Ark. We'd been so close. I knew it.

As we drew closer to the Jaffa Gate, the exit from the Old City, I said, "I want to go back there tonight."

"It's Shabbat."

"There's no more digging to do. That means we wouldn't be working, just going for a Sabbath stroll."

"But we need to open that door."

"How hard can it be?"

"We could be stuck down there till Sunday morning."

"What better place to pray on Shabbat than under the Holy of Holies?"

"You know what *pilpul* is?"

"No."

"Arguing back and forth over the intricacies of the Law. You show a certain talent for it."

We passed through the narrow gate, an example of *mitzrayim* if ever there was one.

"I don't mean to argue," I said.

"What about the body? Don't *you* think we should go to the police?"

"I want to find the Ark."

"Then what?" she asked.

"What do you mean?"

"Once we find it, what do we do next?"

"I don't know."

"Come have Shabbat with me. We'll discuss what to do." She stopped. "I go this way." She pointed to Jabotinsky Street. I'd keep going back on Karen Hayesod for the two blocks back to the hotel.

Casting about for a decisive debate point, I stayed mum.

"Listen," she said. "I know you're thinking things over. You'll do a better job at that after a day of sleep. Come tonight, *kein*?"

"*Kein*," I said, the word for yes. My Hebrew vocabulary was expanding.

Here on Karen Hayesod at eight-thirty in the morning I was reminded of my business trips to Hong Kong. Everyone was in a hurry, and on the sidewalks pedestrians played a game of human pinball. Neither there nor here in Jerusalem did anyone waste breath with an "excuse me." I'm sure I made things worse by having my mind more focused on the tunnel I'd been worming along two hours ago than on the street I was walking down now.

It took a harsh, grinding noise to bring me back to reality. Perpendicular to traffic, a yellow bulldozer was turning right from the road but not at the intersection. I tilted my head and stared. The machine caromed off a parked Mercedes. I'd read about two incidents where terrorists used construction vehicles to kill pedestrians on the streets of Jerusalem. It seemed so unlikely, surreal, that I'd be in the midst of a third that I just stood on the sidewalk until the scoop's gaping maw was just twenty feet away.

The bulldozer, like its namesake, was a powerful beast, but not a nimble one. Heart and adrenal glands pumping at full power, I skittered off to the side like a matador as the bulldozer whooshed by me on the sidewalk and rammed its scoop into the gray stones of a building. A gush of pedestrians was cascading away from the bulldozer. Many of them had cellphones by their ears. Must be calling the Israeli equivalent of 911.

The bulldozer backed up and then came toward me for another go. The driver, dressed in a work shirt and jeans as if for a routine job clearing a construction site, gave me an empty glance. I might as well have been a mound of dirt. I jumped out of the way of the blade, but the machine quickly twisted toward me, and I faced the dark emptiness of that scooped blade again. I let it rush by. It missed by a foot. I turned my back and took two quick steps. Wait. Trying to outrun it wouldn't work. Instead of running away from the yellow beast, I leaped onto its running board.

I heard zinging now. Bullets were hitting the cab, but they weren't making it through the metal and Plexiglas. The driver kept going, his tongue between his lips as if making a particular effort to concentrate. He turned his wheel to the right and then found himself looking right at me. Until then, I don't think he knew I was up there, but the expression on his clean-shaven face didn't change anyway. He turned the wheel—he was going to try to scrape me off on the facade of the building.

Grabbing hold of a yellow bar, I moved down the running board until I was level with the cab. I'd been wrong—at least one bullet had hit the maniac driving the vehicle. A crimson stain was spreading across his right arm, but he kept his left hand on the steering wheel while his right hand worked the gear levers. He paid the wound no mind.

As though I'd been expected, Caterpillar Inc. had placed U-shaped handholds across the back of the bulldozer behind the cab. I pulled myself from one to the next to make it over to the street side of the machine, away from the buildings. When the driver turned to look for me back on the right, I was ready. I reached in through the open door of the cabin and, from behind, put my arm around his neck and began to squeeze. Then I brought my other arm up across the lower part of his face. He tried to turn around. He got far enough that I could see his eyes had popped wide open, whether with surprise or lack of oxygen I didn't know. I squeezed harder and did not let go when the bulldozer's serrated scoop rammed into a building again, stopping forward progress. As the engine roared with effort, the driver tried to pull my arms away. He was probably stronger than I was, but he was wedged into his seat and had little leverage. Thank God for the time I spent on those Nautilus machines back home.

How long do you have to cut off someone's oxygen before he loses consciousness? Two minutes? Help would be here before that. The driver dropped his hands from my forearm. When I turned back, I saw a knife heading toward my belly. Fuck. I tried to jerk out of the way. I didn't make it, but it didn't matter. The point hit my belt. There was no time to reason, but I knew I couldn't let go of his neck to go for the knife. That would free him for a better thrust. I squeezed harder. He wiggled the knife out of the leather. From there, he jerked it back over his shoulder toward my right eye.

The ten-inch blade was swooping toward my face when an

explosion of blood, bone, and brain erupted. I kept squeezing his neck—all that did was force a red gusher out of the hole where his ear had been. I let go and the driver slumped over. With him out of the way, I could see an extended arm, pistol in hand, reaching in through the other doorway into the cabin. Raising my eyes, I came to the face of Professor Rivka Golan framed by her headscarf.

Above the ringing in my ears, I heard her say, "Get down from there."

I followed orders. The bulldozer was between us and the crowd. I looked back up and saw the driver lying across the seat of the bulldozer. His striped green shirt had worked its way up his torso. I saw the hole above his left shoulder blade and the black hair on the back of his head.

My right eye was twitching.

"Listen. What were you doing? He was trying to kill you."

"And lots more people."

"The other people were smarter than you. Next time, if you're unarmed, do what they did. Run away from the person trying to kill you, not toward him."

"Where'd you get a gun?"

"From my pants pocket. I always have one with me. I'm a major in the IDF Reserve."

"Oh." The Israeli Defense Forces. It had sounded like the army was her rival when she'd talked about her son. So that's how she knew her calibers. Back in the tunnel, she'd said she was usually calm in an emergency. She had the training.

"The police will be here in a minute. If the police start questioning us, well, it will lead them back to the tunnel. Can you handle things on your own?"

"I thought you wanted to go to the police anyway."

"Can you handle it?" she repeated.

She'd saved my life. What could I say? "Yes," is what came out of my mouth. Bravado.

Then she reached up and pulled my head down. She gave me a kiss. Not an affectionate peck on the cheek, but a kiss on the lips that, deep as it was, lasted only a second or two.

"Don't worry," she said, when she pulled back. "You were sent here for a reason. If it's meant to be, we'll find the Ark."

She walked around the bulldozer and into the crowd on the street.

Chapter 21

No sooner had the professor—the major?—been swallowed by the crowd than police officers appeared on either side of me.

"You must come with us," said the younger of the two in thickly accented but understandable English.

"Am I under arrest?"

"You must come with us."

A hand grasped each of my upper arms. I wasn't exactly Moses. The sea of people scarcely parted as we struggled through. A lightly bearded man in jeans and parka made a grab for me. I tried to pull away, but the police frog-march prevented that. He started pumping my hand and saying some words in Hebrew. Then someone else pounded me on the back. Shouts hit my ears. Waves of people closed around us as I was pummeled, grasped, and yelled at. Did I now have a fan club? It took another minute to bob down the street and get into a squad car. Then we were surrounded by dozens more people waving and smiling at me. Ignition on, the car crept through the crowd.

"What were they saying?" I asked the crew-cut policeman who sat next to me in the backseat.

He lifted the left side of his upper lip, then his shoulders, and finally his two palms. He didn't speak English.

"Where are we going?" I called through the Plexiglas to his

colleague who I knew could communicate in English. But the driver either could not hear me or chose to ignore me. I yelled again, but again to no avail. So I sat in the backseat of an Israeli police car going who knows where.

What is going on? First, Mitch takes a bullet in the shoulder and now a bulldozer runs amok. And the common factor in both? Me. I was there, a bystander to violence both times. And that doesn't even count the mugging. What the fucking hell is going on?

The car stopped, and my escorts extracted me from the back seat. We'd pulled up in front of what looked like a hotel. It squatted atop a hill in the midst of other hills covered by scrub, sand, and gravel. I squinted. There were no other buildings nearby, but someone figured there would be soon. Amidst the bleak desertscape, I spotted three traffic circles that had been graded but not yet paved.

"Where are we?" I asked.

"The new Jerusalem police headquarters," said the driver.

"We are still in Jerusalem?"

"Yes."

Apparently, the city limits of Jerusalem were expanding.

Far removed from big city crime and squalor, the headquarters consisted of three connected blockhouses adorned only with three rows of small windows. After a brisk walk through bright shining corridors, I was shepherded into an interrogation room. There were eyebolts in the floor for connecting shackles, but my hands and legs remained free. I turned my head to peer into the big mirror to my right. For a moment I thought the figure in the mirror, haggard and drawn, was my grandfather as I'd last seen him. Chimpanzees in the zoo don't recognize themselves either when they see their reflections. Perhaps I'd slipped down a rung or two on the evolutionary ladder.

Time to get rational. In the past two years of sitting in my paisley chair back in Woodside, California, I'd read countless police procedurals. Thanks to what I'd learned from them, I knew I was looking into a one-way mirror and that people were watching on the other side. Again like a chimp in the zoo. I nodded politely. However, I did manage to refrain from scratching my armpits.

Leaving me alone in the room was, crime fiction had taught me, a tactic intended to make me more pliable. But why did they want me that way? I started to rerun the morning's events through the film projector of my mind.

* * *

A hand was on my shoulder. I'd dozed off.

"Mr. Kalman?"

The man before me hadn't shaved in a day or two and wore wire-rimmed spectacles, a blue polo shirt, and a gray polyester-ish jacket. As he sat down on the other side of the metal table, he lowered his head and I could see that the promontory of hair above his forehead would soon yield to the erosion of male pattern baldness.

"Am I under arrest?"

"No, Mr. Kalman. You are a hero. You killed a terrorist."

"It was not me. Do you know who fired the bullet who killed him?"

He shrugged. "So many Israelis are in the army and carry guns. A good reason for an unarmed American tourist not to play hero."

"Perhaps the line between heroism and foolishness is not always clear."

"Have you fought in war, Mr. Kalman?"

"No."

"Oh, that sounded like a soldier's comment." He rubbed his stubbly chin. "In any case it appears that Jerusalem is dangerous for you."

"I was in the wrong place. May I ask your name?"

"Cohen."

"That name must be pretty popular here in Israel." If we'd been in the States, I bet he would have said "Smith."

Ignoring me, he asked, "You were coming from where?"

"I'd been walking through the tunnel under the Wall."

"Just walking through?"

"I would like you to inform the American Consulate that I'm being held here." Mitch *had* said they were standing by to help.

"You may leave."

"Okay. Good. Thank you." I stood. He waved me back into my chair.

"Soon. Tell me what were you doing under the Wall?"

"What any tourist does."

"Does every tourist look for the Ark of the Covenant down there?"

"I beg your pardon?"

"The Ark was destroyed in Babylonian times."

"Perhaps."

"Experts say for sure. So I cannot see why you need to spend any more time in Jerusalem." He leaned forward and his jacket opened enough for me to see the leather straps of a shoulder holster. They reminded me of the bindings of the *tefillin*, but those had been encased a prayer in a wooden box, not bullets in a carbon steel cylinder. "We've been concerned about you."

"Concerned about me?"

"We were concerned you might cause some trouble during your visit."

"I'm causing trouble?" I began, hands extended in a gesture of openness, or maybe of exasperation. "I'm almost run down by a terrorist and that makes me a troublemaker?"

He tilted his head back and looked at me with a mixture of

curiosity, indulgence, and patience. When I realized he wasn't going to answer, I tried another approach. "So you are a police officer?"

"Of a sort," he said.

"Of the Shin Bet sort?" Shin Bet was the Israeli security service.

He smiled without showing his teeth and left the room.

* * *

"Apparently, it's not safe for you here in Jerusalem," Cohen said as he re-entered the room.

"What, someone is after me?"

"You should not take chances, and we cannot guarantee your safety."

"I never asked for a guarantee."

"I do hope you have enjoyed your vacation here in the Holy Land. I'd be glad to drive you to the airport."

"I would prefer to stay. I like it here in Jerusalem."

"Thank you. I'll consider that a compliment. I'm *yerushalmi*—a native of the city. We will go."

As we walked out the front door of the headquarters, I put my hand up to shield my eyes from the beams of desert light. After a few blinks, I saw in front of us a regular civilian sedan, a blue Renault.

I'd enjoyed the hospitality of the Shin Bet or the Israeli police or whoever they were for a total of twenty-four hours of questioning, eating, and sleeping. Now Mr. Cohen opened the passenger side door for me as if I were indeed a guest. No sitting in the back as I had in the police car.

When we were back on the road, I said, "Could you please drop me off at the Sheraton?"

"Why don't we go straight to the airport?"

"I don't want to just leave. I have people to say goodbye to."

"You can call them from the States."

What the hell? "This is all kind of Kafkaesque, isn't it?"

"You think you are being accused of something and you do not know what?"

"Yeah," I said.

"You are not being accused of anything. We cannot guarantee your safety. It's best for you to go home."

"I'm not a child."

"And you have your rights, too." He gave me an indulgent smile that said all Americans were naïve innocents amidst the *realpolitik* of the Middle East.

I looked down at my pants, filthy with the dirt of the tunnel, splattered by the blood of the bulldozer driver.

"Even if I were to leave, I need to stop by my hotel to change clothes and pack."

"Behind you," he said.

I turned to see my rolling bag reclining in the back seat.

"We packed for you. You can change at the airport," he said. "Call it Israeli hospitality."

"I still need to check out of the hotel."

He reached into an inner pocket in his jacket and handed me a hotel bill. "They left the charges on your American Express."

"And a plane ticket?" I asked.

"It awaits you at the airport."

"My passport?"

He reached back into his jacket pocket and handed it over.

We drove in silence for another fifteen minutes. Then he said, "All in all, a memorable way to spend your fiftieth birthday, wouldn't you say?"

I'd lost track of the date.

Chapter 22

"Cohen" was a human garage door opener. As we approached each security checkpoint at the airport, he would flash his ID and a piece of wide cloth tape would lift or a door would open. We didn't go through the standard explosive detectors nor did my bag join its brethren on the conveyor belt through an x-ray machine. Of course, I myself had nothing to hide. Cohen, though, did have that revolver—and maybe more.

Even with a stop at the men's room for me to change into a clean button-down and pair of khakis and toss the clothes I'd been wearing into a trashcan, what should have taken ninety minutes took barely nine.

We stopped at Gate 9E. "Here. This is your flight," Cohen said.

I looked at the board. "It says Flight 001, JFK."

"Yes, your flight."

I looked down at my watch. Flight 001 left at one in the morning. Four hours until takeoff. We wedged ourselves into adjoining plastic chairs, the type so common in air terminals, designed for discomfort.

After thirty minutes of silence, I asked Cohen, "Would you watch my bag? I need to go to the bathroom."

After taking a piss and washing my hands, I came out of the men's room and turned right, away from Cohen and the gate. I didn't really have a plan. Cohen wanted me to stay at the airport, so I wanted to leave. Perverse? Obstinate? Contrarian? Probably all three. I just didn't like being told what to do.

Halfway down the concourse, I saw Cohen, arms folded, waiting for me. God, I hated being so predictable.

"I was looking for something to eat," I said.

"I'll come along," he replied.

"What about my bag?"

"It'll be fine."

After all the security vetting everyone else had gone through, he was probably right.

As a last meal in Israel, I ordered—what else?—falafel and hummus on pita. While the boy behind the counter squeezed the fried balls into the bread's open pocket, I looked up at the LCD screen over his head. CNN International's plastic-haired announcer was moving his lips, but the sound was off. Then the picture flashed up a news video. Wait. The Caterpillar bulldozer was careening into the wall. The caption on the bottom of the screen read "Karen Hayesod Street, Jerusalem." There, there I was on the back of the 'dozer. Some tourist must have aimed a phone to catch the entire business, but whoever it was had been prudent. He or she had stood a hundred yards down the street —too far away for me to be recognizable. Still, the vantage point gave me perspective that I hadn't had while living through the event. Pedestrians were peeling away from the runaway machine. A pan shot showed a khaki-uniformed soldier shooting a handgun toward the cab from across the street. He stopped when I got close to the driver, but a female soldier with a long blonde braid stopped next to him, dropped to one knee, and aimed a rifle. A series of recoils showed she'd been sniping until I was all the way in the cab. It must have been one of her shots that hit the driver's arm.

I watched the action unfold as if at the multiplex back home —I identified with the figure on the screen just as I would

Daniel Craig or Matt Damon. The figure was grappling with the driver. I held my breath. I'd seen this movie before but still held my breath. Would the professor get there in time? I breathed out as the terrorist's head exploded and crimson rain showered down on the pants and shirt now in the airport trash. The unknown cinematographer's artistic pans must have caused the camera to miss the professor's approach. As the action unwound, it might have been the hand of God that reached down and squeezed the head of the driver until it burst.

"You are a lucky man." I turned around and saw Cohen's eyes focused on the screen.

When the boy behind the counter handed me my sandwich, I paid and then moved toward the garbage can.

"I'm not hungry after all," I said, about to fling it away.

"Wait," Cohen said. "I'll eat it."

By the time he'd finished, it was time to board.

As I stood to join the queue, Cohen seized my arm. "It doesn't make sense to come back here, does it? You may not be so lucky next time."

"What are the chances that I find myself in the middle of a random terrorist incident again?"

He shook his head. "Israel doesn't need any more trouble. You belong in America where it is safe."

I walked into the jetway. America safe? Where snipers lay in wait? Or Israel, where one was bait for man and machine, where one tripped over long-dead corpses? I really was a trouble magnet in both countries, wasn't I?

As the plane taxied into the night, I saw Cohen's stolid figure watching me from behind the plate glass of the terminal.

Chapter 23

To my surprise, in its hurry to ship me off, the Israeli government had sprung for a business class ticket. Coach must have been full. It was thirteen hours to New York. My preferences must have been in the El Al database: I had a window seat. But for the first time in my life, sitting between another person—a Russian with no English—and the porthole bothered me. I felt confined. Sure, this was better than being squeezed into a middle seat in steerage, but the aftershocks of the claustrophobia I'd felt in that tunnel were still rattling around my skull.

Somewhere over Greece, I did get to celebrate my birthday, even though in Israel it had ended two hours ago. But the plane ran on New York time where Sunday was still five hours away. Three flight attendants clustered in the aisle by my seat and began singing in Hebrew to the tune of "Happy Birthday to You." That database again.

The passengers around me were good sports and joined in. "*Yom huledet sameach, yom huledet sameach.*"

One of the attendants pulled a bottle from behind her back and popped off the cork. A flute glass was slapped down on my tray table and a few drops of bubbly pale-straw liquid overflowed onto my pants. She put the bottle down on my table, but when I said, "No, please for everyone," the nearby passengers all received a swallow or two of the liquid in their Styrofoam and plastic cups.

I drained my glass to the lilting *l'chaims* of the attendants and the shouted *do dna* of my neighbor, responded to a question in accented English by admitting to a half-century on this planet, and then finally extricated myself from the impromptu celebration by claiming fatigue.

After a minute or two of eyes closed, I peeked. The white buds of an iPod were stuffed into the ears of the Russian next door. His eyes were closed, and his head bopped up and down in rhythm to whatever he was listening to. No one else was paying any attention to me anymore. Good. The bottle was back on my tray table. I was a beer drinker by predilection but it seemed inhospitable to ignore the remaining half inch that swished around. Into my glass it went. Happy birthday to me. Bottoms up.

What next? I fingered the bottle. Gamla Brut. *Méthode champenoise*. From the Golan Heights Winery.

Golan. Rivka Golan. Professor/Major Rivka Golan née Becky Goldschmidt. I shut my eyes and felt her kiss again.

Then my eyes popped open. Cohen had known I was looking for the Ark. He'd said nothing about the professor. But she'd been involved, too. Wouldn't he know about her, too? Had she turned me in? I felt disloyal thinking about it, but had she? What could her game be? If she didn't want to look for the Ark, why smuggle me into the tunnel in the first place? If we'd found the Ark, I could see why the Israeli government wouldn't want the world to know, but we hadn't. If she was just looking for unskilled labor, she could have done better than a fifty-year-old from nine thousand miles away. She couldn't have figured on the man in the bulldozer, could she? Did she want to make herself a hero? No, she'd walked away from any laurels.

In the end, though, it wasn't rational thinking that made me reject her as the one who had sicced Cohen on me. Katie had sent me to her. Through a commutative law of faith, the trust I had in my one child transferred to the person she'd sent me to. Or that's what I told myself. I worried for a few minutes that my reasoning had sprung from the memory of a woman's mouth against mine. So what? I decided it didn't matter and resolved to believe in the woman who'd given me that kiss. A kiss of truth, of *emet*.

Who, then, had fingered me?

Chapter 24

My phone rang. I looked down at the Caller ID before pushing the talk button.

"Yeah, John."

"Alex, sorry to bother you so early on a Sunday morning, but I've been trying to reach you all week."

"I've been out of the country."

"So, how are you? What's it been, three years?"

"Could be," I said. "John, you're calling on a Sunday. What's up?"

"Right to business, huh? How are Veronica and Katie?"

John Burste was a managing director at Everest Partners, a top-tier Silicon Valley venture capital firm. Backing my start-up had added nicely to their oversized returns. If John really cared about my personal life he might have checked in a little more often than triennially. In fact, he'd probably looked up the names of my wife and daughter in some contact manager before the call. I did remember his third wife was Delia, a tall blonde who'd been working in PR when John met her at the Demo Conference a few years ago. I didn't ask about her, for fear he'd moved on. He had divorced his first two wives, both also blonde, before they'd reached their third anniversaries.

"Thanks for asking," I said. "What's up?"

"Well, Alex, when it comes to new technology aimed at

business and infrastructure, lots of the big venture capitalists are like brood hens sitting on their nest eggs right now. There are whole sectors they're not investing in, like enterprise software, for example."

In the old days someone like Arthur Rock would take a real chance on a few chip engineers and end up backing what turned into Intel. Or back two long-haired computer hackers and jump-start Apple. Ancient history.

"There aren't too many old-style venture capitalists left, John. Most VCs today would rather clip coupons or invest in a videogames company whose latest release features talking zebras."

"Yes, Mr. Sweetness-and-Light. Here's the idea. You know our software-as-a-service company, CrucialPoint?"

"There was talk of them going public last summer."

"Well, they're cash-flow positive, and we want to make them the vehicle to buy start-ups around the Valley with good products and employees."

"How much you going to invest?"

"Sixty mill."

Plenty of companies around the Valley needed a stream of capital to make it across the Sahara of starting a business. With sixty million you could have the pick of these corporate refugees.

"I apologize. That sounds like something a venture capitalist should be doing. Congrats. If you're calling to ask me if it's a good idea, I say yes." I had friends I could send John's way.

"I'm not asking your opinion of the idea. I'm asking you to get back in the fray. Enrico tells me he sees you at the gym every time he's there. Enough of that. You want to spend the rest of your life as a gym rat? C'mon, you're an entrepreneur, Alex. Get back in the game. We'll give you options for six percent of CrucialPoint. I know you don't need the money, but that doesn't matter. You don't want to while away your time on a treadmill to nowhere. Your daughter's away in college, right? Time to do something, make a contribution."

John knew how to push the right buttons. He didn't appeal to my greed. He couched his proposal in almost humanitarian terms—we could rescue good companies. He knew, too, that we'd get great prices. The crazy obsessives who started companies in Silicon Valley were motivated as much by seeing their dreams come to market as by mere money.

"You know, if we're too stingy in buying up companies, the employees will have no incentive to stay," I said.

Whoops—I'd said "we," and John's voice got oilier in response.

"Who better than you to do the balancing between incentivizing the employees and getting a good price?"

"Let me think it over, John."

"It would be great to be working with you again, Alex. Could you give me an indication of where your head is at?"

"John, I just got in from Israel. They say it takes a day to recover for each time zone you cross. Give me some time to get over the jetlag."

"You're not trying to put me off? You're really willing to think about it?"

John's partners would want a status report at the weekly partnership meeting tomorrow morning. That's why he'd called on a Sunday and why he was pushing me for an answer.

"I said I would."

"Great. Let's talk Friday then. Alex, it would be great to work together again."

"Yeah, John. It *would* be great to have you beating on my head with a two-by-four like in the old days. Isn't that why they're called board meetings?"

"C'mon, Alex. The company would be yours to run. Maybe we should sit down and talk about it."

"I'd like to, but I'm in Boston."

"So I didn't get you up early after all. Wait. You're not there talking to someone else about a job, are you?"

If I said yes, I could probably get another percent or two of CrucialPoint. "Nope."

"All right. You talk to your wife and get back to me by Friday. I'm calling on my cell. Gimme a call at this number with any questions."

"Thanks, John."

I pushed the end button.

At first, I'd booked a plane for San Francisco from JFK—to go home. Then I realized I had no real home there anymore, so instead I flew up to Logan. By ten, I'd checked back into the Faculty Club at Harvard. I hadn't even called Katie to tell her I was in town yet.

After a few minutes, I plugged in the electric kettle. Five minutes later I'd let the arms of a chintz-covered wingchair enfold me. It was about as ugly as my favorite place to sit back home in Woodside but, like my purple paisley, it made up in comfort what it lacked in esthetic appeal.

Hmm. I'd had other calls from headhunters, VCs, and former colleagues over the past couple of years. I'd deflected them all. The trip to Israel had changed things. John's timing was good. It *was* time to get back into the game. Which game, though?

I let the tea burn its way down my throat and let my little gray cells churn away in the background.

Chapter 25

I tapped the button on my phone's screen to call Katie. I had no desire to surprise her and Elliott *in flagrante delicto*. Once was enough.

"Hi, sweetie."

"Daddy."

"Anything wrong?"

"No, no."

I knew her. I'd caught her in the middle of something again.

"Am I calling at a bad time?"

"No, no."

"Sorry to keep popping up like this, but I'm back in town."

"Uh, great."

"Do you and Elliott want to go out for brunch?"

"Uh, Dad?"

"Yeah?"

"Mom's here, too."

"Oh."

"And we were going to meet *her* for brunch. You should join us."

"I don't want to interfere."

"Don't be silly."

"Only if it's okay with your mother."

"She's taking us to the Faculty Club."

"That's convenient."

* * *

Supposedly, a phoenix sings its sweetest song as, consumed by fire, its life ends. The end of our marriage appeared to have had an analogous effect on Veronica. I looked at her as though I were an art critic examining a portrait at the Museum of Fine Arts. In the last two weeks she'd undergone a restoration to her original splendor. No more purple smudges under the eyes. The lines at the corners of her mouth had disappeared. She wore a crimson coat, fitting for a visit to Harvard, and leather boots with three-inch heels that brought her closer to my own height. She leaned toward me and turned to offer her cheek. I paid her the obeisance of a peck.

Katie stood back, watching the tableau move to completion. Releasing Elliott's hand, she scampered over to me and threw her arms around my neck, just as she used to when I'd come home from the office fifteen years ago.

"Daddy!"

She folded her legs under her just as she had then, too, and I had to strain to prevent her weight from forcing me into an unrehearsed bow.

"Whoa, whoa. I'm not so young anymore, and you weigh more than thirty pounds now." My back still ached from digging in Jerusalem. I was going to pay further penance for that pretense of youth.

I shook hands with Elliott.

"How was your trip, sir?"

Sir? The courtesy contrasted with the picture, still vivid in my mind, of him bare-chested in Katie's room.

"Terrific. Thanks for asking."

At the buffet, I heaped smoked salmon, scrambled eggs, and salad on my plate.

Back at the table, Katie said, "Dad, it looks like you couldn't decide whether to eat breakfast or lunch."

"This is how I ate in Israel. I guess I got used to it." Of course, I wouldn't burn up calories digging all night here. I'd have to be careful.

"Tell us about the trip, then. Was Professor Golan helpful?"

"She sure was. I wouldn't have gotten anywhere without her."

"What did she think of what your grandfather said?"

"She was skeptical."

"What grandfather?" Veronica asked.

I explained.

"So that's why you ran off to Jerusalem," she said.

"I guess so. I figured why not?"

Veronica giggled. "Did you wear a fedora like Harrison Ford's?"

I bristled a little, but then relaxed. I'd thought along the same lines often enough. "Sure. And I carried a bullwhip, too."

"I've done some reading," Elliott said. "Your grandfather is not the only one who thinks the Ark may be below the Temple Mount."

Katie had spilled what she knew to Elliott. Well, I hadn't told her to keep it to herself.

Veronica leaned back on her chair as if distancing herself from the discussion.

It took twenty minutes to recount what I'd been up to in Jerusalem—omitting only the mugging, the clandestine nature of the digging, the Saudi corpse, the attack by the bulldozer, tangling with Cohen, and that last kiss. After the same amount of time catching up with Katie and Elliott, I pushed away from the table.

"What are the plans for the rest of the day?"

"We're going to the Gardner to look around," Katie said. She knew I loved the Isabella Stewart Gardner Museum for its

Italianate architecture, for its collection of John Singer Sargents, and for its notoriety as the site of the largest property theft in history. Stolen by person or persons unknown were paintings by Rembrandt, Degas, Manet, and Vermeer. Katie called my habit of stopping and staring at the thirteen empty frames left behind by the thieves "pathological."

"Why don't you come along?" Veronica asked. In the course of twenty years of marriage, I'd learned the language she spoke often sounded like English, but the meaning could be quite different. If she were forced to pick one more person to join them on their outing, I would have been around her seven billionth choice.

"You love the Gardner, Daddy." Even Katie couldn't interpret Veronica-speak as I could.

"No, thanks. I'm still jetlagged, beat. I think I'll work on the *Times* crossword."

An hour later, though, I was out for a run on the banks of the Charles. Along the riverside pathway of dead, brown grass, I navigated between couples walking, mothers pushing, and bikers riding. Most days I'd be taking in a lungful of car fumes with each breath. On Sundays, though, cars were barred from Memorial Drive. Splayed across the Coke-bottle green of the water, a scattered flotilla of rowing shells jerked forward with each sweep of their oars.

I'd gone out for crew myself freshman year when I'd been a stringbean, weighing in at 148 despite my six feet. A few days in the rowing tanks as a candidate for the lightweight boat convinced me to stick to water polo as my sport and running as my recreation. It wasn't the hard work. It was the sensory deprivation. You didn't know where you were. You weren't supposed to care. You had to focus on bringing the oars toward your chest and then thrusting back on your bench. That was all. In fact, digging under Jerusalem had brought back the same feeling. There, my world had extended no further than a shovel and the dirt in front of me.

As I worked up a sweat in the here and now, I stripped off my black Giants sweatshirt and tied it around my waist. It was February, but my kind of day nevertheless—the sun shining with a cold, distant light, the air crisp and pellucid. I watched the prows of the boats piercing the water. A runner could look around, know where he was, think things over.

Katie and Elliott. Huh. My last two years in college I'd lived with Florencia Mariscal. Both history majors, we'd shared classes, activities, meals, and a bed. What had happened? As a lark, she'd applied for a Rhodes Scholarship. She'd checked with me, and I'd encouraged her to go ahead. She won. She wanted to turn it down. I urged her to accept. I thought our love would triumph over a mere two-year separation. The naïveté of youth. So now she was an avatar for every woman in America with movies in her blood. The mother of three, she headed Hollywood's hottest studio.

As for me, I was pulled into the vortex of Silicon Valley. For the first five years after business school, I'd had no time for relationships with anything other than business plans, sales calls, and money-raising. To celebrate the first million-dollar deal at the company where I was V.P. of sales and marketing, I'd taken myself to the Stanford Theatre in downtown Palo Alto to see the classic film noir, *D.O.A.* When the lights went on after Edmond O'Brien figured out who'd poisoned him, I blinked a couple of times from the sudden brightness and then from what I saw—a woman in the row in front of me, two seats to the right. I said nothing to her but she turned as if I had and stared back at me. The French call it a *coup de foudre*, a lightning bolt. We kept our eyes locked until I said, "Uh, hi. I'm Alex Kalman." It sounds funny, but my fists were clenched shut and my breath came in gasps.

"Veronica Graves." Then she introduced her date, too. The poor slob had no idea what had just happened.

The next night I called directory assistance for Palo Alto and then neighboring cities until an operator found a listing for a V. Graves in Menlo Park. The line was busy—this was over twenty years ago, before voice-mail became ubiquitous, when lines *could* be busy. Five minutes later, I got through.

"Hello. Veronica, this is Alex...."

"Kalman," she said.

"Yes."

"I tried to call you five minutes ago," she said, "but your line was busy."

We were married four months later and had Katie only ten months after that.

The multiverse theory put forth by trendy physicists holds that there are an infinite number of universes. Each time any person makes a choice, a different choice is made in a parallel universe. That, of course, leads to different consequences.

What would have happened if I'd chosen to see *D.O.A.* the next night? What if a noise to my left had caused me to turn in a different direction at the end of the film? What is the Alex in that other universe doing? In that multiverse, he's probably single. Veronica always told me no one would put up with me except for her.

What if the drunk who'd run down my mother had stayed at the bar for a nightcap? In that universe, Aron never becomes Alex. He grows up in Brookline and is carried along by generational inertia to become a bearded rabbi in a white shirt and dark suit.

In *this* universe I'd screwed up my marriage to a good woman, and my dad had screwed up his relationship with his own father, and I did not even remember my mother. That's how the cards were dealt. Katie, though, was a royal flush. And so if I had to choose again, if I could live in any of the multiverses, I'd still pick this one where I married Veronica because our union produced Katie.

I looked up. Where was I? I recognized the Watertown Arsenal. I'd run three miles upriver while mulling over what universe to live in. I turned back toward Cambridge and let my mind wander again.

Now that I'd decided to stick with this universe, what was my next move? Parachuting into CrucialPoint made total sense. There I could do what I did best, use my experience. But I instinctively turned from making the predictable choice. A day after my father had told me I shouldn't leave a good job, I quit to do a start-up.

Dad's advice to me had always been conservative, but, as I'd learned a few weeks ago, he didn't follow the route mapped out by the GPS navigation system of his life either. He'd strayed from the ordained path, leaving Brookline and starting over in California.

I guess my obstinate genes were his legacy. Cohen was not going to keep me out of Israel. Screw him. If he told me I couldn't come back, I sure as hell was going to show up. If that Ark was there, I'd do my damnedest to find it. After two years of sleeping, exercising, and reading—living without feeling—I'd had nine days with a mission, a cause. Thank you, Grandfather.

I came out of my reverie. Across the river sprawled the blue-domed Georgian edifice that was the business school's Baker Library. I sped up and left it behind.

Chapter 26

I sat up in bed.

What time was it? I reached to turn the clock radio toward me. As I twisted it around in the dark, it tumbled over the edge of the nightstand. Despite the clatter, when I tilted its face up, I could see the red LCD lights shining. 2:07.

Then I heard a gentle rapping at the door. So it wasn't only jet lag that had kept me from sleeping to a reasonable hour.

I cracked open the door. There in the hallway stood Veronica, barefoot, belted into the white terrycloth bathrobe supplied with her room.

"May I come in?" she said with her eyes lowered like a little girl's.

Less than half a day after I decide to continue on my odyssey, I hear a siren's song.

"Sure," I replied, pushing the door all the way open. The robe's nubby fabric scraped against my arm as she floated by.

I jumped when the door slammed behind me. I blinked a couple of times after switching on the overhead light.

"Were you awake?" she asked. "I tried to knock softly so you'd only hear me if you were."

"It's okay for me to be up. It's breakfast time in Jerusalem."

Veronica retreated until her back was resting against the end of the four-poster bed. I needed support, too, and leaned against the closed door. We stood ten feet apart, eyes locked, hands at our sides, like two gunslingers in an old Western.

She drew first. "Do you ever think of how we met?"

"Just this afternoon when I was out for a run."

"It was something."

"Sure was."

"Are we going throw that all away?"

"I thought you had someone else."

"It's not like it was at the Stanford Theatre." She scrunched her face into a moue. "Should we try to find it again?"

"I don't think so."

She crossed over to me in three strides and put her arms around me. I hugged her back.

"Can't we try?" she asked. I felt her moist lips moving through my T-shirt. "What we had, what we felt, twenty years ago, we shouldn't throw it all away."

"I still have the memories. They'll always be there. I'm not going to throw them away."

She let me go and took a step away.

Her robe hung open. With each breath her still-firm, ruby-nippled breasts came an inch closer to me and then backed away. Her belly, even flatter than it had been twenty years ago, glistened as downy hairs caught the room light. I could feel blood rushing to my groin. Any man in his right mind would reach out to her.

I extended my arms.

Then I took the two open flaps of her robe and folded them over each other.

I tied her belt.

"I'm sorry," I said, and in a way I really was.

"I guess you'll be hearing from my lawyer, then." Her tone was filled more with regret than vengeance. She pushed by me, opened the door, and slipped into the corridor.

So in one day I'd resolved to turn away from a chance to go

back to what had made my life in Silicon Valley special—my marriage to Veronica and a job as a high-tech CEO. Now, my heart was in the East. What I needed was a plan.

Chapter 27

By Monday morning at eight I was running up the Charles in the opposite direction from the day before. I needed a run to get my subconscious working, to come up with my next move.

Yesterday I'd gone far enough to see the Charles narrow to an overgrown stream. Now, as I passed MIT, it broadened to a third of a mile across. Supposedly, some early explorer had figured it for the Northwest Passage rather than the very wide mouth of a very short river.

Memorial Drive was open again for business today. With each breath I sucked in the flatulence of a thousand automobiles carrying their passengers to work at universities, start-ups, hospitals, and downtown high-rises. I crossed from Cambridge to Boston at the Longfellow Bridge and started galloping down Charles Street until I turned right at the Public Garden on to Beacon Street.

First semester of freshman year, I'd thought of majoring in psychology, but after taking a couple of psych courses, I'd decided the operation of the human mind was better explained by the occult than by science. All this popped into my head as I slowed and recognized where I was. I stood before the house at 63 Windsor in Brookline, home of my late grandfather. My unconscious did not explain why it had brought me here, but I figured it was on my side in life's struggle. So I walked up the flagstone path just as I had a few weeks before and thrust an outstretched index finger at the doorbell.

A dark-bearded, white-shirted, black-suited young man—what else?—answered the door. "Ah, Mr. Kalman. Welcome. You'll want to see the rebbe." It was as if I'd been expected, but I doubted too many callers showed up at the front door of the Bialystoker Rebbe in running togs. My escort, though, did not even give a second glance to my Foothill College sweatshirt with a hole in the left sleeve, cotton running shorts with some logo too faint to read, or my relatively new Air Max 95s. We walked through the living room where my grandfather had died. The man gestured toward a heavy, dark oak door.

A quick knock and I heard a muffled "Enter."

Rabbi Natan Zweiback looked up from unraveling leather straps from his left arm as we walked in.

"Aron, I'm so glad you've returned." He spoke as if I were expected.

"Yes, here I am again. Thank you."

He laid what I'd learned in Jerusalem were called *tefillin* into a red velvet-lined box and gave me a bear hug that would have done Hulk Hogan proud.

I tried to pull away. "I've been running. I'm sweaty."

"Cousin, who cares? Sit. Sit. Please. This house is yours. You are welcome." He gestured over to a chrome pitcher on a round table. "Would you like some tea?"

This time I was ready for the thick sweetness of the beverage, but not the heat that burnt my tongue and throat.

After we'd sunk into the threadbare cushions of two chairs, he asked "You were off on your quest?"

"That's what you called it before. Do you know where my grandfather sent me?"

"No."

"I want to keep it secret."

"I have nothing to tell anyone," he said.

My grandfather really hadn't told him? Huh. I needed to shake off the cynicism of Silicon Valley. "I trust you. But I don't want you telling anyone else," I said.

The rabbi spent most of the forty minutes it took me to go through the story sipping his tea, pinching the bridge of his nose, and stroking his beard. He did interrupt twice, though. The first one came after fifteen minutes when I told him about finding the body in the tunnel. He muttered a few words of Hebrew.

At the thirty minute mark he interrupted again. "Wait. You were there in Jerusalem at the incident with the bulldozer?"

"Yes."

"I saw videos on CNN. People were running away as fast as they could. Praised be *ha-Shem* that you got away. It must have been terrifying. Were you close by?"

"Close enough, but I didn't have time to get terrified."

"It happened too quickly?"

"Yes, and afterwards I didn't have much time to reflect because I was picked up by two policemen."

The rabbi raised an eyebrow, and I picked up my narrative.

"Why did this Cohen ask you to leave?" he asked when I'd finished.

"You know as much as I do now." I lifted up the mug of tea for a last sip. Lukewarm. "He said I was causing trouble."

"They didn't want you looking for the Ark?"

"Apparently not."

"What are you going to do?"

"Go back to Israel."

"But Cohen sent you back to the States."

"Yes."

"So you return why?"

"Because my grandfather asked me to."

"But wouldn't there be trouble, even war, if the Ark were discovered?"

"My grandfather said to seek *emet.*"

"Who is trying to stop you?"

"The same people who tried to stop him. The Israeli government. Cohen."

He tugged at his earlobe. "Yes, Cohen sent you home. But Cohen was not driving the bulldozer."

"I'll be more careful. I was in the wrong place at the wrong time. Lightning won't strike twice." No sense telling him about the muggers on Ben Yehuda. He'd just get more worried.

"Perhaps, but there are others besides the Israeli government who'd prefer that the Ark remain lost." The rebbe took another sip of tea. "Why are you doing this? You hardly knew your grandfather, may his memory be a blessing."

"What would you do if he'd asked *you*?"

"But I knew him all my life." I shrugged, and in response he stroked his beard and said, "Perhaps you knew him, too."

"I beg your pardon?"

"Perhaps you carried him inside your *nefesh*, your soul."

I'd been reprogrammed like the Manchurian Candidate? "That's a stretch, don't you think?" I asked.

"Who knows? You must follow the path that *ha-Shem* sets out for you."

Was he saying I *had* been reprogrammed, not by my grandfather but by God?

"Thank you for listening," I said.

"The Talmud says 'When two people listen patiently to each other, God listens to them too.'"

I changed the subject. "And you, Rabbi, what is new with you?"

He smiled. "Tziporah is pregnant."

"Wonderful."

"One life departs, another begins."

"This is your second?"

"Yes. If it is a boy, we will name him Yitzhak."

"Nice," I said.

"I do have a favor to ask of you."

"Of me? Anything."

"Nothing in your parents' bedroom has been moved since your father left."

"Like my grandfather was waiting for Dad to come back?"

"Or perhaps for you."

I started rubbing my own chin, beardless as it was. "Now you need the room for your kids?" He nodded. "You want me to go through what's there?" I asked.

"Thank you for understanding."

* * *

I tried on the jacket of one of the dark suits I found in the closet. My arms were half an inch longer than my dad's. The other half of the closet was filled with long skirts, long-sleeved blouses, and long scarves. Of course, I didn't remember my mother—she'd been killed before I was a year old. I held a blouse up to my nose. The clothes had been in the closet for close to half a century, and logic told me it couldn't be, but I swear I caught a whiff of a clean, baby-powderish scent that must have been my mother's. I covered my face in the garment, slipped to the floor, and tears started running down my face. I hadn't cried when my father died, nor when Veronica told me it was time for a divorce. The last time I remembered crying was when Katie was born. Why now? How could you cry over something you'd never had?

When I finally stood, I took the wet blouse and threw it on the bed. I strode over to the photo of my parents and me I'd seen on my last visit and placed it on the bed, too. I opened the top drawer on the right of the bureau and came to nylons. Mother's side. I moved to the other side and opened and closed the drawers with underwear and socks. Further down I came across two neatly folded prayer shawls. I chose the one with perspiration stains around the neck and deposited it on the bed. The next drawer contained a box of cracked leather; inside were my father's *tefillin*. There had been a time when he'd strapped them on each morning. I didn't know why but I placed them on the bed, too.

Next, I sat down on the Windsor chair in front of the desk and started going through papers drawer by drawer. I came across fifty-year-old statements from Cambridge Trust and Savings. I chose one envelope at random and found a canceled check dated four weeks after I was born, made out to Boston Lying-in Hospital for two-hundred thirty-six dollars and eleven cents. Healthcare *had* become a little more expensive over the years.

In the last drawer, I found my mother's passport, issued when she was twenty-one. I'd always figured my daughter got most of her looks from Veronica. Now in the black-and-white passport photo I saw the resemblance in eyes, nose, mouth, and expression that had passed from my mother through me to Katie. Leafing through the blue booklet, the only two stamps I could find were from Lod Airport on March 12, 1958 and Idlewild two weeks later. My parents had honeymooned in Israel? Yes, the airports had been renamed, but they were the same Ben-Gurion and JFK I myself had just taken off from.

Below the passport lay a birth certificate with the space next to "name of child" filled in longhand with *Aron Kalman*. Born on February 15 at Boston Lying-in Hospital. No surprise anymore that my father was listed as Chaim or that the occupation box said *Clergy*. There was no space for the occupation of my mother, but there was one that listed my color as white. A gold star marked the certificate as authentic along with the stamped signature of Joanne Prevost Angalone, City Registrar.

A knock on the door and it swung open. Natan again.

"How are you doing?" the new rebbe asked.

"I only want a few things." I gestured toward the bed.

"Shall we send them to you in California?"

"That would be great. Thank you."

"And the rest for *tzedakah*, for charity?"

"Yes, that would be fine, too.

"Take as much time here as you'd like."

"I'm done."

"So you found what you were looking for?"

"Yes."

The first glow of an idea was starting to throw off sparks in my brain, and I was anxious to see if I could get a fire going.

Chapter 28

"You look good," I said.

"No bullshit."

"Okay. You're in better shape than I expected."

"All right. I'll accept that."

Mitch Samuelson and I were back in the walnut-paneled study of his house in suburban Virginia. We sat in two chairs pulled up to the fireplace. Like Moses' burning bush, the ceramic logs were enveloped in flames without being consumed. Mitch's arm was in a plaster cast that, with the help of aluminum struts, held it halfway up to his forehead as if on its way to a salute.

Mitch sipped from a snifter of Hennessy, and I took baby gulps straight from a bottle of Dominion, a hoppy pale ale that slid down smoothly. I didn't want to drink too quickly. Belly space was at a premium after Sarah's dinner of strip steak, onion rings, and apple pie. I'd offered to help with the dishes, but she'd scooted me out of the kitchen.

"Who knew they taught cooking in business school," I commented. Sarah had been a Baker Scholar at Harvard.

"Yeah. For the last couple of weeks, I've watched her turn into her grandmother..."

"Where a thin husband is an insult to her as a cook."

"And as a nurse," Mitch finished.

The room bore witness to the places Mitch and Sarah had lived in his years in the Foreign Service. The walls were adorned with the vibrant stripes and squares of fabrics from Ghana, some sort of Toltec or Aztec masks, and a dagger of over eighteen inches with a jeweled hilt that must have belonged to some desert sheikh. The floor was covered with four oriental rugs. A rogues' gallery of framed photos on the wall showed Mitch with secretaries of state going back to Lawrence Eagleburger.

I walked over to Mitch's desk and hefted a wedding picture. "Sarah looks beautiful. You? You look young."

"Twenty-six years ago. We thought we knew everything, but we didn't know shit. Hey, you want a cigar?"

"Sarah allows them in the house?" I used to smoke maybe half a dozen a year, but Veronica put an end to that.

"Right now I can get away with anything, and I'm taking advantage."

"I don't have the same excuse. Only if you're having one."

"That's what I had in mind. We sinners enjoy company. She bought me that humidor on the desk."

After cutting off the ends of the cigars, I lit Mitch's, then my own.

"So I hear they kicked your butt right out of Israel," he said.

"That was newsworthy?"

"I guess things at the consulate were slow that day. They did kick you out though?"

"Hey, I thought you were on medical leave."

"I keep in touch."

Of course, the Israelis would have let the State Department know. "Let's say they encouraged me to leave."

"They didn't want to celebrate your heroism?"

"Oh, is that what they call trying to save your own ass nowadays? What would you do if a bulldozer was trying to run you over?"

"Get out of the way."

"That's what I did."

"By moving closer to the terrorist?"

I shrugged. "One does stupid things when under stress."

"One does." Mitch took a healthy swig of cognac.

"Mixes well with the Percodan you're taking for the shoulder?"

"I recommend it. Was your trip a success? I assume if you'd found the Ark, I would've read about it."

"Yeah, some blogger probably would've picked up the news."

"So what do you want to do?"

"Go back to Israel."

"After they've already kicked you out once?"

I tried to change the subject. "Any idea who shot you?"

"No. The locals say random violence. The Bureau's still poking around, but they don't have diddly-squat. Back to you, then."

"Okay. Don't the Israelis have to let me in 'cause I'm Jewish?"

"Yeah, I remember from college how Jewish you were—your Sabbaths were spent wolfing down bacon cheeseburgers at Mr. Bartley's."

"With you."

"But I'm a lapsed Episcopalian. Yes, the clergy at my childhood place of worship would have been just as shocked as any rabbi, but I would not have been violating any dietary laws, just the laws of good taste as understood in Haverford, Pennsylvania."

I laughed. "Seriously though, bacon cheeseburgers or not, I'm Jewish enough for The Right of Return and all that. They have to let me in, don't they?"

"No. They could put you on some kind of watch list of undesirables."

"Really? What if I got a passport, one they didn't recognize?"

"You're asking me? C'mon. I work for the State Department. I can't say 'great idea, Alex' to your buying some forgery on the black market."

"No, no. I want to get a new passport issued."

"Don't play innocent with me. You're up to something, aren't you?" he asked.

Mitch had known me a long time. I shrugged.

"What good will a new passport do you?" he asked.

"How fast can one get a new passport issued?" I parried.

"Well, there's a special program for getting expedited service if you're leaving the country within two weeks. You can make an appointment with the Passport Agency here in town. On Nineteenth Street, I think."

Mitch took a puff on the cigar and sent a series of smoky doughnuts up toward the ceiling. "Now, if I were trying to get into Israel," he continued, "and the Israelis maybe didn't want me there, I wouldn't try checking in with El Al at Kennedy and landing at Ben Gurion."

"What would you do?"

"Well, I'm not saying, but if I were, I'd say enter Israel at Eilat."

"At the southern tip of the country?"

"Yeah, there's a crossing there from Jordan. The guards are pretty laid back. They're mostly dealing with tourists taking a shortcut across Israel on their way from Jordan to Egypt."

"No kidding," I said in a flat voice.

"You know your next move?" he asked.

"Think so." Thanks to him I now had a plan I was burning to try.

I took a puff on the cigar and tried to copy Mitch's perfectly symmetrical smoke rings, but instead emitted a series of misshapen pears, hearts, and crescents.

Chapter 29

"Do you have an appointment?"

"Yes. At ten."

"Your name?"

"Aron Kalman."

"Here's your ticket. Please go to the window indicated when your number shows up on the TV screen." She pointed toward the kind of old-fashioned tube you see with arrival and departure information at airports. The whole system for getting a passport worked just like the one back in California for getting a driver's license at the Department of Motor Vehicles.

I went over and sat on the one available plastic chair. I was wedged between a besuited, Hermès-tied man about my age and a frizzy-haired backpack-toting girl around Katie's. A quick scan of the waiting area showed it to be pretty evenly divided between the two groups they represented—businesspeople and itinerant wanderers.

"I'm going to Panama."

"Huh? Oh, sorry." I'd been back in Jerusalem searching and digging before the backpacker snapped me out of my reverie. "Anything special down there?"

"My boyfriend's found a cool place called Hostel Heike on Isla Colon. That's an island off Panama. Around twenty dollars a day. I'm going to meet him there."

"Sounds like fun."

"I don't know."

"Sounds pretty good to me."

She cocked her head and gave me a quizzical look. Then, of all things, she grasped my right hand in both of hers. "But I don't know if it is. Should I be looking for something? I don't think I really love Harold, but I'm going anyway. What am I going for? What am I looking for?" We sat silently and companionably, holding hands, for a few minutes.

"Uh. Look, uh, what is your name?"

"Monica."

"Monica, my number's come up on the screen."

"Okay. Thanks. Talking to you helped, got me thinking. Do you have a daughter?"

"Yeah, around your age."

"She's lucky. My parents would have told me what to do."

"Maybe I had no good advice."

"Maybe you were letting me work things out on my own. Tell me, are you looking for something, too?"

"Isn't everyone?" I said.

"God bless."

I strode up to Window 15 and flashed a woman in her forties the same kind of friendly and open smile I'd used when opening negotiations on a big deal back in Silicon Valley.

She responded in the mechanical voice of an automated attendant, "Mr. Kalman, what can I do for you?"

"I've lost my passport and need a replacement. I have a ticket for a flight in four days." I handed over the passport application.

Her hands flew over the keys of a terminal.

"Your social is connected to a passport for Alex Kalman."

"Right."

"But this birth certificate is for Aron Kalman."

"Yes, that's my birth name. I'd like the passport issued under my birth name."

"How did you get a passport under Alex, then? Did you have your name changed?"

"My father always called me Alex and he arranged for my first passport when I was a little boy. Since then I've just been renewing." I spread out my hands.

"We require that name changes be backed up by documentation like a marriage certificate or court order. Sorry."

She looked down and was about to push the button to call the next person up to her cage.

"So..."—don't get mad or frustrated, friendly smile again—"...what do you suggest I do?"

"Well, I guess I could issue you another passport under the name Alex Kalman. Fill out a new form and go back to the reception desk and get a new number."

Shit. What now?

"But I'm not changing my name," I said. "This *is* my birth certificate with my birth name. We're fixing a mistake."

"You make a good point. I guess that means I can't really authorize a passport for Alex Kalman either now that I know it's not your real name."

Great. I was even worse off than before. "May I ask your name?" I said.

"Mrs. Schmidt."

"Okay, Mrs. Schmidt. It sounds like I can't get a passport under either name now. Does that make sense?"

For the first time she looked at me like I was a person and not a blue booklet.

"You know, it doesn't."

"And I really need to catch that flight."

Chapter 30

I'd planned on spending a big chunk of the eleven hours from Kennedy to Amman sleeping. Early in my career, when I ran Asian sales for a start-up, I'd learned to sleep in planes—failure to snooze on a trans-Pacific flight meant zombie-dom the next day in a Tokyo or Hong Kong conference room. Anyway, after I'd pushed away the dinner tray, just as I was about to shut my eyes, the man next to me asked, "Do you mind if I borrow your *Journal*?" He spoke with a British accent.

Of course, I'd noticed him already. Clad in a charcoal suit, striped shirt with white collar, and a keffiyeh with a red band, he was an atavism who still dressed for flying as if it were a special occasion. His bearded face was turned toward me, but his eyes were hidden behind his sunglasses' mirrored lenses. What was it about Arabs and their omnipresent dark glasses?

I extended my hand across my chest, and we shook.

"Alex Kalman," I said.

"Mohammed al-Harbi."

His grip wasn't the loose, hospitable grasp I'd felt from other Arabs, but Western-style firm.

He saw the way I was looking at him and said, "I am sorry for the dark lenses. I suffer from photophobia. Too much falconry in the desert sun." I didn't know whether he was kidding or not, but his tone didn't convey any levity. He whisked the glasses off, and I saw irises nearly as dark as his pupils. With his aquiline nose, he looked like a raptor himself. He blinked slowly one time and then put the glasses back to rest on his beak.

"You are from the desert?" I asked.

"Arabs are people of the desert, Mr. Kalman."

"But now you live in Amman?" I pressed.

"Me, a Jordanian?" He shook his head so violently I wonder if he took my question as an insult. "No. I'm a Saudi."

He was putting together an investment fund and was on his way to a meeting with a potential investor. When I told him of my own background, he peppered me with questions on the world of venture capital.

"Is Silicon Valley still a good place for investing?" he asked. "Or am I too late?"

"You're an outsider. You'd be at a disadvantage there if you want to chase the same deals everyone else chases."

"So you say we need to be contrarian. What kind of deals should we be looking for?"

He was new to the VC world, but asked intelligent questions. Saudi Arabia had to do something with the unending spate of petrodollars pouring into its coffers. Why not an ownership interest in that Xanadu of high technology, Silicon Valley?

After I finished expounding on the need for real risk capital in the Valley, al-Harbi wanted to know my business in Amman.

I didn't like lying for no reason, but I couldn't exactly tell him I was sneaking into Jerusalem to dig up the lost Ark.

"I'm retired. I've always wanted to see Petra." I didn't say I was on my way there now.

He nodded. "A place that inspires awe. I would like to see it again. It's a reminder of what Arabs can do."

I hadn't thought of the Nabataeans of two millennia ago as Arabs, but they must have been. "Yes," I said.

"Yes," he echoed. "Once we Arabs controlled all the territory from India to France. While your ancestors lived as serfs, we made discoveries in medicine, philosophy, mathematics, and science."

No sense arguing. I didn't really know what my forbears had been up to, but the thrust of what he said was true. "Why no longer?"

"Our leaders grew greedy. But with guidance from our king, we can reassert ourselves again."

"What about democracy?"

"We Saudis are members of a desert tribe. A king's strong hand is required to bring our people back to where they once were."

He never took offense at my questions. I'd never met any monarchist before, let alone one who believed in the divine right of kings.

We'd end the conversation, and I'd begin reading the *Forbes*, *Atlantic*, or *Sports Illustrated* I'd bought at Kennedy. But within fifteen or twenty minutes, we'd pick up the thread again. I never did get my nap.

We exited the plane still discussing whether oil prices should continue to be set in dollars.

As we approached baggage claim and the border checkpoint beyond it, he said, "Perhaps I can look you up next time I am in California?"

"I'll look forward to it," I said. "Let me give you my email."

"Wait." He snapped his fingers and twisted his head toward me. When I looked back at him, all I saw was my own reflection in his lenses. "Alex, I told you I would very much enjoy seeing Petra again. My meeting is not for two days. Why don't we drive down together today, spend the night there, and tour tomorrow?"

I guess we were on a first-name basis now. "Most generous, Mohammed, but I would not want to put you to any trouble."

"Trouble? No trouble. I have a car and driver waiting for me. I would enjoy your company."

"Thank you, but..."

"No buts. It would be rude to say no to desert hospitality."

We were in an airport, not a sheikh's tent. "All right," I said.

"Good." He clapped me on the back. "We can finish our discussion on how to solve the world's problems. The car has plenty of room and a big boot for all our luggage."

"All I have is this," I said, nodding toward the small rolling bag. "I guess you do have checked luggage?"

"Yes."

"Well, I have some calls to make. Let me make them and meet you in front."

"Fine, fine."

The Jordanian border guard didn't look up as he stamped my passport. I passed through the lobby of Queen Alia Airport where the doorways had domed tops like mosques. Outside the air was cool. I strode by a massive black panther of a car crouched by the curb. Two minutes later I was alone in the back seat of a cab on my way to Amman's bus depot.

* * *

"No, no, I'll get it." I handed over ten Jordanian dinars to the cab driver.

Along with my traveling companions, Phil and Eden Berring from Rochester, Minnesota, we walked up to Jordanian border control past a beret-topped soldier to a smiling man who stamped our passports. We passed another soldier who waved to half a dozen of his Israeli counterparts cradling Uzis. We were being handed off like principals in a Cold War spy trade.

As we moved westward down a gravel path toward the international border, a bright southern sun burned my eyes and pounded on my skull. I put my hand above my eyes to help my Ray-Bans with the task implicit in their name. Then I rubbed my five-day-old beard.

From twenty yards away the Israelis looked formidable, modern-day Maccabees. As we passed them, I saw they were no more than teenagers—boys who had to shave only every third day and girls who still wore their hair in pigtails.

Human mice, we entered an opening in a labyrinth.

"When we crossed at the King Hussein Bridge on our last trip, it took four hours to go through border control," Eden said as we twisted between concrete barriers. I'd met her, a travel agent, and her physician husband on the bus ride from Amman to Aqaba. They'd flown into Amman rather than Ben Gurion because she had free tickets.

I took a deep breath. No wonder the Berrings were planning to begin their Israeli vacation in Eilat. It was sunny and a good fifty degrees warmer than in Minnesota.

At the end of the maze we saw eleven people in line. The couple directly in front of us pulled out Egyptian passports.

"Crossing here between Aqaba and Eilat is like crossing between Tijuana and San Diego," Eden said. "They're twin cities separated at birth."

"The problems of the West Bank do seem pretty far away," Phil said.

"Are you going to have time to see Petra?" Eden asked me.

"No, not this trip," I said. What's up with this? Everyone wants me to go to Petra.

"You really should. We went a few years ago. Spectacular."

"I guess I could look into rearranging my itinerary." Like hell I would.

She handed me a card. "Just tell my office that I said to call."

Thanks to my own dark glasses, Eden assumed I was looking at her, not over her head, when I expressed my gratitude for her offer. The Egyptians were called to the little booth. The guard waved one through and then, after a two-minute dialogue, the other. He didn't stamp their passports.

We'd made it to the front of the queue.

"So Aron, you first," Phil said with a courteous gesture.

"No, please. After you."

Eden and Phil's stop at the Israeli booth lasted less than thirty seconds.

"*Shalom*," I said as I handed Aron Kalman's passport over to the border control policeman.

"*Shalom*," he said. "Take off your glasses, please."

He squinted as he examined my face and then looked down at my passport.

He typed in my name on a keyboard marked with both English and Hebrew letters. A drop of sweat rolled into my left eye. Shit, it stung.

"Is this trip for business or pleasure?"

"Pleasure." Blink, blink.

The phone on the guard's desk rang. I couldn't understand the Hebrew, but the guard looked up at me.

Would my heart break through my ribcage? Could it be Cohen telling him to send this man back to Jordan? He hung up. He raised his arm and a heavy stamp came down on my passport with a squeak and a thump.

"Welcome to *Eretz Yisrael*, Mr. Kalman."

Chapter 31

The first two hours of the bus ride from Eilat to Jerusalem were spent crossing the Negev Desert. Even through the darkened bus windows, even with Ray-Bans still resting on my nose and ears, the brightness of the desert sun burned. Twice alongside the road, we passed Bedouins on camels. I didn't understand why people who lived in this inferno wrapped themselves in headdresses and robes. Mark Twain once said he was so hot he felt like taking off his skin and lolling in his bones. So what did the Bedouins know that Twain didn't?

When Katie, Veronica, and I had walked the Freedom Trail in Boston on a family trip a dozen years ago, Katie would say, "I can see Sam Adams standing there" or "I can see the lanterns in North Church." Standing in the footprints of the patriots transported her back in time. Here under the unrelenting sun, cruising through the Negev, passing camels and caravans, I felt as Katie had. I was wandering in the desert with the ancient Israelites. The driver's voice on the loudspeaker jerked me back to the present.

First in Hebrew and then in accented English, he announced, "We are making a small detour to admire the gift that Hamas sent us from the Gaza Strip."

I looked out the window as we swerved around a missile crater. Yes, I had definitely returned to the twenty-first century.

By the time the bus had finished wrestling with rush hour traffic in Jerusalem and pulled into the smoky glass and concrete Central Bus Station, it was almost five-thirty. The blanket of darkness would spread over the city in an hour. I had made no hotel reservation. Going back to my last hideout at the Sheraton had seemed risky. It would be too easy for Cohen's people to find me there. Anyone else who was looking for me, too.

I reached down into my roller-bag and pulled out the laminated Streetwise Jerusalem map. The case clattered over the uneven stones as I hauled it through David's City.

Forty minutes later I rolled up in front of the house on Masaryk. I rang the bell. And rang again. She wasn't home. Before I could give the doorbell a third push for good luck, I heard a voice call out in Hebrew. There, thirty yards down the street, strode the professor. I held up my hand in a half wave, but that gesture only engendered another torrent of inscrutable words.

There was nothing for it but to doff the Ray-Bans. Rivka broke into a run.

"Hello, Alex, *shalom.*"

She crashed into me and encircled me with a squeeze that would have done a python proud.

"*Shalom*, Rivka."

She let me go and looked at me from the distance of her outstretched arms.

"The beard, it makes you look like a rabbi. I didn't recognize you."

"Good. I don't want to be recognized by anyone in this city." She pulled back. "Except you," I finished.

"I knew you would be back. I prayed for it."

I kind of felt that I'd made it on my own, without divine intervention. Still, in the end Mrs. Schmidt had issued me a passport as Aron Kalman, and that *was* sort of a miracle. "Yes, here I am," I said.

"Come in, come in. Tell me about your trip. Are you tired? Are you hungry? Would you like to stay here?"

Ten minutes later, settled in her living room with a Dancing Camel in my hand, I asked her if the authorities had questioned her about the bulldozer incident on Karen Hayesod Street.

"No. I made a clean getaway, but..."

"They wanted to know about you and me in the tunnel."

"Sure."

"You had to tell them something. Other people saw me down there."

"I told a man named Cohen you were the father of a student of mine and I showed you around."

"And helped me tunnel under the Temple Mount?"

"Well, there's the truth, and then there's the whole truth. What about you? Tell me what happened."

"I, too, had the pleasure of meeting Mr. Cohen."

Rivka alternated nods with "hmms" as I recounted what had happened since I saw her walk away from the dead terrorist and me. When I was done, she leaned well over halfway across the coffee table that separated our chairs. "So the government doesn't want you here and you snuck back in anyway."

"I guess."

"Why didn't you tell me you were coming?"

"After reading how NSA could listen to any call, read any email? I figured Shin Bet could do just as well."

She nodded. "If you came back, it must be to finish what we started."

"Must be. What's happening at the tunnel, with our diggings?"

"Nothing. No one has found what we did."

"So did anyone come looking?"

"Not really. Every week or two some bureaucrats from the

Department of Antiquities come through. Last visit was pretty thorough. They might have been looking. They didn't know we'd replaced two of the meter-thick stones in the wall with ones of only a few centimeters. A single person could have moved them out of the way."

"What about the dead Saudi?"

"I haven't seen him since you did."

"We let some new air in there now. I'll bet he's really starting to stink."

"That's not a good way to talk about a human made in God's image, but..." She half-smiled. "I think he was already pretty dried out."

"Did you come up with any ideas about what he was doing down there?"

"Sure, some hypotheses. We can discuss later. In the meantime I'll cook some dinner."

"No, no, I don't want to put you out."

She stood and put her hands on her hips. "Okay, don't put me out. What's your plan?"

"Uh..."

She leaned over the table and put a strong finger against my sternum. "We're in this together, partners, or you're on your own."

Of course, my hope all along was to stay with her, but I needed to make sure she was ready to incur the risk. It was a lot to ask.

"You're a professor," I said. "You work for the Department of Antiquities. You're in the army. I don't want to ruin your professional and military career while I go chasing after rainbows."

"If the Bialystoker Rebbe says chase rainbows, you chase rainbows."

"Okay, so *I* chase rainbows."

She pressed her finger harder and pinned me against the back of the chair. "Partners or nothing."

"What about your job, the army, the university?"

"I can make my own decisions."

As I stood up, she kept her finger pressing against me. I held out my right hand. She lowered her hand from my chest and grasped it.

"Partners," I said.

"Partners," she said.

We shook.

Chapter 32

An apparition stood at the doorway of Rivka's bedroom and shouted, "*Shalom, Ima.*" Backlit by the hall lights, the figure had no features.

Awake now, I wrenched my arm free and turned to see Rivka rolling away.

After my jostling, together with a second "*Shalom, Ima*," from the ghostly figure, Rivka leaped to her feet and ran toward it. She was wearing an oversized teal, orange, and white Miami Dolphins jersey that reached down below her knees. Throwing her arms around the nocturnal intruder, she turned him sideways. I could see the visitor was clad in olive drab. I could see, too, his eyes narrow as he looked at the stranger in his mother's bed.

He spat out a quick question in Hebrew. She raised her index finger to her mouth. They walked into the hall and shut the door. I was still more or less in my traveling clothes. After dinner, I'd told my new partner that I'd stay on the couch. She'd said fine, but she had hours of work at her desk. I could go to sleep on her bed, and she'd wake me so I could move into the living room when she was done. She hadn't.

Before going outside to meet the IDF, I went into the bathroom and threw some water at my face. The mirror showed why Rivka hadn't recognized me. Six days were enough to have given my face a stubbly gray-brown beard. Smudges gleamed purple-black under my eyes. The face gazing back at me did look more like that of a rabbi than a high-tech CEO.

Okay, let's face the music.

I found my shoes with socks folded on top at the foot of the bed. I opened the door and found Rivka and her son next to each other on the couch where I was supposed to be sleeping. Their heads were bowed toward each other, and they were going back and forth in machine-gun Hebrew.

Rivka was facing me. She stood and said in English, "This is my son Ori Segel, and this is..."

"Aron Kalman," I said and stuck out my hand. He grasped it and squeezed. I squeezed back and I could see the tendons on his neck pop as he upped the power of his grip. I was not interested in a contest—I'd lose to this young warrior anyway—and let go. He was inspecting me and I did the same. He had about three inches on my six feet, a sinewy build, and a haircut so short his skull shone under the room light.

"The life of a soldier," Rivka said.

"Yes, I just got leave this evening and was able to catch a ride with the captain." Ori's English was fluent, but accented.

"I never know when he's going to show up," his mother said to me.

"And you are visiting Jerusalem?" Ori asked.

"I'm interested in your mother's work," I said.

"So I noticed," Ori said, shifting weight from his left foot to his right and back again.

"Mr. Kalman is a gifted amateur archeologist," Rivka said. "We're investigating a theory of his together."

She sounded a little stilted, but that must be because she was talking to her son in English.

"Great. Nice to meet you," Ori said. "I'm tired. I started on patrol this morning at five."

"How long are you here?" his mother asked.

"I'm driving back with the captain tomorrow evening at six," he said, still dancing from foot to foot. I wondered if he needed to piss after his long ride.

"So you go to sleep now. I need to get some work done first thing. I'll be back before lunch and then we'll spend the afternoon together."

Ori pecked his mother on the cheek and headed to his room.

"I thought you were going to wake me so I could move out to the couch," I said to Rivka.

"I tried, but you just turned over. You were exhausted. There was no sense waking you."

An Orthodox woman in Brookline wouldn't touch my hand. This observant Israeli showed no sign of embarrassment in sharing a bed. Huh. The only one embarrassed was me.

"I'll sleep on the couch now if that's okay."

She picked up the bedclothes that she'd laid out on the end table and threw them at me. "Suit yourself."

I lay on the couch. I'd caught my daughter's boyfriend stripping in her room. Now I'd been caught in the bed of this boy Ori's mother. The screw turns.

* * *

I heard the clinking of food preparation in the kitchen. The last time I'd looked at my watch the glowing hour hand had just passed four. Now it was almost eleven.

Still in the clothes I'd slept in, I padded into the kitchen. Ori was taking two mini-casseroles out of the oven.

"*Boker tov*," he said. "You slept well."

"I guess so."

"My mother prepared breakfast for us before she left."

I saw the yellow pupils of two eggs looking up from atop a mixture of peppers and tomato sauce. "What is it?"

"*Shakshuka*. It's my favorite. You want coffee?"

"Please."

We sat across from each other. I took a first bite. "It's great."

He shoveled an oversized spoonful into his own mouth, and while chewing, smiled for the first time. After a moment, he thought better of it. "Mr. Kalman," he said.

"Aron," I said.

"Mr. Kalman, my father has been dead for many years."

"Yes, your mother told me. I am sorry."

"In all that time she has never had a, um…"

"Relationship?" I suggested.

"Yes, a relationship. She still loves my father."

"I understand."

"She has her work. She has no time for this. She is not a frivolous woman. She has a position of importance."

In his mind proximity equaled guilt. Even though I'd made nothing close to an advance, I still had to stifle the impulse to explain. I felt guilty anyway. After the incident with Elliott in Katie's room, I was more on his side than my own.

"I understand," I said again. "Your English is impressive."

"Yes, yes. My mother spoke to me in English while I was growing up." He narrowed his eyes. "What kind of partnership are you and my mother undertaking?"

"Ah, she told you of our partnership?"

"Yes."

"An archeological partnership," I said.

The doorbell rang.

"Are you expecting someone?" Ori asked.

"No."

A second ring.

Ori went to answer the door and I retreated to the bedroom.

Through the open door, I heard a Hebrew conversation between two familiar voices.

After a minute, the caller said, "*Todah*," Hebrew for thank you.

Ori replied, "*B'vakasha*," and closed the door.

When he strode into the bedroom, I held my finger to my lips and made a shushing sound. He closed the bedroom door.

"The guy at the door wore gold wire-rimmed glasses and had a widow's peak?" I asked.

"Widow's peak?"

I raised my index fingers to my forehead and made a vee. "A piece of hair like this."

"You know him, then."

"Did he say his name was Cohen?"

"You do know him."

"Thank you for not saying I was here. I'm sorry to have caused you to lie."

"I did not lie. He asked for Alex Kalman, not Aron Kalman."

"And you said?"

"*Emet*. Never heard of him."

Chapter 33

"He is a wonderful son," Rivka was saying between bites of her fish. "But he might be a little overprotective."

"He did have quite a surprise when he got home."

"Yes, he did."

"I guess you explained."

"Explained what? Pfft. None of his business. I told him you were our guest. That's all he needs to know."

Great. I wouldn't be looking for a magical attitude transformation from Ori anytime soon, but in fairness I had to give him credit for not turning me over to Cohen. Who had told Cohen I was back? Was the guy at the border savvier than he'd let on?

I'd convinced Rivka to let me take her out to dinner. We were sitting outside under a tarp at Kafit, which was around the corner from her place on Emek R'fayim, the main street of the German Colony. Huge metal mushroom heaters kept us warm.

"Is there this kind of security at all the restaurants?"

Rivka's purse had been opened and I'd been patted down before we'd been buzzed in by a guard.

"Yes, pretty much. But this one especially. Back in 2002, a bomber tried to get in here, but someone in the restaurant saw the electrical wires and tackled him before he could blow us up."

"Us?"

"Yes, those of us who were eating here."

I stared at her for a moment. She paid no attention, spearing a cucumber with her fork and placing it between her lips.

"I don't know how you can do it," is what I ended up saying.

As she conveyed some greens to her mouth, she shrugged and said, "Because it is home."

We ate without talking for a couple of minutes, and then I asked, "What did you and Ori do this afternoon?"

"We stopped by to visit a couple of his friends and then visited a couple of mine at another excavation in the Old City."

"A postman's holiday."

"I don't know the expression."

"It's English. A mailman goes for a hike on his vacation..."

"And an archeologist looks at ruins." She clapped her hands. "Yes, we wandered around where I work every day. And you, what did you do this afternoon?"

"I went for a run."

"To?"

"To the Knesset and *then* to the Old City."

"We can't stay away, can we? So what are we going to do?"

"That's what I was thinking about on the run."

"Let's take a walk and talk things over," she said. "Maybe we're alike and think better when we're moving."

I won the tussle over the check. She claimed she should pay because she was my host in Jerusalem. I trumped that argument by saying I'd invited her. I paid cash.

As we ambled down Emek R'fayim past boutiques and restaurants, she linked her arm in mine.

"I now have a Hebrew name," I said. "I'm Aron Kalman and have the passport to prove it."

"I heard you introduce yourself to Ori as Aron."

"Why did you change from Becky to Rivka?" I asked.

"As a sign I'd changed my life."

"Okay then, call me Aron."

We finalized a course of action before we'd walked three blocks.

Chapter 34

"We're just grave robbers, aren't we?" I asked.

Rivka laughed between gulps of air. "It's an occupation with an illustrious history here in the Middle East."

At first the body of the dead Saudi had smelled worse than two weeks ago. But either I was getting used to it or the tarpaulin we'd wrapped him in took the edge off his eau de rotten meat cologne.

"Can we take a break?" she asked.

We lowered the two ends of our six-foot green roll in the tunnel. I turned my head toward her, and the miner's light on the helmet lit the oblique planes of her face.

"We're almost out."

"What time is it?" she asked.

"Just the right time for grave robbers. Two-fifteen." I held up the watch so she could see the hands herself.

"You changed your watch."

"Yeah, I did." On my last trip, I'd added ten hours to figure local time. On the bus through the Negev I'd reset it. Switching the subject to the matter at hand, I asked, "What do you think this guy was doing here?"

"Wouldn't you figure the same as us—looking for the Ark?

"So he could destroy it?"

"Maybe if he was working for the Palestinian Arabs. Arafat

denied the Temple was ever here. Finding it would undercut their claims to Jerusalem and the credibility of the PLO, too. But if he is a Saudi..." The shadows played up and down her face as she shook her head in the yellowish lantern light. "The Koran calls the Ark the *'Tabut E Sakina'* and treats it as holy and powerful since it holds relics left by Moses and Aaron."

"So if this guy was a Saudi or was working for them, he would have wanted to find the Ark?"

"Yeah. The Saudis view themselves as the protector of Muslim holy relics."

"Makes sense. Maybe we should get back to work."

Half a minute later, I was hunched over, walking backward, with my fingers grasping folded furls of the tarp and my knuckles twisted into the covered skull of the mysterious Saudi.

"Do you know what *kavod hamet* is?" she asked.

"No." I almost went on to ask if I should, but I was saving breath.

"Respecting the dead," she explained. "Even if this man was a Saudi agent, he was still made in God's image and deserves respect. Wait. Stop. We are at the wall."

"You go through the hole," I said. "I'll pass him to you."

"Right."

The tunnel was too narrow for her to walk around the body. Given her belief in respecting the dead, she couldn't really walk on top of him. That would break up the skeleton anyway, something we didn't want. Rivka put her back against the right side of the wall and pressed her feet on the opposite side. It took a couple of minutes for her to sidle up to me.

"Good work," I said.

She slid through the hole I'd dug weeks ago and called out. "Okay. I'm ready."

I picked up the end of the tarp and leaned it against the edge of the hole. I reached underneath at what must have been around the body's chest and tried to push it through. No go. The tunnel wasn't wide enough for me to get the right angle.

"Just a minute." I called out. "I've got to get back to the other end."

"Okay." I knew Rivka was only a few feet away, but she sounded a lot farther.

Then I reversed the route Rivka had taken, propping back and feet against the wall and edging along.

When I got to the other end of the tarp, I lifted and pushed. It didn't work. The skull was in the hole, but it must have been stuck around the neck. And the package was sagging in the middle. Hmm. Rivka wanted to respect the dead. Okay for her. It was going to work better for me if I thought of the load as cumbersome camping equipment.

I lifted the end of the tarp so that it was the same level as the skull in the hole. Then I crouched and put the end of the tarp on my back. With my arms over my head, I worked my way up to the middle of the roll. I could feel the indentation of a waist. Taking a firm hold, I thrust my hands forward. Whew. Over half the length of the tarp had made it into the hole.

I heard Rivka's hollow voice say, "I see the head."

After two more pushes, the tarp began to move on its own. I shivered. Rivka was dragging him through. Then I followed the body and snaked through the hole myself.

We had plenty of room on the other side.

"You okay?" I asked.

"Spotting a dead person's head coming through the passage." She shivered. "It was like a stillbirth."

"Yeah, something for the screenplay of a horror movie. Where to?"

"About ten meters ahead is the opening to the chamber we talked about."

When we'd talked the night before, Rivka had insisted we get the authorities involved. At the same time, she wanted to keep the tunnel—the route to the Ark?—secret as much as I did. So we'd move the body to where it could be found—the area where Rivka's team was excavating. Seemed simple when we'd said it, harder as we hauled a desiccated corpse in a labyrinth under the Western Wall in the wee hours of the morning.

Chapter 35

The day after our body-transporting adventure, Rivka slid *Haaretz*, the morning paper, across the breakfast table.

"Look at the picture below the fold," she said.

There was a photo of a body sack being put into an ambulance by a couple of paramedics.

"That's the customer of Darwish's Tailor Shop?"

"The very same."

"Your plan seems to be working. You've got the authorities involved, and they don't know about the tunnel."

I was watching her nod as I reached for my mug of Wissotzky tea. My hand closed around its handle—almost.

"Shit." As it hit the tile floor, the mug became an antipersonnel bomb, exploding into dozens of porcelain shards.

"I dropped one, now you have," Rivka said. "We're even. Let me get the broom."

"Wait, I'll clean it up," I said to her retreating back.

"You wait."

But I didn't. I started picking up the larger pieces with my right hand and laying them on the palm of my left. The last time I'd cleaned up spilt tea was when Veronica came into my office to ask for a divorce.

When Rivka returned, she shook her head. "You are more Israeli than I am."

"What do you mean?"

"You may not speak Hebrew, but you are stubborn and hard-headed enough to fit right in here. Listen. Sit down. Let me sweep up the pieces."

She held out a dustpan, and I deposited the larger pieces I'd gathered.

"Open your right hand."

I did. A bubble of blood was swelling on the meaty part of my thumb.

"I told you to wait," she said.

I turned over her left hand and pointed to a three-inch slash of scar tissue on her palm. "Maybe I'm not the only clumsy person."

"*Touché.* That's from a dig in Caesarea when I was in graduate school."

"Looks like you chiseled your hand."

"Because that's what I did. Two over-anxious, stubborn Israelis. That's us. Let me see the thumb again."

She leaned down to inspect my hand. I started to look down, too, but my eyes stopped when they reached the neckline of Rivka's blue work shirt. The way she was bent over had caused her shirt to fall away. I found myself looking at a lacy black bra that both cupped her round breasts and separated them with a shadowy cleavage. Dirty old man. I forced my eyes to end their rest stop and resume traveling down to the hand Rivka held in hers. A translucent crimson balloon was inflating and deflating on my thumb in harmony with my pulse.

Rivka thrust my hand under the tap, washed it with dish soap, poured some hydrogen peroxide over it, and put on a bandage. Field dressing. She sat me down and swept up the wet detritus of the mug. Then I insisted on mopping the floor. Why? To show I was no invalid? Or to focus on manual labor rather than what I'd seen under my partner's shirt?

"Want to take a chance on another mug?"

"Sure, let's live dangerously."

The tea scalded my mouth and throat on the way down. It hurt, but I figured I deserved it.

"So," she said from across the table.

"So, your plan worked."

The tunnel had been closed to tourists yesterday after Rivka notified the police of the body.

"Tell me what the paper said."

"That the decayed body of someone long dead was found in a closed-off chamber under the Western Wall."

"Do they mention you, that you notified them?"

"No, it only says that an archeologist came across the corpse in an unexcavated chamber."

"Does it say anything about foul play or it being an Arab?"

"No. They wouldn't want to do that. There could be riots."

"What are the police going to do?"

"What can they do? That man was killed years ago. The story implies he's been there since the Old City was under Jordanian control."

"Anything else in the story?"

"A lot more words. No more information."

I changed the subject. "So what do you think Mr. Cohen was doing here yesterday?"

"Looking for you."

"But he'd never been here before."

"No."

"Logic says he knows I'm back."

"Or suspects it. But how?"

"Maybe they really did recognize me at the border crossing in Eilat."

"Then Cohen would have not been so polite. He would have come with a team and searched the place."

"Do you think he has the house under surveillance?"

"Not that I could tell."

"Oh, you looked." Of course, she *would* reconnoiter. She was a major in the IDF.

"I'm not sure anyone would recognize you anyway. The beard, the sunglasses."

"I'd rather not run into him."

"I agree," she said. "Follow me."

* * *

I raised my head from the sink and looked into the mirror. When I'd met Rivka, my face was clean-shaven and my crown covered in hair. Now it was the other way around. Rivka had cut my hair short with a scissors and finished the job with soap and razor, leaving me with a gleaming white skull. And after Rivka's ministrations with the contents of a translucent brown bottle, the color of my beard had changed from gray-brown to auburn.

"You dye your hair?"

"A fine question to ask a lady. But no. Look." She bowed the top of her head toward me. "You see the gray in there?"

I did spot a couple of light strands curling down from the streak of her part. "I know better than to answer that question."

"My mother spotted gray hairs on my last visit to Florida and displayed no such reticence."

"I'll bet the one thing that can make you feel older than finding your first gray hair is having your daughter find hers."

She laughed. "She wanted me to go right down and see Gretchen at her hair salon. I wouldn't go. So when I got back here, what was waiting in a FedEx package?"

"The dye?"

"Well, Mom prefers to call it hair coloring, but you got the basic idea."

"But you didn't use it."

"No. I must have been saving it for you."

I looked back in the mirror. "I don't recognize myself."

"Good. Maybe the Shin Bet won't either. Now let's go get you an ID so we can get back to work in the tunnel."

Chapter 36

"Those are Arabs?" I asked Rivka. I didn't want to make any assumptions.

"Yes."

I had my new ID, but apparently I wouldn't be using it anytime soon. A couple of hundred demonstrators stood between us and the tunnel entrance. Like waves against the shore, they rolled toward a blue line of helmeted and shielded police, only to retreat and then, a quarter minute later, roll in again.

"What are they saying?"

She cocked her head. "That Jews are desecrating the bodies of the sacred guardians of the Haram esh-Sharif."

"The body we moved."

She nodded.

"I thought you said no one could tell he was an Arab."

She shrugged. "Rumors. In this city, if something can be interpreted in a way that insults Islam, it will be."

Drowning out the end of what she was saying, a great shout of "*Allahu Akbar*" came from the protesters as they pushed against the police. As they retreated, the noise ebbed as well.

I yelled in her ear, "A sacred guardian who gets his uniform at Darwish's Tailors?"

"Professor Golan?" A woman, whose face was hidden

behind a mask of mascara, rouge, and lipstick, beckoned to a man with a video camera that was labeled with some Hebrew as well as "Channel 2" in English. She stuck a microphone in front of Rivka. I moved behind the cameraman. The last thing I needed—new look or not—was to have my face broadcast around the country.

The wave of protestors started in again, and the rolling rumble of their voices crested as well.

It was going to be great television. The head of the dig under the Wall shouting to be heard against the Arab protesters in the background. After two minutes, Rivka concluded her response to a question with a quick chop of her arm. She was done.

The reporter and cameraman each shook her hand.

I took her arm and guided her a hundred yards away from the tumult.

"What did they ask you?"

"Who the man was."

"And you said it's up to the police?"

"Yeah. That's about it." Seizing my arm, she marched back to the screaming crowd. She screamed back. I don't know how, but I could tell she was speaking Arabic and not Hebrew. A ring of a couple young men formed around us.

Now *this* interview was not being recorded for later broadcast. Rivka would shout out a sentence or two and then one of the crowd would shout back. The circle of men around us grew like rings on a tree, but minute by minute instead of year by year. In the middle of ten concentric circles, Rivka called out a few sentences, and a majority of the crowd nodded. Then an unshaven, olive-skinned but blue-eyed man of around twenty-five pushed his way to within two feet of us and started yelling. I hooked my arm in Rivka's as if to pull her away, but she didn't budge. It didn't matter since there was no place to go. We were surrounded.

Rivka gave every indication of giving the man her full attention. He kept up his argument or invective or whatever it was for three minutes. The crowd that had been nodding at Rivka's professorial reasoning started doing the same at their colleague's spouting. They came closer, shrinking the circle around us. I was jostled by people behind me, but I didn't turn around. I kept my eyes on the confrontation.

When the man had to pause in his shouting to catch his breath, Rivka launched into an oration of her own. Even at high volume, she sounded reasonable and authoritative. When the man tried to interrupt, to drown her out, a couple of arms emerged from the crowd to pull him away from her.

Another man stepped forward and asked something in a voice only a couple of dozen decibels over normal.

Rivka's reply lasted no more than fifteen seconds.

The innermost ring of people turned around and started to push the next ring away from us.

Only now, after the danger was dissipating, did it occur to me to be frightened. What if Rivka had said the wrong thing? Would the crowd have turned to violence? Would we have been ripped limb from limb? Anyway, she had said the right thing.

She took my hand and walked away.

"Ooh." Rivka staggered, and I saw a small, plum-sized rock fall to the ground at her feet.

I hoisted her back up just as I had when Katie was three and she'd stumbled on the way to the park.

Once she was upright, I tried to shake my hand away, but Rivka's grip was tight. I knew she had protection in the pocket of her cargo pants.

"Let go. They threw a rock at you. I'm going to get your gun."

I hadn't realized that the term "seeing red" meant just that. I looked back over my shoulder and saw the crowd through a crimson mist.

"Let me go," I said.

"What are you going to do, shoot the whole crowd?"

The rock had opened her forehead. The stream of blood flowed over her eyebrow, past a closed right eye, and down her cheek onto ancient cobblestones.

"Give me the gun. We need protection." I tried to pry her fingers off my wrist.

"No. Look."

Three policemen were running toward us.

From behind we could hear some of the Arab crowd trying to catch up, too.

Now Rivka did let go of my hand and held both of hers palms out to the police as if *she* were the cop and she was stopping oncoming traffic. They slowed and lowered the batons they held.

Then she turned the other way. There were three Arabs as well. When about ten feet away, they bowed. Rivka listened to a short speech, blood still streaming, and then said, "*Salaam.*"

"*Salaam*," they said and moved back.

"What did they say?" I asked.

"They apologized. They were ashamed that someone had struck a woman."

"Let's get you patched up."

For the second time, I'd been ready to turn to violence to protect Rivka. First the yeshiva boy who'd thrown the bag of shit at her, and now the protesters who'd hit her with a rock. We've been human for millions of years, and civilized for, what, four thousand? A threat to the woman I was with, and I'd shed civilization's thin skin like a molting snake. Rivka had demonstrated she had courage but still knew when to walk away. Me, I'd tried to grab her gun, which didn't make sense in any context. If it came to gunplay, we were far better off with her finger, not mine, on the trigger.

Chapter 37

"You think it's going to leave a scar?" I asked.

Rivka and I were sitting the next morning at the Square Cup, which I now considered "our" café in the Old City.

She answered my question with one of her own. "Do you care?"

"No, but I'll bet if your mom cares about three strands of gray..."

"That she'd care about seven stitches. You'd win the bet."

"Can we talk about yesterday?"

"Yes, I'm ready."

After our confrontation, she'd spent a few hours at the hospital and then ten more sleeping. I'd tried to discourage her from going to work today, but here we were on our way to the tunnel, just stopping for tea and the triangular rolls stuffed with salty cheese called *borekas*.

"What did you say to the crowd?" I asked.

"I told them I was an archeologist."

"And they said?"

"That the dirty Jews were desecrating Muslim holy places."

"And you said?"

"That I was a professor who seeks the truth."

"What convinced them in the end?"

"I'm not sure I did convince them, but I offered to take them on a tour of the tunnel."

"All of them?"

"No, ten." She smiled. "A minyan."

"Where did you learn Arabic?"

"Before the first intifada we worked with Arabs all the time on digs. They'd come in from the West Bank or Gaza. I have lots of Arab friends from back then."

"They can't come in anymore."

"No. The government says it would be unsafe. You know, it's like Cain and Abel or Jacob and Esau. The biggest feuds are never between strangers. They're among family. Let's go."

* * *

My new ID worked like a charm. The Israeli guards called me "Professor Kalman" as they inspected the laminated card—a logical assumption given that I was entering the tunnel with Rivka. At her staff meeting, she introduced me as an American from Harvard. I sat through the meeting, understanding none of the Hebrew, but still able to glean that Rivka was explaining why her forehead sported a bandage, why I was there, and why an Arab delegation would be touring the tunnel.

After the meeting, the dozen archeologists on Rivka's team —six Israelis, two Americans, and a representative each from England, Canada, Holland, and France—came up to shake hands and welcome me. The group wasn't only multinational—given that the Englishman's last name was St. John and the Frenchwoman's first name was Christine—it was interfaith as well. As Rivka instructed, I told one and all I was there "just to look around." As Rivka figured, they took that as code: I was there to decide whether Harvard would co-sponsor the dig. Like any group of academics, they were bloodhounds, always sniffing around for the scent of grant money. I hadn't lied. What they inferred was their business.

Five minutes after the meeting I was following Bertrand St. John—"Call me Bertie"—down a ladder toward a pit. He was thin-faced, yellow-blond, and wispy-mustached. Give him an ascot and a pipe, and he could have been sent over from central casting to play his namesake in a P.G. Wodehouse adaptation of *Masterpiece Theatre*.

"Kalman?" St. John looked up at me and said, "When I was in the States last, Rivka introduced me to a student named Kalman. Ph.D. student in Egyptology. Katharine Kalman. Rather a smasher."

"I believe she's an undergraduate."

"That right?" He tilted his head. "I've put my foot in it, haven't I? Your daughter?"

"She *is* a smasher, isn't she?"

At ten-thirty, ninety minutes before noon prayers, a group of ten Arabs came down. They must have gone through the metal screeners, and I'd bet they were patted down as well. Nevertheless, two uniformed guards trailed after them with their hands on holstered handguns. It seemed wrong to be overtly armed in this realm where professors and worshipers searched for truth—the former via archeology, the latter via faith.

"*Salaam aleikum.*" Rivka bowed.

"*Aleikum salaam*," said a bearded man in flowing robes. The other nine men were dressed in jeans, khakis, button-downs, and work shirts.

When the tour group passed the women praying near the Holy of Holies, Rivka stopped to explain. I couldn't understand the Arabic, but I could see the impatience of her audience. So could Rivka. She cut her lesson short, and we resumed snaking through the tunnel toward the place where we'd laid the body.

One man—he was the blue-eyed agitator from the day

before—stopped at the concrete plug in the wall. He called out a question to Rivka.

"Do you understand English?" she asked him.

"Yes."

"Fine, then. Aron, would you explain to our guest while the rest of us go ahead?"

I stuck my hand out. "Aron."

"Suleiman."

"How perfect," I said.

"Yes?"

"Suleiman is Arabic for Solomon, isn't it? You know, the builder of the first temple."

"Come, do you really believe there was a first temple here?" He looked past me. One of the guards had stayed with us. He watched from a respectful distance.

"Your English is very good."

"Yes. I lived in the States for twelve years."

"Where?"

"Dearborn, Michigan. I went to Wayne State." He ran his hand over the concrete. "This is where the rabbi was drilling to find the temple."

"You are well informed. I believe so."

"All this excavation is intended to support Israeli claims to Jerusalem."

"Or maybe to just find the truth."

"No. Jerusalem is not a Jewish city."

"Why do you say that? This is where the temple stood."

"Zionist propaganda. But even if I concede there was a temple here, it was destroyed in Year 70 of the Western calendar. If we are basing claims on religion, then we Muslims have a more recent claim. It was from here that Mohammed left for his trip to heaven."

I hadn't read the Bible before my first trip to Israel. But I had taken a semester-long course on the Koran back in college.

"Hmm. How could that be? The Holy Koran says Mohammed left from the furthest mosque. Jerusalem had not yet been conquered by his armies when he took that journey, so the furthest mosque cannot have been here."

"You believe your legends about the temple, and you say this to me about ours? What about this fact? For over twelve centuries, until it was stolen by the British in 1918, Jerusalem and all Palestine were Muslim. The Old City has been Jewish only since it was stolen again in 1967." He leaned forward to bring his face closer to mine. "You Zionists twist the facts to suit you."

"I don't think we're going to resolve this. Wouldn't it be nice if Jews and Muslims could share, though?"

"Zionists don't share. Jerusalem is ours." Then with an abrupt change of subject, he straightened up and asked, "What do you think is on the other side of this hole?"

"I'll bet Professor Golan and the other archeologists would love to know, but the government does not want to offend Muslims by digging under the Dome of the Rock."

"Which is another way of saying they do not wish to face rioting," Suleiman said. "The Zionists understand force and nothing else."

"Shall we catch up with the others?" I asked.

He walked in front of me, the fingers of his right hand brushing over the beige stones of the wall. I turned my head to the left to see St. John and his team down in the excavation area I'd visited thirty minutes before. Smack. I ran right into Suleiman.

"Sorry."

"No problem."

He'd turned and was facing the wall. His fingertips pressed against the stone, the very stone that hid the opening to the tunnel where we'd been digging.

How much do you think this stone weighs?" he asked.

"I don't know. A ton? Two tons? Why do you ask?"

He rapped on it with his knuckles. Then he rapped again with his ear against the stone.

"I wonder what is on the other side."

Chapter 38

When we caught up to the other nine of our visitors, they were just outside the chamber where we'd placed the body.

Give and take was going on in Arabic, but now I had Suleiman to provide a running translation.

"She"—he pointed down at Rivka—"said, 'This is an area where excavations have not yet begun.'"

"Did you recognize the person?" asked one of the guests.

"I'm told he had been dead for too long to recognize him."

"But was he an Arab?"

"Can you tell if someone is an Arab just by looking?" asked Rivka, answering a question with a question.

"But he was not one of the people working on your project?"

"No. Nobody has gone missing. We would have known a long time before a body started decomposing."

"If he was an Arab, what would he have been doing here?"

For a moment there was no reply. Then, from where we stood, Suleiman stopped translating and called down in English. "Did he find out something that the Zionist authorities did not want known? They would have killed him then."

Rivka looked up and answered him. "What might he have found out?"

"That there was never a temple here."

"It is true that we have found little evidence of the First Temple, of Solomon's Temple, here," Rivka said. "Any evidence of the First Temple lies beneath the Dome of the Rock, and our rules do not allow digging on the Temple Mount. But we have discovered remnants of the Second Temple. I am as certain as an archeologist can be. The Second Temple was here and was destroyed by the Romans."

* * *

Our guests left in time for the muezzins' prayer call. Rivka was busy the rest of the afternoon. I occupied myself checking out what her team of archeologists was up to. Part of the price of living in Silicon Valley is listening to obsessive friends who prattle on about their latest breakthrough at work. Archeologists, it turns out, are no different.

I headed back to Rivka's office around five.

I was starting to relax in the chair on the other side of her desk when she said, "Shin Bet was by this afternoon."

I reversed my momentum, leaned on her desk, and asked, "Was it Cohen?"

"No. One of his minions, I suppose."

"They don't know about me being here?"

"At least they didn't mention you. He said one of the ten Arabs who toured this morning is a known provocateur."

"Was it Suleiman? I swear he knew there was something on the other side of the wall."

"I asked what Suleiman might be up to, but the guy they wanted to talk about is an Al-Fatah operative, a guy about five-ten with a beard."

"Boy, that helps a lot."

"Yeah, well, they wanted to know what this Al-Fatah guy saw."

I leaned even closer across the desk. "And you said?"

Rivka didn't react to my invasion of her space. "No, I didn't tell them about our tunnel." I moved back a few inches. "C'mon, I wouldn't do that without talking to you first. But maybe we should go back to Cohen. We've found a dead body. Now we have evidence that professionals on the other side are sniffing around. I'm an academic, you're an entrepreneur. Neither one of us is exactly James Bond. We're way over our heads. We need help."

I crossed my arms. Of course, she was right. The problem was that going to the authorities meant the end of the search for the Ark. They'd stop us just as they'd stopped my grandfather and the other two rabbis three decades ago.

When I'd started my company, plenty of VCs had ridiculed both the business plan and my ability to manage a company. Determination to prove our investors right and those who didn't invest wrong had driven my compulsion to make the company a success. Once we'd been within fifteen minutes of not meeting payroll. We persevered.

As if reading my mind, Rivka said, "You are a stubborn man. That might be good in business, but more's at stake here than material success."

"You're right," I said. "If this blows up, I don't want anything to happen to you."

"But you don't care if anything happens to you?"

"I'm committed," I said.

"How committed?"

"Here's how we explain commitment in Silicon Valley. When you order a bacon-and-eggs breakfast, the chicken participates. It's the pig who's committed."

"So we're both pigs," she said.

I reached across the desk to put my hand on her arm. "You sure?"

In reply, she reached down and pulled something out of her

backpack that looked like a homemade hairbrush—a strip of wood with a couple of metal prongs sticking out.

"What is it?" I asked.

"A skeleton key for a three-thousand-year-old lock," she said.

One by one, the other archeologists stopped by to say goodnight. When they saw our heads leaning toward each other over her desk, they must have assumed we were negotiating the terms for Harvard's participation in the dig.

Rivka carried a virtual sheaf of time cards in her brain. When the Frenchwoman left at a little after six, she sighed and said, "Last one." She reached into her canvas bag—which looked like the offspring of a beach bag and a valise—and extracted a pita sandwich, yogurt, orange, and apple water for each of us.

"I guess we don't need refrigerators down here," I said.

"No. Thirteen degrees summer or winter."

I did the quick mental arithmetic to convert the temperature into Fahrenheit. Fifty-five degrees.

I started to peel an orange, but after watching for a moment or two, she seized it from me. The skin fell away under her fingers, and she handed it back to me, stripped naked, in about five seconds. One more proof of female superiority.

"So, professor?" I asked.

"You sound like *my* grandfather. He'd say, '*Nu, liebchen*?'"

"Okay then. *Nu*?"

"You think this Suleiman knew about the tunnel?"

"He stopped at the exact point where our tunnel started and asked me what was on the other side."

"Could be coincidence."

"And if it wasn't?"

"Okay then. If Suleiman did know, how did he know?"

"Why does Cohen keep sniffing around?"

She squinted and looked at me like an art appraiser examining a lost masterpiece. "Do you think I'm telling them?"

"No." But I'd hesitated for a moment. Mistake. Big mistake.

She stood up on her side of the desk. I saw a scarlet flush rising from her neck. "You asshole. I thought we were partners. You suspect *me*, don't you?"

"Slow down. No. I don't."

My junior year of college I'd taken boxing lessons from Ben Boal, a rock-hard former light heavyweight who had been in his seventies. He'd told me my reflexes were great, but if I wanted a career in the ring, I needed to find a knockout punch.

Anyway, before I even registered that an open palm was flying toward my left cheek, muscle memory went to work. My forearm went up and stopped Rivka's hand three inches short of its intended destination. She dropped it back down, but her lips, a compressed bloodless white, indicated a fierce desire to try again.

"Wait," I said. "Wait. Instinct made me block you. I deserved that slap. Let me get ready. Take your best shot." I closed my eyes and scrunched up my face. After ten seconds of suspense, I felt rough fingertips trail across my cheek.

"*That's* your best shot?" I asked and opened my eyes. She had her hands palm up in exasperation. "Can we sit down now?"

She nodded. "I guess I have a temper, too."

"But you obviously don't hold a grudge for long."

"I'm an Israeli. But you did wonder whether I informed on you?"

"Are you going to slap me again?"

"I didn't slap you the first time."

"Okay. Are you going to *try* to slap me again?"

"Maybe, if you don't give me an honest answer. Did you suspect me?"

"Yeah, a little. I have that kind of mind. I even thought

about my own daughter, her boyfriend, and my college roommate who's my oldest friend. You know Andy Grove?"

"The former CEO of Intel was your college roommate?"

"That's not what I meant. Well, Andy says only the paranoid survive."

"That may be a good way to live your business life, but it's not so good for your personal life."

Caesar crossed the Rubicon, Cortez burned his ships. There are points in every life where there's no turning back, where commitment to a course of action is required.

I reached across the desk and took her hand. "You're right, partner. Let's figure out our next move."

Chapter 39

Rivka looked at the proto-key she held in her hand and then at the lock that had stymied us last time we'd gotten this far.

"Come on," I said. "Let's open up and see if the Ark is here."

"Patience," Rivka said. She took a deep breath. "I want to remember this moment."

My heart was pounding, my head was pounding. I tried deep breathing.

Rivka said, "In junior high we read *Uncle Tom's Cabin*. Mr. Huskey told us when President Lincoln met the author during the Civil War, he said, 'So you're the little woman who caused this big war.'"

"You don't think we should open that door?"

"I'm an archeologist. Opening a door like this is what I do. But we're partners, too. So I need to ask if you're sure, if you want to live with the consequences."

"Maybe nothing is there," I said.

"Maybe."

"And maybe if the Ark is there war will come."

"Maybe."

"What is there for sure is *emet*. We'll only find out the truth of what is there by using your key. Let's do it."

I pointed my flashlight at the door. Rivka inserted the

hairbrush key into slits in the wooden lock. She jiggled it and then pushed with her palm against the door itself.

"It's unlocked?"

"I'm not sure."

"What can I do?"

"The bar should slide to the right once I unlock it. Push it that way and I'll keep moving the key around."

Ten minutes later I was still pushing, and she was still jiggling.

"We should have brought an axe."

"Patience," Rivka said.

My patience didn't last too much longer. I threw my shoulder against the door. An immovable object against an all-too-resistible force. No movement.

"Shit. Shouldn't wood this old be rotten?"

"It's cool and dry in here with no air circulation. If we hadn't opened things up, this door would be just as strong in a few thousand more years."

"How do you know this key will fit?"

"I have pictures of similar locks found in the Fertile Crescent. This should work. It fits."

"Try it again."

I held the flashlight over my right ear and got within three inches of the infernal lock. I could see the prongs slotting into the wood. Maybe the door was stuck. My bathroom window in Woodside jammed every spring after not being opened for the four rainy months after Thanksgiving.

I ran my fingers around the lock. Maybe the wood was rotting—I felt a pit on the underside. Lying on the floor and pointing the flashlight upwards, I could see a round hole no more than a half inch across. I reached into my pocket and pulled out a pencil and inserted it.

The bar on the door moved. Rivka knocked it with the heel of her hand and it pulled out of the way.

"What did you do?"

"There was another keyhole in the bottom."

"Those clever devils. We've never seen a lock like this before." Rivka lay down and looked up at the extra hole.

"Someone must have. Come on."

She stood up and slapped the rear of her cargo pants a couple of times to get the dust off.

"Yeah. I guess a paper on ancient Middle Eastern lock technology can wait."

We pushed the door open and sprayed our beams around once and then again.

"No Ark in here."

We stepped inside a room with sand-colored blocks running around its circumference. The domed ceiling had been cut out of rock. A stone igloo. It took nineteen paces to walk straight across the room, over fifty feet.

"Is this where the Ark was kept?" I asked.

"If it was, it's not here anymore, but I don't think so."

"Why not?"

"I remember touring Leeds Castle. It was surrounded by a moat and then a wall, but that wasn't enough. The castle keep, the medieval counterpart to the Holy of Holies, had another wall and moat around it."

"So we've reached the inner defenses here but not the keep?"

"Apparently. Besides…" She looked down at her compass. "…I'd guess we'd be right under the Holy of Holies in about fifteen meters that way." She pointed. "I sure wish GPS worked down here."

I slammed the narrow end of my pick between the two blocks on the wall—as featureless as any other—she'd indicated. Nothing except for the vibrations transmitted from the tool up my arm.

"Frustrated, huh?" she asked.

"Disappointed?" I asked in response.

"I am. I think we should go back. We need better tools."

"This sounds stupid, but I think we're on track."

"Why?" she asked.

"Just a feeling."

"Okay. I can go with that. But we'll still need more equipment and more time to get through all this. That's enough for now. She looked down at her watch. "It's nine-thirty. We can get out of here and still get a decent night's sleep."

"You go ahead. I want to stay," I said. "You've got a couple of more sandwiches."

"Yeah. Lots more. Drinks, too."

"Come back and get me tomorrow night, okay?"

"I'm not sure it's a good idea. I'll stay, too."

"*You* need to be at work. No one will miss *me*."

Chapter 40

I crossed my legs on the floor of my limestone igloo and closed my eyes. I hadn't wanted to tell Rivka about my sense of déjà vu before she left. It was too silly. Embarrassing. Had I been in this room before? Or maybe it was that I was meant to be here. My grandfather had been here. I knew it.

I opened my eyes. A few days in the Holy Land and I was turning into a Jewish mystic. But if my grandfather and his colleagues had been in here, they'd figured out how to get to the Ark. And they'd been in their sixties.

I pulled out a pita stuffed with hummus and tomatoes and munched. Just as I stuffed the last piece in my maw, I remembered Rivka's trick of the thin block that looked thick.

With the broad end of the pick, I started working my way in widening circles from the block I'd marked when Rivka was still here. Tap, thud. Tap, thud, Tap, thud. And then on a block about twenty feet to the right of the one Rivka had pointed at. Tap, tap. A hollow sound. I couldn't be sure if it was a natural variation, but the color of the stone looked lighter than the others.

I went into the bag and out came hammer and chisel. The blocks had been fitted without mortar. Pulling one out could make the whole room collapse. The hollow-sounding block measured about five feet long and three tall, reaching from my waist to my head. A half hour of work and I'd made a hole in the block about twice the diameter of the flashlight. I shoved it through and took a peek. I was looking down a dirt passageway. A wormhole. Narrow, but with enough room for a pretty fat worm.

It took me two hours to chip out a hole in the stone about twenty inches across, a little wider than my shoulders and as wide as the crawl space beyond. Then, as though I were getting ready for the guillotine, I stuck my head through the hole. I couldn't see much, since ten feet into the passage it hooked to the left.

Well, there was nothing for it but to climb in.

* * *

My breaths come in short bursts.

I scratch my fingernails into the dirt and pull myself forward another fraction of an inch.

Now in this tunnel I experience true panic—what passengers strapped into their seats feel as their plane plummets to the ground, what people in a burning nightclub sense as they yank on the handle of a locked fire door.

The narrowness of the passage and the lack of traction for my pushing feet and pulling hands make each inch gained a victory over throbbing muscles, broken nails, and silent screams.

Pull harder. Dig the toes of my boots into the floor and push. Shrug my shoulders to keep from getting wedged in. I raise my head and knock a clod of dirt from the ceiling that skids off my nose.

Now I am bargaining with myself. I'll see what's around that corner before yielding to claustrophobic terror. Only a foot to go. Scratch nails in and pull. Dig in feet and push. Breathe deep. Calm down. Feel walls pressing in. Shut eyes. Look down on self. Dig in again. Six more inches. Three. One last push.

My heart pounds so fast and so strongly that my chest bounces off the dirt floor as if on a trampoline. Please, God, let there be a way out. I open my eyes. I have a telescopic view into the room, unable to see its ceiling, floor, or side walls. But it doesn't matter. For in the bull's-eye of the opening floats a box covered with animal skins. A corner of tarnished gold peeks out. I close my eyes and hold my breath.

Chapter 41

Eyes open, deep breath. Not blind, still alive. My grandfather had extended a mirror on the end of the pole to see the Ark. He wouldn't look at it directly. Here I was though, wedged in a tunnel, looking right at the box—covered by animal skins and made of beaten gold—he'd described.

The impulse to move forward overpowered the instinct to panic. Two feet to go before my hands were in the room that contained—could it be?—the Ark of the Covenant. The receptacle where the ancient Hebrews had placed the two stone tablets Moses brought down from Mount Sinai.

I did remember my pledge to Rivka. We were partners. I'd wait for her before touching the Ark. But no reason not to inspect the room. It didn't matter whether Edmund Hillary or Tenzing Norgay *saw* the peak of Everest first. What counted was who *reached* it first, and it seemed fair that the archeologist should do that here. But maybe it was dangerous. Maybe there'd be something like the curse of King Tut's tomb. No sense worrying about it now. Arguments could be postponed until we were both here.

No longer able to snake forward, I had to twist. The passage narrowed, and I was on my side wriggling. Like a diver in pike position, I was bent at the waist, hands extended. Like that same diver who saw himself as a knife blade about to cut through water, I was ready to slice into the room that held the Ark. I shifted the flashlight to my left hand and dug the fingers of my stronger hand into the ceiling. Then the nails of the three middle fingers of my right hand were out of the tunnel, in the room. I wriggled my shoulders. I thought of the times a tailor had held a tape across my shoulders to measure me for a suit. Whatever width he measured was the exact diameter of this tunnel. I wriggled again. Some crumbles of dirt fell onto my neck. My right elbow reached the end of the tunnel. I twisted again and dangled my arm down to reach for the floor of the room holding the Ark. I dug my boots into the sides and then pushed against the new footholds. Another inch. My hand brushed against a flat rock that must have been sitting on the floor. Another push. Now I held that rock in my fist. Dig my boots in again. Twist my shoulders. Push.

I put my left hand on the outside of the hole to pull myself forward. Shit. My shoulders are wedged tight. A few more inches, that's all I ask. My hand, my fingers are a claw locked on the outside rim of the hole. I pull again. Then harder.

But I didn't propel myself forward. Instead, my shoulder popped, my hand flew backward, and clods of dirt started raining down.

Chapter 42

Couldn't breathe. Why try? If oxygen didn't make it to my brain, the terror would end. Mouth and nose were clogged with dirt. I shook dirt out of my eye sockets. Some small pieces scratched at my corneas as I blinked. I could see the top of the Ark or whatever it was. The Maglite must have rolled out of the tunnel into the room during the dirt avalanche. The black dots in front of my eyes? Soil or impending unconsciousness?

I tried to bring my left hand back to unstuff my nose and mouth. A thunderbolt of pain shot across my shoulder and back. God help me, I was awake now. I gagged and tried to find the saliva I needed to get the dirt out of my mouth. Spit. Nothing. Playing whale, I blew out through my nose. My left nostril stayed clogged but I could feel dirt particles spraying out of my right one. Through the cleared nostril, a deep breath brought the oxygen I needed to my lungs even while it compacted the dirt further on the left side. I guessed I wouldn't die of asphyxiation. Terror maybe, but not asphyxiation.

My right fist was clenching the rock fragment. I attempted to move my left hand again, this time leaving my shoulder as immobile as I could. I bent my arm at the elbow and brought it toward my face. Not a thunderbolt this time, just a miasma of pain spreading from my shoulder. I stuck an index finger into my left nostril to try to clear it. No go. The angle wasn't good. I was pushing the dirt further in. Okay. I stuck the finger into my mouth and excavated my way to the back of my throat until stopped by a muddy plug. I pushed the index finger right through the middle to clear the airway. When I gagged this time, a stream of phlegm and dirt and partly digested pita found an opening on the side of my mouth. I spit out more.

I took inventory. Right nostril—cleared. Left—clogged. Mouth—operational again.

I tried to move forward toward the presumed Ark. No go. Then I dug the heels of my hands into the dirt and pushed. Let's run the movie backward, come out the way I came in. Nope. Stuck. The glowing hands of my watch told me it was two-twenty. I cursed the minute hand crawling around the dial.

Like any two-year-old, I'd had a jack-in-the-box. Turn the handle and it played "Pop Goes the Weasel." After the monkey popped out, I'd had to concentrate to push it back down into the box and snap the lid over its head. Here I was doing the same thing. I'd take some breaths and then count to a thousand. Focused on the counting, I'd try to keep my respiration even and calm. I knew the panic was inside me ready to pop, but I kept pushing it back down.

After I finished each deliberate count, I'd look down at my watch, expecting an hour or even two to have passed. No. Each minute was a day, each hour a month. I hadn't even known I was claustrophobic until I came to Jerusalem. Now, wedged in a tunnel under the Temple Mount, twenty feet from what might be the Ark of the Covenant, I was living the nightmare I'd been destined to have.

* * *

"Aron! Are you in there? Alex?"

I looked down at the watch hands. Seven-thirty. What? I'd fallen asleep?

"Yes, in here."

Rivka's voice again. "You're in the passage?"

"I'm stuck."

"Here I come."

I checked my watch and started counting the seconds.

As she came closer, the beam of her flashlight bounced off the dull brown walls and brought some reflected light around the corner.

It had taken me two hours to get myself wedged in like this. It took a tenth of that time for her to tap on my boots. As with gymnasts or jockeys, size was a disadvantage when it came to tunnel-crawlers.

"How are we going to get you out?" she asked.

"Don't you see that hole at the other end?"

"There's time for that later."

"I can see a box of about three by five covered with skins. Is that the right size?"

"Oh, my God. Be careful."

"You think I'll be struck blind?"

"I guess not. Torah says the Ark was one-and-a-half cubits high and wide and two-and-a-half long. Sounds right."

I heard her murmuring in Hebrew.

When she stopped, I asked, "There's a prayer for finding the Ark?"

She ignored the question. "It's okay. I can see how you're wedged in. What do you suggest?"

"Why don't I push with my hand and you pull on my feet?"

"Okay. On three."

I pushed down on my free right hand. My shoulder. I wanted to scream, I would've screamed, but not with Rivka six feet away. I tried to stifle it, but a moan leaked out. She stopped pulling.

"You're hurt."

"Nothing serious. Can you get me outta here?"

"Listen, my angle isn't right. With you extended, I don't have any leverage to get you out. Let me think. I have a hammer and chisel in my bag here. If I got them to you, you'd be able to widen the hole a little, but you'd need to move forward. Then you could be in the room with the Ark with no way out. I'd have to get help."

"I don't think calling out the cavalry is a great idea. We're under the Dome of the Rock, for God's sake."

"Let me see. Could you bear it if I lay on top of you? It still would be easier if you could move backwards."

"No. There's hardly enough room for that. We can't both end up stuck."

She didn't answer. "What are you doing?" I asked.

"Taking off my sweater. Every millimeter is going to count."

"Wait."

She didn't. I felt her torso sliding up the back of my legs. Then her hands were around my waist as she pulled herself up. What would have been exciting in a bed was terrifying in a tunnel. She stopped when the compressed flesh of her breasts was splayed over my shoulder blades.

"Stop," I gasped. "Get off. You're going to get stuck."

"No, I won't."

"But if you do, we'll rot here."

"Turn away." She laid her head on my back and started chipping away at the stone around my left shoulder. Each tap sent a signal of agony to my brain. I put the back of my right hand in my mouth and bit down.

"Can you move your shoulder out now?" she asked.

"Maybe if I pushed again and you pulled."

She grabbed the sleeve of my shirt and pulled.

I wasn't ready for that. "God."

She didn't stop until she'd ripped off the sleeve. Then she

started rubbing something onto the exposed flesh of my shoulder.

"What is that?"

"Pita bread."

"You're rubbing me with pita bread?"

She slithered back down the length of my body.

"You're ready? One, two, three."

She pulled as best she could. I pushed. Agony. I didn't stop. My left shoulder moved. Skin tore. I twisted. I moved, two inches maybe, but I moved.

"Alex, you okay?"

I couldn't talk for a few seconds. I had no reserves.

"I'm okay," I said. "You freed me up. Let me see what I can do."

Pushing with my right hand and sparing my left as much as I could. I made slow progress. So long as I was moving the black dog of claustrophobia was held at bay. Then I felt strong hands around my ankles.

"Shall I pull again?"

"I can make it out."

"But what if I want you out this century?"

"Go ahead and pull, then."

She placed my feet on the floor and I took a few steps backward until my head was out of the passage. I stood up and turned.

There was Rivka buttoning up her blue work shirt, a thick sweater at her feet. She put her arms around me and her head on my shoulder, the left one. I flinched.

"You're hurt," she said.

She lifted my arm. My body quaked. I bit my lip.

"You've dislocated your shoulder. I can put it back."

"Okay," I said.

"You're too tall. Lie down."

I did as I was told.

"Take some deep breaths. Relax."

With her right hand, she anchored my bent left elbow to my side. She took my left hand in her right and rotated my shoulder outward. The muscles around my shoulder tightened.

"Take slow deep breaths and make sure you fully exhale," she directed.

Then she guided my wrist outward, further rotating my shoulder. With a jarring clunk, the amount of pain plummeted from a sharp stabbing to a dull throbbing, from nearly unbearable to almost tolerable.

"Ah."

"Try to move your arm now," she said.

I stood and rotated it. "I'm fine. Thank you. Army training?"

"Of course."

"I thought you weren't coming back till tonight?"

"Good thing I came in early." Then her index finger was pressing against my sternum again. "That was pretty dumb to go in there yourself."

"Yes."

"You were going to wait for me."

"I wanted to see where the tunnel was going."

"A great thing for a claustrophobic to try on his own."

"Claustrophobic?" Her green eyes were locked on mine. "Well, it was a little tight." I changed the subject. A sandwich was ripped open on the floor. "You were getting something to eat? Why did you rub my shoulder with pita?"

"Some olive oil was floating on top of the hummus. I used the bread to sop it up. I figured a little lubricant couldn't hurt."

I put my hands around hers, the one against my chest. "That's good thinking. Thank you. You've saved my life twice now."

"You do seem to require some looking after."

"You were saying a prayer in there because we might have found the Ark?"

"Uh, no."

"Then for?"

She dropped her eyes. "Your safety. Seems to have worked." She shrugged. "Can we stand back to back?"

I turned around.

"Good," she said. "I'm about six centimeters narrower than you at the shoulders. I'm going in to see what you saw."

I started to say something, looked at her, and stifled it.

She leaped up into the hole and started snaking her way down it.

She kept up a running commentary as she progressed. About twenty minutes after she started, I heard her hollow voice call out, "I don't know if it's the Ark, but it sure could be. There are skins on top. The Torah says from *tachash*, but we don't know what animal that is. Wait. Oh, my God. I'm coming back."

"Are you okay?"

"Fine, fine. I'll be right back."

The return was slower because she was moving backward.

She emerged from the hole feet first.

"What?" I asked.

She turned. "What did you see in the room?"

"I could only see the box. I got stuck. I didn't see the whole room."

"I did. The box sits on a platform which King Solomon supposedly built."

"But?"

"At each corner of the platform on the ground there's a, uh..."

"A what?"

"A skeleton."

"Oh, shit. Not again."

Chapter 43

"*Boker tov*," Christine said. She said nothing about the coating of dirt we both wore or my missing sleeve.

"*Boker or*," Rivka and I replied.

It was baked into the characters of Israelis to one-up each other. They had to trump a simple "Good Morning," with a highfalutin' "Morning Light." It's just the way it worked.

"I wonder what she thought," Rivka whispered after she'd passed.

She was French. She'd probably think it was romantic if we'd been rolling around on the floor together before eight-thirty in the morning.

"Come on," I said. "She's an archeologist, too. She knows it's a dirty business."

"Exactly," Rivka said.

I followed her over the catwalk in the hollowed out room and sat across the desk from her.

"You should go back to my place and get some rest," she said. "How's your shoulder?"

Its aching and throbbing seemed distant.

"Fine," I said. I reached into my pocket and pulled out the rock fragment. "Can you read what's on here?"

"What's that?"

"A piece of rock."

"I can see that. Where did you get it?"

"From the floor of the Ark room."

"You couldn't get in. You were stuck."

"But I could reach down to the floor."

"Nice of you to mention it." She held out her hand. "Never mind. Let me see."

She turned on her desk lamp. "There's writing on here."

"Hebrew, isn't it?"

Rivka went into a desk drawer and pulled out a magnifying glass. The examination commenced. If a deerstalker had covered her head rather than a scarf, she could have been Sherlock Holmes's younger sister.

"Sort of," she said.

Her hand went back into the drawer and came out with a pencil and scratchpad. She pulled the light down closer to the rock. Hand into the drawer again, emerging with a pair of black, plastic-framed glasses that I'd never seen before. She looked up, stuck out her chin, and slipped them on. Then she peered at the fragment for two or three minutes. Finally, she picked up the pencil. She stared, muttered, wrote, and erased for twenty minutes before looking up again.

"Do you know what this says? Am I supposed to believe this is real?" Her tone mixed incredulity and defiance.

"I have no idea what it says or if it's real."

"Well, it's a fragment, so it's fragmentary. Do you know the Ten Commandments?"

"Kind of."

"Well the second one says, "*Lo yeeh-yeh l'cha eloheem a'chereem al panahy.*"

"I know the English. Something like 'You will have no other gods before me.'"

"Very good. Literally, it's closer to 'You shall not have other gods beside my face.'"

"That's what's written on the shard?"

"Yeah, in a kind of proto-Hebrew, halfway between the old Hebrew alphabet and hieroglyphics. Canaanite is what we usually call it. Here let me show you what it would look like in English."

Her hand raced across the scratchpad. Then she held it up.

You sh...
have n...
gods...
my fa...

"Of course, the letters on here don't run from left to right like this," she said.

"Even I know Hebrew is written from right to left."

"Not this. It's both. Boustrophedon is the technical term."

"Boustro-what?"

"Boustrophedon. It's Greek for 'as the ox plows.' The lines alternate left-to-right and right-to-left. Even the letters face opposite ways from line to line."

"So the scribe wouldn't even have to lift up his hand."

"If there was a scribe."

"What do you mean 'If there was a scribe?'" I looked at her. Even through the dirt smears, I could see two red points on her cheek. Her eyes glistened. "*Really*? Come on. You think—uh, God—inscribed these letters?"

"Listen, do you remember the story of the Golden Calf?"

When I was in college, my girlfriend Florencia had dragged me to see Schoenberg's *Moses und Aron*. Who knew it would prove useful thirty years later? "Sure. When Moses went up to Mount Sinai to get the Ten Commandments, the Hebrews melted down their jewelry to make an idol."

"And what happened when Moses did come back?"

"He was pissed."

"Yeah. So pissed that he threw down the two stone tablets and shattered them."

"I thought the Ark was where the two stone tablets were kept."

"Right. Remember, Moses went back up to Sinai and got a new set."

"Yeah. Then what's this?"

"There's a rabbinic legend that the pieces of the first set were kept in there, too."

"Seriously? You think this might be one of them?"

"Who knows? Probably not, but we need to find out."

"How? By carbon dating?"

"That's for organic material. If the fragment was from a clay tablet we could try thermoluminescence. But on rock, really the one way to date the writing is by the inscription itself."

"Can't you do that?"

"I can guess, as you saw. But this is a little before my time. The leading expert on Canaanite inscriptions is at Hebrew U."

"When can we see him?"

"Let's go," she said.

"Now?" I asked. "What about your day job? What if your team needs you?"

She stood. "Now."

Chapter 44

The door swung open, and a soil-stained Rivka emerged.

"He's on the phone. He signaled he'd be about ten more minutes."

We settled into a leatherette couch, alone in a waiting area in Hebrew University's Institute of Antiquities.

"We're at the Mount Scopus campus of the university," I said.

"Right," Rivka said.

"And this area of Jerusalem was occupied by Jordan after the War of Independence in 1948?"

"Almost right. Mount Scopus itself remained an Israeli island."

"So how did students get here?"

"They didn't. The institute moved to Giv'at Ram in the New City and only came back here after Jerusalem was reunited in 1967."

I stood and moved over to the windows to look down at the panorama of Jerusalem. Whether I looked to my left at the nearby graves on the Mount of Olives or to my right at the faraway Knesset, my eyes would wander back to the Golden Dome on the Temple Mount, reflecting the rays of the pale lemon winter sun.

Rivka came up and stood next to me, but said nothing for two minutes.

Only after we sat back down did she ask, "You saw Christine's face when we left together?"

We'd passed the Frenchwoman for a second time that morning on the way out.

"Yes."

"She gave me a knowing smile," Rivka said, smiling herself.

"Okay. She thinks we're sneaking around, but I doubt she's guessed what we're sneaking around doing."

"Oh, I doubt she's guessing at all. She thinks she knows."

The light bantering allowed us to avoid the big subject. To hell with that. "My grandfather says he saw the Ark with a mirror."

"I had a mirror in my bag but you never gave me the chance to use it. Anyway, that's why the Ark was covered in skins. So there'd be no inadvertent glimpse."

"Now that we've seen an exposed corner and not been struck blind, we should be safe."

"If it's not the Ark, we're safe. But if it is..."

"Then we're not?"

"Not completely. It says in the fourth chapter of Numbers, 'They must not touch the holy things, or they will die.'"

"And it's clear the term 'holy things' includes the Ark?"

"Oh, yes. In Second Samuel, when David was having it moved from here to Jerusalem, the oxen pulling the cart stumbled. Of course, the driver, a poor schlemiel named Uzzah, reached out to steady the Ark, to make sure it didn't tip over. He was instantly struck down."

"Yeah, I read that. Do you believe that really happened?" I asked.

She shrugged. "Might have. Might not. Who am I to say?"

"So getting wedged in the tunnel saved my life?"

"Could have if it kept you from touching the Ark."

"All I was going to do was look."

The door opened, and a tall man in a white lab coat entered and went through the Continental ritual of air kisses on both sides of Rivka's face. Then he took her hands in his. Even after they started talking, they stood uncomfortably close—not uncomfortable for them, but for me.

Drowning in the spate of Hebrew words issuing forth from them, I took a closer look at Professor Amit Ben-David. Tall, lean, dark, with a dimple in his chin. If the good professor ever tired of archeology, he could always make a pretty good living as a male model.

I heard my own name, and Ben-David turned toward me.

"Pleased to meet you, Professor," I told him. He gave me a white-toothed smile. And to aggravate me a little more, he had a firm grip, too.

"You came across a piece of stone with Canaanite carvings?" he asked in an Israeli accent.

I pulled it out of my pocket and handed it over.

"You might have something here, Aron. The lettering looks Canaanite from, oh, three thousand five hundred years ago."

"That's what Professor Golan figured," I said. "I guess the boustrophedon writing is a real clue."

He gave a jerk in surprise. Well, more of a tremor. "Yeah. That's right."

He looked over at Rivka. "And you want me to estimate when the letters were scratched in the rock?"

"Right," she said. "Also your guess on the kind of tool the carver used. And can we identify where the rock is from, too?"

"How about if we just climb back in to the university's time machine and watch the person carve the letters?"

"Amit, I know we're asking a lot."

"When do you need this back?"

"This afternoon," she said.

"The time machine really would be easier."

She gave him two more air kisses and said, "We'll be back at five."

Chapter 45

"Aron, Aron. Wake up."

Rivka was shaking my shoulder, the good one, not the scraped, just-popped-back-into-its-socket one. "What time is it?"

"Four."

I sat up, and a book fell on the floor.

Rivka picked up the book I'd bought on my last trip. "A little Bible study?"

"Better late than never. I guess you know my namesake, Aron, went right along with the crowd in making that golden calf."

"And he was the first high priest. That's what I like best about the Torah. Even the heroes are far from perfect. Shall we get back to H.U. and see what Amit has figured out?"

"Wouldn't it be easier to call?"

"Easier, yes. Better, no. Let's go."

I'd showered and put on clean clothes when we got back from the first meeting with Ben-David. "Let me wash my face and brush my teeth."

Fifteen minutes later we caught a bus on Emek R'fayim. In forty-five, Rivka was waving her ID at a sensor by the door of the building on the university campus where we'd visited Professor Dimple Chin that morning.

She was reaching for the stairway door when it swung open as if by mere proximity. No magic was involved. A man in khakis and a blue Hebrew University sweatshirt said, "*S'licha*" without even looking up.

The man could not have been a native Israeli. The courtesy he demonstrated in holding the door for us showed he'd learned his manners in a country where Israel's every-person-for-himself ethos did not prevail.

Rivka was taking the stairs two at a time. She waited at the landing, palm slapping against her cargo pants. "Let's go."

She did not hold the door for me on the third floor—she was an Israeli convert—and I had to race-walk to pull even as we approached the office. I did hold the door for her.

"Amit?"

No answer.

"He's probably in the library."

"Okay."

We went down a floor.

"Amit?" she called out.

No answer.

"Let me go check in the back room," Rivka said.

I looked at the shelves filled with bound issues of journals, mostly in English, but with a sprinkling of German and Arabic.

"Aron!"

I ran to the opening at the back of the reading room.

"Rivka, where are you?"

"Here."

I hadn't seen her because she was crouching behind a table. Crouching over the unconscious form of Professor Ben-David.

Chapter 46

"We'd better call 911," I told Rivka.

"He's breathing."

As if in response, Ben-David fluttered his eyes. His irises swam for a moment and then clicked into focus on Rivka's face.

"*Cheres*," he said and stood up.

I looked at Rivka. "The fragment," she translated.

Once he was standing, Ben-David's head started to weave and his pupils disappeared under his upper lids. I grabbed one arm and Rivka the other. He slumped and we eased him back down, his back against the wall.

"I'm okay" he said

"What happened?" Rivka asked in English this time.

He shook loose, stood again, and trotted back into the other room with Rivka and me following.

"*Uf la'azazel*," Ben-David said in the same tone an American would say "Aw, shit."

"The fragment is gone?" Rivka asked.

"*Kein.*"

"What happened?" Rivka asked again.

"Yeah, sure. I was working on the fragment here under the ultraviolet lamp."

"Right," Rivka said.

"A man came up and asked me how to find Professor Ben-

David's office. That's the last thing I remember until I saw you."

"Was he wearing a sweatshirt and khakis?"

"How did you know?" Ben-David asked.

"We passed him on the way up here," Rivka said.

Here I was again rubbing up against unexpected violence. "How did that guy anticipate us?" I asked. I turned to Rivka. "We should call the police."

"He's long gone," she said.

"I don't think the rock he took was worth too much anyway," Ben-David said.

"Why not?" Rivka asked.

"The letters looked like standard Canaanite to me, but they were perfect. Duplicate letters matched exactly. So the workmanship was my first clue."

"To what?"

"To when the inscription was done. The second clue was the lack of chisel marks or any cutting at all."

"But the letters were carved into the rock somehow."

"Not carved. Burned."

"What do you mean 'burned'?"

"Etched with a laser or something. The sides of the indentations showed the rock had melted."

"So whoever did the inscription could have used a heated arrowhead or something," I suggested.

"Granite melts at around six hundred degrees."

"Celsius," Rivka said.

"If this were genuine, the work would be rough," Ben-David said. "I'd even say the laser was computer-controlled. I'm telling you the duplicate letters were exact matches. This was done pretty recently, then. Maybe not last week, but in the last twenty or thirty years for sure." He gave me a grin meant to be sympathetic. "I think you fell for a line from a street vendor. I hope you didn't pay too much for it."

Any last drop of sympathy I had for Ben-David vaporized. If he'd revived enough to poke fun at a stupid American tourist, he counted as being in good shape.

"Could you tell where the granite came from?" Rivka asked.

"Well, that was peculiar, too. I wanted to send it out for analysis."

"Do you have a guess?"

"I'd say it was from an achondrite."

"From a meteor?" she asked.

"That's what it looked like."

Rivka ignored me and laid a hand on Ben-David's wrist. "Shall we take you to see a doctor?"

"No reason. I'm fine. My head doesn't hurt. I don't know why I fainted."

"Probably gave you a whiff of some anesthetic," Rivka said. "Something odorless and fast-acting. Maybe Sevoflurane. Easy to get."

The things you learn in the Israeli Defense Force.

"I'm sorry I lost the stone," Ben-David said to her. Turning to me, he said, "Maybe you can pick up another one in the Arab market."

"We're sorry to have put you through this," I answered. "Kind of a wild goose chase."

"A what?"

Rivka rattled off some Hebrew, and he nodded.

When we got outside, Rivka put her hands to her head. "This is too much."

"The fragment being stolen?"

"Yes, and I should never have gotten Amit involved. He could have been killed. He was my husband's best friend. I would have never forgiven myself."

"How long has he been carrying a torch for you?"

As a pinkish flush climbed from her neck to her cheeks, she said, "He's a real expert in his field."

If she didn't want to answer a question that was none of my business, fine. So I asked, "You think he was right about the inscription being recent?"

"Come on, we'll catch the bus and discuss this back at the flat."

* * *

"There's got to be a logical explanation. We know my grandfather and his rabbi friends were down there."

We were sitting at the dinner table. I poured some Dancing Camel down my gullet. Rivka sipped her merlot.

"So they left behind that fake fragment to mislead people? Your grandfather was the Bialystoker Rebbe. He would never do such a thing."

"Okay, he wouldn't have. He couldn't. He didn't even get into the room with the Ark. Perhaps one of his colleagues did."

"You told me you were looking for truth." She drained her wineglass and poured another one. "You're not even considering the most logical explanation."

"You're saying the rock fragment was from the Ten Commandments?"

She jutted her chin out. "Here are the choices. The ancient Hebrews had lasers, it's a hoax, or it's a piece of the Ten Commandments. I pick Door Number Three."

I stood up and looked down at her. "You're saying God wrote perfect letters on a rock not from this world."

For me the existence of God was an unprovable possibility, and I was content to leave it that way.

"You don't have to shout," Rivka said. I focused on her hand as it lifted the freshened glass to her lips for another swallow. Rock steady. "Why not?" she continued. "It confirms what the Torah says."

For Rivka, God's existence was a certainty.

"So after thousands of years of searching, it fell to you and me to prove God's existence to a world of skeptics?"

She folded her arms across her chest. "Perhaps that's what your grandfather meant by *emet*."

"Can you imagine what would happen if it were announced that pieces of the Ten Commandments had been found under the Temple Mount?"

"The parties on the right here in Israel would call for control of the Temple Mount. With proof of the Ten Commandments, they would win elections in a walk. There would be rioting in Arab countries demanding the Temple Mount remain under Muslim control. The Iranians would ratchet up their threats to use nuclear weapons. American evangelicals..." She stopped and looked at me. "What?"

"The chain of events you described, well, your words were about the same as my friend Mitch Samuelson—he works for the State Department—used. Wait a minute. What time is it in Washington?" Looking down at my watch, I subtracted seven hours. "It's two in the afternoon there."

I took out my iPhone and picked his home number off my contact list.

"Hello?"

"Hi, Sarah, Alex. How is he?" Without a thought, I'd changed identities from Aron back to Alex.

"He's right here." Her tone told me she still blamed me for Mitch getting shot.

"Hello, Alex?"

"You sound good, Mitch."

"Yeah, I'm almost ready to get back to the office. What's up? I was about to call you."

"Yeah? Shall I go first?"

"No, let me," Mitch said. "I heard a body was found in the excavations under the Wall."

"Yes, it was all over the papers here." No lie in saying that.

"So you made it back in?"

"Yeah, through Petra," I said.

"I figured. Anyway, here's what wasn't in the papers—the Israelis figured out who the person was."

"Go ahead. Who?" I held my breath.

"A Professor Al Ghamdi from King Saud University in Riyadh who was supposed to have disappeared in the desert twenty years ago."

"Was this professor's field archeology?"

"Good guess. Want to guess his specialty?"

"The ancient Holy Land?"

"Not far off. The Jewish tribes of Arabia in Mohammed's time. This guy was connected, too. His mother was a daughter of Ibn Saud."

"She was a princess?"

"You got it. And his younger brother, well, really a half-brother, is a colonel in Saudi intelligence. He'll want to take vengeance on whoever killed his brother."

"That professor's been dead for a long time."

"I met the colonel once. He's scary. When he looks at you, you don't have a clue what he's thinking."

"How can a person with a good poker face be scary?"

"When you can't see the person's eyes behind dark glasses."

Shit. "The kind with mirrored lenses?"

"Yeah, how'd you know?"

"And this colonel speaks English like he was at Eton and Cambridge?"

"Marlborough and Sandhurst, actually." After a few seconds, Mitch said, "Dammit, you have come across him."

I swallowed down a caustic mouthful of bile and said, "Maybe." God, what if I had taken that ride to Petra?

"He's dangerous," Mitch said. When I said nothing, he took his voice up a dozen decibels. "I know you're stubborn, but this is no game. Listen to me: it's time for you to get out of Israel for good."

"Uh, Mitch, when I originally met with you, you had a briefing book on the search for the Ark."

"Yeah. So?"

"And it came from our consulate in East Jerusalem?"

"Yeah. I told you I asked them to get something together for our meeting. Any problem with that?"

"Just that you've got a spy in the consulate."

Chapter 47

"It makes sense," I was saying to Rivka after I'd hung up with Mitch.

"I only heard your side of the conversation," Rivka said. "Take me through your theory."

"Okay. We'll start with everyone I spoke to about what my grandfather had asked me to do."

"Okay."

"Katie," I said. Rivka held up her thumb. "You." Index finger. "Mitch." Middle finger. "Next, the people they might have told. My daughter's boyfriend." Ring finger. "Did you tell anyone?" She shook her head. "I don't think Rabbi Zweiback knew but he might have." She did not stick up her pinkie.

"He's the Bialystoker Rebbe chosen by your grandfather. I don't think he should be on the list."

"I trust you, Katie, and Mitch, too. You raised fingers for them."

She raised her pinkie. "I thought you didn't trust Mitch."

"I do trust *him*. But people in the American consulate in East Jerusalem knew Mitch was meeting me to discuss the Ark. What happens right after we meet? A sniper's waiting for us."

"What sniper?" Rivka asked.

I explained.

"You didn't think to mention this before?"

"The sniper shot Mitch."

"But you were the target, right? You knew that."

"Suspected it. We're the same size and Mitch was sitting in the passenger seat where, by all rights, I should've been."

"So who would want to stop you from coming?"

"We've been through the possibilities."

"Not us, not Israel," she said.

"Probably not. On the one hand, Mr. Cohen seemed to know what I was up to. On the other, he wanted me out of the country. That doesn't quite jibe with assassination, but we're not going to cross them off the list."

"The United States government. They're pushing for peace and don't want their efforts to explode in their faces."

"Well, given Mitch's involvement, if it was the United States, I'd like to think it was a rogue operation," I said.

"Okay, what about the Arabs?"

"Finding the Ark... Well, that would call into question the legitimacy of Muslim control of the Temple Mount. It would bring strong Christian support to the Israeli side in negotiations, especially in the United States but in Europe, too. Hamas, Hezbollah, the Palestinian Authority, Iran—all would do most anything to make sure the Ark is not found. Including shooting at me and stealing a rock fragment."

"Yeah."

"And Mitch said the consulate in East Jerusalem is largely staffed by local Arabs."

"But nothing we've said is conclusive."

"There is that matter of the Saudi archeologist."

"But you were shot at before we found him."

I threw up my hands. "We'll figure it out eventually. In the meantime, I want to see that Ark again."

"We know that there's no harm in looking," Rivka said.

"But no touching, huh?" I asked.

"It'll be like fooling with the gators back home in Florida. We'll bring a stick and poke at it from a safe distance."

"Let's go tomorrow morning."

"Right. We'll start early before the team shows up. Can you be ready at five?"

"Sure."

"Let's go to bed, then."

I started taking the cushions off the back of the couch.

"Come on, you can use half of the bed in my bedroom," Rivka offered.

I shook my head.

Chapter 48

I opened my eyes, completely awake. A shadowy outline glided by on the other side of the living room. Rivka's son Ori on leave again? No. Ori would head to his own bedroom, not slink along the wall toward Rivka's. I could yell and hope Rivka could get to her gun before the phantom opened her door, but I didn't know how heavy a sleeper she was or how close she kept the gun. Bad odds. I started groping along the floor, my fingers trailing across shoes, sweatshirt, belt, flashlight. Perfect.

I sucked in a chest-full of air and pushed it back out by shouting "*Salaam*" as loud as I could. My thumb flicked the Maglite's on-switch. The figure raised his left arm to shield his eyes. At the end of the limb dangled a small carbon steel instrument, but I was moving fast by the time I registered what it was. I was almost to him when the arm of our midnight caller described a graceful arc, a powerful, perfectly timed backhand swing that would have done Roger Federer proud. My head must have been harder than he expected—the collision between my noggin and his gun was a draw. I started falling and the gun went flying. Even as I was dropping, my momentum carried me forward. I heard him go "Oof" as my good shoulder crashed into his midsection. At the same time I heard the gun clattering across the floor.

On my knees, I was surprised to find the Maglite still in my hand. I didn't have room for a good swing, but I still found the crack the flashlight made against the outside of his left knee gratifying. I shined the light up into his face. His skin glowed ghostly white, and a grimace revealed a missing eyetooth. I tried to get up, but the heel of his hand sent me back to the floor. Knocked supine, I could see him lurching toward the flat's entrance. Just as he disappeared into the front foyer, Rivka flung open her bedroom door, both hands on her service revolver, the reflected glow of my Maglite outlining her form. The downstairs door slammed shut.

"You okay?" she asked.

"You'll be able to see him out the front window," I said.

"So what? You want me to start spraying bullets in the dark down Masaryk Street?"

This time she'd been sleeping in an oversized University of Miami jersey. Number 18. The synapses of my brain flashed with an incongruous thought—in this lighting and from this angle, Rivka's legs looked marble smooth and impossibly long. She crouched and prized the flashlight from my hands and then held it up to the left side of my face. "Your cheek looks like an overripe *chatseilim*—an eggplant. Tell me what happened."

"I woke up and saw a guy skulking around."

"And you attacked him with a flashlight? You're fifty years old. Do you think maybe God gave you more courage than brains?"

"What else was I supposed to do?"

She shook her head as if at a headstrong child. "I don't know. What now?"

I pulled her head close and whispered, "They know what we're doing and where we are."

She nodded, turned the lights on, and looked around.

"There's nothing missing," I said at conversational volume.

"How do you know you woke up right when he came in?"

"I don't know. I just do. Maybe I heard him open the door."

Twenty minutes later we emerged from the flat on to Masaryk Street laden with backpacks. Rivka had her hand in the pocket where she kept her gun.

"So you think someone has a listening device in there?" Rivka asked.

"It would explain a lot."

"Did you see who it was?" she asked.

"Yeah," I answered. "I'd met him before, and we both saw him again this afternoon on Mount Scopus."

"The guy in the khakis who opened the door," she said. "But where had you met him before?"

"On my first trip here someone tried to mug me on Ben Yehuda."

"What? Are you sure this guy in my flat was the same person?"

I flashed on the missing right eyetooth. "I am. I thought it was a random mugging, but..." I stopped and took her arm. "Listen, these guys are relentless. Maybe it's time to give up."

"Are you giving up?"

"Yes, I'll give up," I said.

"You'll break your promise to your grandfather?"

"Yes."

"Then let's go to the police."

"No, no. I don't want to get you in trouble."

"I'm not sure who'd get into more trouble. But I do know they'd kick your ass out of the country. Which is what you don't want. Get off the bullshit about giving up. You won't get rid of me that easily."

"Why not?"

"Because we are two strips of bacon on the plate next to each other. We are *partners*, and we are committed." She took a deep breath. "Okay, back to the alleged listening device. How long do you think it has been there?"

"A while, I think."

"Then why did they decide to move now?"

"It's not the first time. I think they heard us before the bulldozer and again before the theft of the rock fragment yesterday."

"Who is 'they'?"

"I'm putting my money on the Saudis, but it's only a hunch."

"If they were listening, wouldn't they have known you were there on the couch?"

"No. Remember, you asked me to share the bed."

"But you said no."

"I didn't *say* no. I shook my head."

"So they figured we were both in the bedroom, asleep and exhausted, and you surprised him."

Right. If I'd been a normal healthy guy, Rivka and I might have been lying in her bed with matching bullet holes. Partners in death.

Chapter 49

In the light cast by an electric lantern, I could see Rivka's face nine inches from my own. The tendons in her neck were popping with exertion. By her ears, tendrils of hair had escaped from her scarf only to be recaptured and pasted down against her face by perspiration. Her eyes were closed—whether as a way to summon more strength or to avoid my stare I did not know. Her hands had reached over my head and shoulders and into my armpits. Her feet were propped against the wall under the hole where my head was emerging. She heaved again.

"Any movement?" she asked.

"A fraction of an inch to go."

"Okay. This time instead of steady pressure, I'm going to try to jerk you through the hole."

"I'm ready."

"One, two, three."

"Fuck." Again the pop, followed by the dagger of pain piercing my left shoulder. Rivka's hands slipped off mine, and she flew backwards. Her behind hit the cobblestone floor, and she skidded in a seated position for another two feet. When she stopped, she was between two of the skeletons at the corner of the Ark platform. Twelve more inches and she would have crashed into the Ark.

I used my right arm to pull myself the rest of the way into

the room. My left was useless. Again. I walked over to where she sat, held out my good arm, and pulled her up.

She turned her head and looked back at the Ark.

"Thanks," she said. I saw something on her face, in her green eyes, that I hadn't seen before—fear. She'd screamed when she'd fallen on the corpse when we'd been down here the first time, but that was not fear: it was fright, the thing that makes you scream in a horror movie. Being that close to touching what might be the Holy Ark, violating a Biblical prohibition, terrified her beyond screaming.

"Thank you. You got me through the hole this time."

We looked at each other for a moment and then she said, "Come here. I'll put your arm back."

Less than a minute later she had, leaving an afterglow of pain where the dagger had been withdrawn.

"I've read Houdini got out of straightjackets by popping his shoulders out of their sockets," I said.

"And in a breakthrough in the art of escape, you've applied his technique to ancient tunnels," Rivka said.

"Only with some help."

Rivka went back to her backpack and pulled out a camera the size of a cigarette pack.

With a sunburst of light every few seconds, she started to make a methodical photographic record of each square foot of the room. The animal skin-clad box stood on a wooden platform. The room itself was maybe twenty by twenty-five feet. The floor where the four skeletons were splayed was solid rock, as were the walls and the ceiling. We were in a cave.

"Look." She pointed to a rock fragment about the size of a note card in the farthest corner from our entrance hole.

Then she went back to the magician's bag of a backpack and pulled out a pair of latex gloves.

My flashlight hovered over the shard.

"How good were you at jigsaw puzzles?" she asked.

"I always tried to put the border together first."

"I think this fits with the fragment that was stolen. It's the rest of the second commandment." She said a prayer in Hebrew. "That's a *shehechiyanu*. It thanks God for letting us live to see this day."

"Amen," I said. "Why do you think there were only two fragments on the floor?"

"I don't know," she said, still peering at the fragment.

"May I hold it?" She handed it over. "Do you think the other fragments of the first stone tablets are in the box?" I asked.

"I don't know that either."

She moved back toward the skeletons. I followed. Unlike Professor Al Ghamdi, these were not the bodies of contemporaries who'd made a wrong turn. The little flesh that remained was dried like rawhide. The bottom jaws of each of the quartet were open as if they'd died in the middle of a conversation. The gray of old bones poked through the remains of clothing. What was most peculiar was the position of the bodies. All four jutted out from a corner of the stand at a forty-five degree angle.

Rivka was the professional here. In both archeological digs and army duty, she must have come across a fair number of dead bodies.

She crouched and rubbed the cloth covering one of the men between thumb and index finger.

"Feel," she ordered.

"Rough," I said.

"Not done on machine looms," she said. "Could you shine the light here on his face?"

The only flesh remaining was around his lips. The dark brown streaks over and under the yellow teeth made it look as though a smile were painted on.

"Keep the light there," Rivka said, as she pulled on the latex gloves.

I'd been so intent on the expression of the dead person, I'd missed what Rivka saw. She moved the fabric away from the shoulder bone, and then I saw it, too—a leather string around what had once been a neck.

After a few pulls, she held up her prize like the winning angler in a bass-fishing contest.

"Look," she whispered.

An amulet—not metal but clay—dangled from Rivka's gloved hand. On it was imprinted a candelabra with seven arms.

"The Temple Menorah," Rivka said.

We stood. "So how long have these people been lying here?"

"I don't know. Since 587 BCE when the Babylonians conquered Jerusalem? The good news is it's a lot easier to date bodies than rocks."

I swallowed my doubts that these skeletons were going to ever show up in a lab. "Did they die because they touched the Ark?" I asked.

"Maybe they were guards," she said, pointing to the short sword that peeked through the robe of the skeleton nearest to us. She shuddered before starting to talk in a voice of exaggerated reason. "I don't like to give up. People are trying to stop us, but now I'm *here*. Maybe with the Ark of the Covenant. You know, I feel like Moses when God spoke to him through the burning bush. 'Hey, God, you made a mistake. I am not the right person for this.'"

"Didn't God tell Moses he was the right person after all?"

"Yes, but he promised him a partner, his brother Aron." She looked at me. "And here you are, his namesake."

"So?"

"Yeah, I want to leave but I can't. If this is the Ark, the

Torah stops being a book of stories. It becomes history. I'm a professor. It's my job to discover truth."

"You're also a major in the IDF. It's your job to protect your country."

"I think that includes protecting the Ark."

"Those four there on the ground thought so, too. Okay. Next move?"

Rivka went to her backpack and took out a round wood dowel with the diameter of my thumb and what looked like a tire iron. Both were about eighteen inches long. She started approaching the Ark like Dorothy walking up to the Wizard the very first time.

"Here, give them to me."

"It's my job."

I held out my hand. She yielded and gave me the metal rod. Ah, not a tire iron, a crowbar. I left my hand extended and with an exasperated sigh, she surrendered the dowel, too.

Stepping over one of the bodies, I went up to the exposed corner of the Ark. Because it sat on a wooden platform a couple of feet off the ground, the top reached the middle of my chest.

"I want to move the skins off the top," I said to Rivka.

"We should wait, get an entire crew in here, use robot arms to move the skins, and video the whole thing."

"We are under the Dome of the Rock on the Temple Mount, and guess what? The Muslim authorities who are in charge in the surface world may not look too kindly on a full archeological expedition down here."

She didn't answer.

"Sorry, that was obnoxious. But look," I continued, "if this is the Ark and seeing it was fatal, we'd be dead. That corner with the gold is exposed already."

"Okay."

Using the crowbar, I pushed the skins off the box onto the

ground. "What kind of animal do these skins come from?" I asked.

The hides were antelope brown, except near the legs where they morphed into zebra stripes. I dangled one of the skins from the end of the bar and ran my fingers along it. No seam. A single skin. "What do you think? Some extinct animal?"

"The Bible calls them *tachash*, but no one knew what it referred to. Rabbi Yehudah said it was an animal with a horn, a six-colored hide, and the split hooves needed to make it kosher. This comes close to fitting. Okapi."

While continuing to move the skins aside, I asked "Aren't okapi from central Africa?"

"There's a twenty-five-hundred-year-old carving of one in Iran. Jerusalem is on the way from central Africa to Iran."

"You know this would be easier if I picked up the skins with my hands."

"And if you should touch the Ark?"

"Then if I drop dead, you'll know it's really the Ark."

"Not funny."

"Trying to release tension, I guess."

She gave me a shrug that went beyond her shoulders. Her whole body curled upward and then relaxed. My father had shrugged the same way after a visit to the principal's office with me. He just didn't know how to handle a first-grader who talked back to his teacher.

When I pushed the last skin off, I asked, "So is it the Ark?"

The question turned Rivka back into an archeologist.

She stepped over a skeleton. Between clicks of her camera, she said, "I don't know. It's the right size. It has rings to slip poles through to carry it. It fits the description from Deuteronomy of a plain box made from acacia wood. But in Exodus it says a craftsman named Bezalel covered the ark he built with solid gold. On top he put two gold cherubs with outspread wings and, um, a gold judgment seat. Biblical gilding of the lily, I guess."

"Almost literally. A box with that much gold would be awfully heavy to cart around the desert," I said.

"Especially for forty years. Once the Ark was moved to the Temple, no one would have really known what it looked like since only the High Priest saw it."

"Which would make it easy for legends to grow around it."

While Rivka kept snapping her camera, I walked around the box holding my Maglite in one hand and the steel rod in the other. On the long side, away from the hole where we'd entered, there were two leather straps running between the lid and the box—sort of primitive hinges. The lack of humidity and air circulation had preserved the leather just as it had the vestiges of flesh on the bodies.

"There's no sign of any lock anywhere," I said. "It looks like you can pull open the top like a child's toy box."

"Wait."

"For what?"

She was breathing hard and came over to me. She put her hands on my head and murmured in Hebrew.

"What did you say?"

"May the Holy One bless you and keep you." She retreated a few steps and then came right back to press against me. She looked up. "Be careful."

I pried off the arms encircling me and took a few paces to stand in front of the box. I put the thin end of the crowbar under the lid and began to open it. A light erupted. My arms jerked in surprise, and the lid slammed back down.

"Sorry." It was the flash of Rivka's camera. I blinked away the stars and started to open the lid again.

"Be careful not to touch the box," Rivka whispered.

For a box that might have been closed for a couple of millennia, the lid opened easily. Inch by inch I raised it with the end of the crowbar. When the lid had opened a foot and a half, I propped the rod between the lid and the box.

I stepped over a skeleton and moved to the side. Rivka moved to the opposite end. I looked in and swung my flashlight's beam into the box. Rivka was doing the same.

"Wait," I said.

Chapter 50

"What?" Rivka asked.

I flicked off my flash. "Move a little closer to the box and then turn off your flash, too."

She didn't ask why. She came half a step closer to her end of the box. Click. Total darkness.

"Keep your eyes on the inside of the box," I said.

It took about twenty seconds before Rivka said, "I see it. The glow. Like the light from a gas burner."

In eerie pulsating blue I made out a rough rectangle and scattered irregular pieces. "It's the letters on that big piece that are glowing," I said.

"Yeah, there is writing on the big piece," Rivka whispered. "But I can't make it out."

We stared for a while. I could hear Rivka reciting the prayer she'd called the *shehechiyanu*.

"Close your eyes," I said. "I'm going to turn on my flashlight again."

Through my blinking, I saw her doing the same. I leaned in. In the box lay two rough-hewn rectangular pieces of rock and twenty or thirty more broken pieces like the two we'd found on the floor.

"Am I really here?" Rivka asked. "Am I alive at all? I can't believe it."

"Can't believe what?"

"That these are the tablets Moses brought down from Mount Sinai," Rivka said.

"This is where they hid them when the Babylonians conquered Jerusalem?"

"Must be."

"What do you think is making the letters glow?" I asked. "Some kind of phosphorescent mold? Or if it's from a meteor, maybe it's radioactive. We didn't check for that."

"Or maybe it's an artifact of the hand of the Holy One."

Rivka closed her eyes. I could see her chest swell and deflate and hear the air sliding in and out between her lips.

I went back to the hole I'd come in through. The prospect of going back out through that devil's channel speeded up my own pulse and respiration. I poked the flashlight into the opening. My shoulders had made it through thanks to the extra force supplied by Rivka and the willingness of my clavicle to slip out of its joint. How then had the Ark, if that's what it was, come in here? Had it been unassembled and put back together once *in situ*? Given its holy status, that didn't seem likely.

Fuck. A murmuring of voices tumbled out of the tunnel. The opening was the end of a giant ear trumpet that brought the sound of two men—no, three... no, four—talking. I couldn't make out the words. The four were not yet in the tunnel, or even in the anteroom, but they could be here with us in minutes.

I put my hand across Rivka's mouth. She emerged from her trance with a jerk.

"Men are coming," I whispered.

"You could hear them through the tunnel?"

"Yes."

She moved to the hole to take advantage of the acoustics.

"They're speaking Arabic. We should have known from the dead Saudi that there was another route down here."

I didn't need a translation for what came next—a muffled

shout that came out of the tunnel. "Mr. Kalman, are you there? We will join you in a moment." The words were English, the accent upper-class British. The voice of the man who'd sat next to me on the plane to Amman. Was he Dark Glasses from Ben Yehuda Street, too? Didn't matter. Colonel Al Ghamdi.

"Shit," I whispered. "We've led them straight to the Ark."

"They're not sure you're here, though."

"They'll confirm it soon enough if we don't do something. Do you have your gun?"

"Yes."

"It won't do much good, will it? Even if we start shooting, all they'll need to do is close off the tunnel, and we'll run out of air like our friends over there." I flashed my light on the four skeletons. What a death. Suffocation in a cave. Maybe someone else would come across our remains in a couple of millennia. The powerful arms of claustrophobia were snaking around my chest. And beginning to squeeze.

"They can't let us live," Rivka said in a calm low voice. She was a soldier. "We've found the Ark of the Covenant."

"What I wonder is how the Ark got in here." I started running my fingers along the walls. Then I shot the beam upwards. "The Holy of Holies is up there, right? It was moved down here, but how?"

Ten feet above us was the craggy gray ceiling, hollowed out along with the rest of the room, the cavern. Like twin floodlights at a Hollywood opening, our beams played back and forth.

We could hear the voices from where we stood. They were in the room on the other side of the tunnel. We had ten minutes, fifteen tops.

Chapter 51

A month ago, if Dr. Zweig had found some fatal tumor during my physical, I might have shrugged my shoulders. Yeah, it would have been a bad break. Sure, I would have been scared. Yes, I would have desperately missed being there for Katie and watching the spool of her life unwind, but I would have known my best days were behind me. No more. Now I had a mission not yet fulfilled. Was this really the Holy Ark that held the Ten Commandments? I had to find out and, if it was, bear witness to its discovery.

"No," I said.

"What?" Rivka whispered.

"We're getting out of here."

"How?"

I stepped back from the platform, took two running steps, and leaped.

I was still in midair when Rivka emitted an urgent whisper, "No."

But her voice was not the last thing I heard in this world. I landed on all fours on the lid of the box.

Unlike the unlucky Uzzah in the Bible, I was still breathing.

Amidst the indistinct chattering of our prospective guests, an Arabic sentence came through clearly. Someone had made it into the tunnel.

"He said he can't see anything yet," Rivka reported. "What are you up to?"

"Better struck dead by God's hand than by a human's."

The ceiling extended about four feet above the top of the Ark. I crouched and raised my hands above my head. The place to start was the middle. What I was looking for I wasn't sure. What I felt was cold rock.

The beam of Rivka's flashlight wavered. I looked down. With her left hand she was still pointing the flash upwards, but she'd reached down with her right hand and was unzipping the pocket on the thigh of her cargo pants. Then she was flexing her fingers around the gun that had saved my life on Karen Hayesod Street.

The hole in the wall began to glow with light from an electric lantern. The man in the tunnel was reaching the first S-curve. I slipped and grabbed on to a rocky protuberance in the ceiling to regain my balance. What I was holding onto moved down. I let go and it snapped back and rejoined the rest of the ceiling. What the hell? I put both hands around the rock and pulled hard. The outline of a rectangle just larger than the Ark itself appeared, and then the left end of the rectangle began to swing down. I hadn't seen a thing to show that the ceiling was anything but solid rock until that trapdoor opened. When it was perpendicular to the floor, I jumped down from the top of the Ark.

"We have to move the Ark."

Sacrilege it might have been, but I tilted one end of the Ark and put my ten fingers underneath. I lifted. Rivka hesitated for a fraction of a second before touching the box, but then raised her end. I'd guess we were each supporting forty pounds.

"Where to?" she asked.

"In the corner to the left of the opening."

We laid the Ark, or whatever it was, in the corner and came back to the platform where the box had lain.

I jumped up, but my fingers only grazed the opening above.

"Here." Rivka interlaced her fingers. I put my boot in the stirrup she'd made. I took my hands off her shoulders and teetered for a second, but managed to get both hands over the ledge of the opening. Pull, you sucker. My left shoulder throbbed, but I was getting closer. Then I felt a push on the soles of my boots. That made the difference.

"Thanks," I whispered.

I lay prone and reached downward with my right arm.

"Here, take this," she hissed. "The camera." She swung it up and I caught it. "Now the flashlights. Now the backpacks."

"Do you want to try to take the stone tablets?"

"Out of the Ark?" Even in low tones, I caught the unstated *Are you crazy?* Then she murmured, "No."

She passed up her gear and then we were ready. Rivka jumped. The tips of her middle fingers made it to the first joint of mine.

"I'll get you this time."

I did. I started pulling her upward by the one hand I'd grabbed and then found the other. Shit, the pain in my shoulder. I shut my eyes and heaved. I could feel her wiggling her legs. Then she was in. Thank God for the gym visits.

"There has to be a way to get the door back up," I said.

From below came more Arabic, each word distinct this time. I asked, "What's he saying?"

"He's at the second S-curve. Look."

The disc of light from her Maglite played over what was a huge lever. The rock I'd pushed on was laced with leather thongs to one end of a long piece of wood—a tree trunk twenty-five feet long and a foot around, stripped of bark and branches. At its midpoint, the pole balanced on a rocky outcrop three feet high jutting up from the floor of the chamber where we stood. Another rock was laced to its far end.

"A teeter-totter," I whispered.

Rivka pulled down on the end over the hole and the naked trunk tilted down over the hole as the far end rose. Air pressure offered more resistance as the rock fitted into the opening.

When the crack was only a few inches wide, our wannabe companion in the tunnel called back to his colleagues. Rivka hopped up and straddled the trunk. The rock began to nestle back into the hole we'd climbed through three minutes before. Then there was a whoosh that cut off the speaker in the middle of a word.

We froze. The only sound I could hear was Rivka breathing.

After thirty seconds, Rivka said, "The engineering here, just amazing. By balancing the two rocks and providing a long lever, a single person can open and close that trapdoor.

"Archeology later, survival now," I answered. "What was the guy down there saying?"

"That he saw a room and the opening was too narrow for him to fit through. You figured on that, didn't you?"

"Not figured—hoped."

"So if he can't get in, he'll not be able to see where we put the Ark."

"That's my hope again."

"And even if he gets in the Ark room, he'll not find the trapdoor."

"One more hope."

She pulled my head down and kissed my forehead. "Okay, here's hoping."

We took the flashlights and looked around another room hewn from rock.

"We were, what, seventy feet below the surface down there?" I asked.

"A fair estimate."

"So now we're fifty-five."

Chapter 52

"There was a way out of the Ark chamber. So there has to be a way out of here, too. Let's start with the ceiling again." No answer. "Rivka?"

My flashlight caught her running her hands over the fulcrum of our primitive seesaw.

"Rivka." My voice was sharper this time.

"I can't get over it. If we hadn't just found the Ark of the Covenant, this would be the discovery of the century. No one had a clue our ancestors could use levers this way."

"Well, over in Egypt they built the pyramids. So why not?"

"The pyramids? Yes, it's assumed levers were used to move the giant blocks of the pyramids into place." She shook her head. "Enough. Back to business."

I cast the beam of my flashlight toward the smooth and rounded ceiling. This cavern was bigger than the Ark chamber, the shape of a Churchillian cigar, a mammoth stogie, eighty feet long and fifteen in diameter, not too different from the cabin of an airplane. No portholes here, though.

For half an hour Rivka sat on my shoulders probing the ceiling for another granite handle that would open a door. We were playing a video game and needed to get to the next level. No luck.

"Shall we try the walls?" I asked.

"You take this side, and I'll take the other. We'll meet at the end."

"At Loch Lomond?"

"What?"

"Never mind."

I ran my fingers along the rock faces. Every few feet I'd come across a fissure and waste a few minutes investigating before conceding its natural origin.

"I'm at the end," Rivka said. So she did get to Scotland before me. "Should I keep coming around till we meet?"

"You have matches and candles in that bag of yours?"

"To see if air is coming in from somewhere? Good idea."

While I continued my inspection, Rivka walked hither and yon holding up a candle like an ancient philosopher searching for truth.

"Okay, I'm done, too," I called out. "How's the flame?"

"As steady as a neurosurgeon's hand."

"So we're going to run out of air?" I asked.

"It'll take a while. And we can always get more by opening the trapdoor."

"Oh, great," I said. "And let those guys know we're here."

"I guess that's what they mean by being stuck between a rock and a hard place."

"We can't be stuck. The Ark came through here. If it came in, we can get out."

I sprawled out on the ground. Rivka joined me, shuffled through her pack, and pulled out two energy bars and a bottle of water.

Between chomps on the honey-almond-oat concoction, Rivka asked, "You know that old Zen koan about a tree falling in the forest with no one around?"

"Yeah." I was playing the beam of my flash on the floor where I knew the trapdoor opening was hidden.

"Did we discover the Ark if no one ever knows we did?"

Peculiar. My hand was tilted a little.

"Does the floor slant downward toward the trapdoor?" I asked.

"Yeah, maybe."

"That would make it easier to push the Ark and platform from the high end of the room to over the trapdoor."

I stood up and started reexamining the tip of the cigar, the room's highest point.

"This wall here seems a little too flat to be natural," I said. "It's what, four feet wide?"

"Wide enough for the platform and Ark to fit through," Rivka said.

"Exactly," I said. "Open sesame."

The incantation did nothing. Rivka took a more practical approach. She extracted hammer and chisel from her pack and took a couple of swings at a rocky protuberance in the upper right corner of the flat area. I held my flash up for her.

"Watch out for flying chips."

"I'm not really chipping at the rock. It's kind of wedged in here. I'm trying to pound it out."

She was right. Half the rock stuck out from the wall, and the other half was wedged in.

I moved my flash beam.

"Hey, I can't see."

"Look," I said. "There's another rock sticking out at the left corner."

"Okay, we'll get that one next."

Rivka hit the chisel into the crevice between rock and wall, then moved it an inch clockwise and hit it again. It took just a couple hundred strikes of steel against stone for the rock to fall out. We didn't need a candle to feel the rush of air into our cavern through the small hole she'd opened.

"Well, we're not going to suffocate," Rivka said.

"Good work." I held my hand up for a high five, but got a

hug instead. "Let's not celebrate too soon. We don't know what's out there."

I gave Rivka a boost and she looked through half the hole with her right eye while her flashlight shined through the other half.

"It's a passageway. Dark. Can't see much else."

"I'm going to let you down, then. My turn to pound. I'll get the rock in the other corner out."

She handed over the hammer and chisel. Fifteen minutes of work and we had another hole.

"What do you think?" I asked.

"This wall is a door held in place by eight rock wedges. Since the thicker ends of the wedges face us, they were hammered in from this side."

"So the people who hammered the rocks in place would have had no way out," I said.

"Which explains the four skeletons down below," Rivka said.

"They hid the Ark down there and lay down to die?"

"The Babylonians were right upstairs and would have killed them anyway. Keeping the Ark out of the hands of the enemy would have been a good reason to die." She drew her right index finger across her throat. "Probably one killed the other three and then lay down and killed himself."

"Let's go to work," I said.

After two hours of alternating at the hammer and chisel, the door stood ready to open. We had eight tennis ball-sized holes to the other side, but a stone face still stood between us and potential passage to the surface world.

I took a flashlight and ran it down the sides of the door. I could barely detect the line that ran between the holes even when I was looking for it. Putting my fingers in a hole and pulling did not move anything.

"I have an idea," I said.

"Me, too."

"Go ahead."

"We each take a piece of rope," she said. "We tie the chisel and the crowbar to the end. You get it?"

"Yeah." The same idea I'd had.

We pushed the tools through a hole and fiddled with them so they held flat against the wall on the other side when we pulled on the rope. The door budged. My head pounded, my shoulder blazed with each pull. Millimeter by millimeter the top of the door swung inward. Once out of the hewn opening, the door balanced on its bottom edge. I moved my rope and chisel to a hole on Rivka's side of the door and tugged with her. Ten minutes of work swung the door open two feet. We threw our equipment through the gap and then squeezed through ourselves.

We stood in a dark passageway high enough for Rivka to stand. I had to bend down.

"And let's see where this goes," Rivka said. Her voice quavered with the prospect of archeological discovery.

"First, let's pull the door from this side and put it back to where it was." If my voice quavered, was it with the thrill of discovery? Or was it the prospect of being in another dark tunnel?

Chapter 53

We were inspecting our handiwork. The door had been wrestled back into place. To someone following the tunnel past the secret opening on their way to who-knows-where, the holes could be seen only when a flashlight was shined right at them.

"Which way?" I asked. "Up?"

Some ancient monarch—Solomon himself?—had ordered construction of this six-foot-wide tunnel through the rock of Mount Moriah.

We leaned forward as we trudged up a steep path.

"You okay in here?" Rivka asked.

"Yeah. The tunnel's pretty wide. I can stand up, and we are moving."

"We're moving in a circle," she said.

"But upwards."

"Right, in a spiral."

I held my light up to a few twisted strips of black iron attached to the rock by primitive spikes. "What's that?"

"It's not from my period, but it looks like a holder for torches from medieval times. When the Crusaders conquered Jerusalem, they converted the Dome of the Rock into a church."

"And when Saladin drove out the Crusaders..."

"The Arabs converted it back."

We passed three more torch holders and then at the end of the tunnel came a door. I chuckled.

"What?"

"It's not stone this time. It's wood and has a knob." Arched at the top, the door had been assembled from planks about six inches wide and sat inside a wooden frame attached to the rock with nails, still hand-crafted, but more modern than those securing the holders.

Rivka leaned forward and tried to turn the black metal knob. Locked.

"Ah well," I said. "It's got to be easier to get through than the stone door. Turn around."

I reached into Rivka's pack and pulled out the crowbar. As I slipped the thin end between the door and the frame, she said, "Be careful."

"Careful not to ruin the door or careful 'cause we don't know what's on the other side?"

"Yes."

Following Rivka's sensible advice, I applied the pressure gradually. Then came a loud snap like a branch breaking in an ice storm, and the frame broke away from the door.

Shit. We might as well have announced our presence over a loudspeaker. We stood stock-still for half a minute. I pulled the door toward us. On the other side hung a pleated black curtain. I felt to the right and left for its end. No go.

"We'll have to crawl underneath," I whispered to Rivka.

"Okay, let's have a look," she said.

We lay on our bellies and lifted the bottom of the curtain. The room was gloomy, but not Stygian dark as I'd expected. On the opposite side of the room, spilling onto wrought iron steps twenty feet away, I could see light coming from above.

Rivka turned on her flashlight. The room was another cave, but one in regular use this time. Oriental rugs covered the floor, and curved divans ran along the walls.

"Oh, God," Rivka murmured.

"You know where we are?" I asked.

"We're in the cave under the rock."

"What rock?"

"The rock that stood in the middle of both temples. It's now the centerpiece of the Dome of the Rock."

"So we can just walk out."

"We'll need to walk through the Dome and across the Mount to get out."

"Okay."

"Not okay. The guards on the Mount work for the *Waqf*, the Muslim authorities."

"Shit. Well, you've got a scarf. You can pass for a modest Muslim woman."

"Wearing IDF-issue pants?"

I shined the light on the divan. There were some sort of throws on them. I picked up the drabbest-looking one.

"Wrap yourself in this."

"We can't steal something from the Dome of the Rock."

"What does the Torah say about saving lives?"

"Well, the doctrine of *pikuach nefesh* says you can do almost anything if a life is at stake."

"Put it on. We're not stealing it, anyway. We're borrowing it. I'll mail it back. I promise."

Watching her twisting and tying the fabric, I asked, "What can we expect out there?"

"I don't know. I've never been here before. Lots of rabbis say only the High Priest can enter the Holy of Holies, and since we don't know where it was, the entire Temple Mount is off limits."

"And you believe that?"

"I'm not sure, but better safe than sorry."

"Okay then, first time here for us both. Well, we might win

the prize for the most dramatic entrance to the Mount in the last few centuries."

Rivka pirouetted. "What do you think?"

To my inexperienced eye she could pass as an Arab. "You're not going to have to pass inspection. We need to get out of the building and off the Mount."

We walked up the metal stairs and ducked under a gate. A man in his forties was taking a photo of his companion against the series of archways that encircled the chamber.

"Oh, Max, can we go down there?" Americans.

The man looked at us somewhat apologetically. "Hello. I'm Max Holliday and this is my wife Peggy. Can you tell us what's down there?"

"I'm sorry. It's a restricted area. She's an archeologist," I said, nodding at Rivka.

Peggy spoke up. "Who do we have to ask if we can go down there?"

"I don't think you can get permission," I replied. "Nice meeting you."

We started walking around the perimeter of the dome past other camera-laden couples and school groups.

"I didn't know tourists were allowed in here," I said. "Maybe you didn't need to pass as an Arab after all." Looking up, I could see we were under a golden cupola, about seventy feet high, etched with intricate geometric designs. Spectacular, but no time for sightseeing.

"Wait," Rivka said. I guess she didn't feel the same urgency. She was gazing at a huge irregular piece of granite that covered most of the floor space under the spectacular dome.

"The Rock of Moriah," I said.

"Where *ha-Shem* rejected the idea of human sacrifice."

I gave her about three seconds to reflect—she wouldn't be coming back here again. "We should get going."

"You're right."

"What do those inscriptions say?" I asked.

"They're from the Koran. '*Allahumma salli ala rasulika wa'abdika 'Isa bin Maryam.*' In the name of the One God, pray for your prophet and servant Jesus, son of Mary."

"So they're denying the divinity of Jesus."

Before she could answer, I saw two uniformed guards running toward us.

Chapter 54

The guards ran right past us.

We turned to watch them and saw our new friend Peggy ducking under the gate on her way to the cavern under the rock.

"This will mean trouble for sure. Let's boogie."

After eighty more feet, we'd reached the front entrance to the Dome. I took another look back. Peggy was gesticulating in front of the guards while Max looked on.

We were outside. The area around the Dome on the Temple Mount was a huge khaki-colored plaza enclosed by trees. Through them, I spotted another building—the minaret gave it away as the al-Aqsa Mosque. Tourists strolled, snapping away. Pairs of security guards chatted or spoke into walkie-talkies.

"There." Rivka pointed at a stream of people trickling out from what looked like the security barrier at an airport. We headed that way. Three hundred yards to the Israeli checkpoint and sanctuary. Two hundred. One hundred fifty.

It was not meant to be easy. A whistle blew from behind us, then another. A megaphone blared an Arabic order.

We broke into a run. I knew what had happened: Petulant Peggy had demanded to know why she couldn't go into the cavern as Rivka and I had. I cursed her with each step.

With thirty-five yards to go, I heard a gunshot. And another warning through the megaphone, this time in English. "Stop, please. We have guns drawn." No shit, Sherlock. I dropped back to stand between the guards and Rivka.

A third guard, fumbling to get at his gun, was coming from the side to cut us off before we reached the security station. He made a grab for Rivka and instead got a hand on the camera strap and ripped it from her neck. It hit the ground. She reached for it, and he reached for her and stepped on the camera. As he looked down, I lowered my shoulder—the good one—to knock him over before he could unholster his weapon. Flat on his back, the man was lying right on top of the smashed camera, the camera that held the pictures of the Ark. God damn.

"Go," I yelled at Rivka.

Almost at the station, Rivka was screaming in Hebrew and holding up what looked like a credit card. Two Israeli soldiers hightailed it out of their little huts and ran toward me. They used the stocks of their Uzis to prod me the fifteen yards back toward their stations, but we got only halfway there before three Arab security guards caught up with us.

One of the Israelis said something to the guards. It must have been Arabic because the guards understood well enough to shake their heads and put their hands on my arms. Then Rivka popped up, accompanied by another soldier—no, not just a soldier: an officer, a captain, according to the six-leafed branch on his epaulet.

He barked out something in Hebrew and then Arabic. The Israeli soldiers grabbed me by my upper arms and started dragging me away. The guards did not release their hold on my wrists and the one who had my right wrist started to unbuttoned his holster. A handgun versus the Uzis? Shit, I was about to start World War III.

Then I heard the sound of gears shifting and looked up to see a jeep with three armed guards cutting across the Mound toward us. The Israeli soldiers yanked harder on my upper arms, but the guards ratcheted up their resistance by pulling on my wrists the other way. God, the screaming pain in my shoulder made me close my eyes. When I opened them two seconds later, I saw an Arab, wearing a gold braid, jump out of the jeep. I turned my head and spotted the fence that delimited Israeli jurisdiction a mere ten feet away.

The Israeli captain and the new arrival knew each other. They shook hands. The Arab officer pointed at me and then Rivka. I took a quick peek at her, and, of all things, she winked. Oh, we *were* going to be okay, or at least get back to Israeli protection, whatever that was worth.

We stood in the cold glare of the winter sun for five minutes while the argument in Arabic went on. Then the captain barked something out to his subordinates. The Israeli soldiers clamped handcuffs on me. Out of the frying pan.

Rivka marched back to the security hut with the captain. I was dragged, facing backward, by the Israeli soldiers. I watched my boot heels etch wavy lines in the dirt of the Temple Mount. Looking up, I saw another jeep roaring toward us. It was driven by a man in glasses with mirrored lenses. Fuck you, Colonel Al Ghamdi.

The line at the checkpoint had grown to a hundred people while the soldiers dealt with me. The tourists must have chalked up the incident to a little extra local color as the soldiers hauled me past them and into the hut.

Chapter 55

The captain fingered Rivka's military ID. So that was what she had shown the guards, what had brought help on the double. I sat in a straight-back chair, mute, during the rapid-fire Hebrew conversation between the two Israeli officers. After fifteen minutes, I was excused. Rivka stayed. Judging from her posture, I don't think it was by preference. As I stood up to leave, she took off the purloined wrap and handed it over to me. I walked down the ramp off the Mount alone.

What now? Fourteen hours ago, that uninvited visitor had broken into Rivka's house. Returning there was not a good idea.

Back in the street, I was in a haze, both literally and figuratively. The atmosphere was gauzy, rendering the city even dreamier, less of this world, than ever. And my own brain seemed detached from the situation. I walked to the Square Cup Café and the same old waiter shuffled out. "Will Madame be joining you?"

"Maybe later."

"Tea then?"

"Triple espresso, please." That ought to burn off the mental fog and chase away the shoulder pain.

The first sip of the bitter, muddy brew did get me thinking. God, I hoped I hadn't landed Rivka in too much trouble. The flutter of a butterfly's wings could lead to a hurricane in another hemisphere, and an email to a well-adjusted, brilliant woman six thousand miles away could lead to this tempest. I might have hit the trifecta, jeopardizing Rivka's archeological career as well as her university professorship and her military commission. Knowing me was just that toxic.

My iPhone wiggled in my pocket. I looked at the screen. A hidden number.

"Hello."

"You're right, and I owe you big time."

"Mitch?"

"Yeah. The security procedures in the East Jerusalem consulate weren't what they should be. We found our guy."

"The guy who passed on that I was looking into the Ark."

"Yup. The Israelis stopped him in his car in East Jerusalem. He'd packed up his wife, mother-in-law, two kids, and some furniture and was on his way to the West Bank."

"He'd been warned, then."

"Yeah, we're looking for someone else, too."

"You don't need to. Professor Golan's apartment was bugged. I'll bet he was working for whoever bugged it, and they warned him. I presume the Israelis let you question the spy."

"Yeah, the Israelis did give us a shot at him, and it turns out the number two guy in the consulate wasn't doing too good a job locking up his laptop. This male secretary, he was reading everything."

"And he was working for the Saudis?"

"Good guess," Mitch said. "When we questioned him about his handler, he described someone we didn't know. But a few weeks ago he had a one-time meeting with a man we think was that Colonel Al Ghamdi, the one with the archeologist brother."

"How could a Saudi colonel get past Israeli security into Jerusalem?"

"How could you? It doesn't matter. The point is we think Al Ghamdi is in Jerusalem."

Well, he was a few minutes ago. "And so?"

"Please, please listen to me this time. You do not want to meet up with him. He lives by different rules than we do. He'll kill you if he thinks you're a threat to his tribe, to the Saud family. He'll kill you if he thinks you had anything to do with his brother's death."

"But his brother died over twenty years ago."

"You won't get a chance to reason with him. Don't put me in a position where I have to tell Veronica and Katie that something's happened to you. We have to get you out of there."

"I hear you, Mitch." I let out the air I'd been holding. "How's the shoulder today?"

"To hell with my shoulder. You are a stubborn bastard. We figure the sniper was trying to stop you from looking for the Ark. Thanks to the leak in the consulate, they knew you were coming. Did you know that?"

"If I hadn't driven for you, I'm the one who would have been shot. I'm sorry."

"Don't be sorry. I asked you to drive. Whether Al Ghamdi is there or not, *you* must be in Jerusalem?"

"Yeah."

"Then do what I tell you. Go to the consulate…"

"Are you kidding?"

"No, the spy was in the East Jerusalem consulate and now he's a guest of Shin Bet. Get your ass to the one in West Jerusalem."

"I've passed it. It's on Gershon Agron."

"Right. Go in and tell them you are Ivan Logue."

"Repeat the name."

"Ivan Logue."

"Okay, the consul general is expecting you. He'll take precautions and get you back to the States safely. We've told the secretary of state what we think the Saudis and their Colonel Al Ghamdi have been up to and, boy, he is pissed. I didn't know they taught language like that at Yale."

"Yeah, I wouldn't think he'd look too kindly on potshots being taken at one of his senior aides on American soil."

"I'm just collateral damage. Today he's sending the assistant secretary to call on the Saudi ambassador to warn them off you."

"The Saudis are really taking this cock-and-bull story about the Ark seriously, aren't they?"

"God, Alex, you can be an arrogant SOB. Listen to me. The colonel's brother was found dead. He *has* to do something about it. It's the desert code. You understand what I'm saying? Don't get yourself killed."

"I didn't have anything to do with his brother."

"Just get out."

In a soft voice I said, "I understand."

"Okay," I could hear Mitch breathing into the phone. "You didn't have anything to do with Professor Al Ghamdi. So don't get yourself killed over nothing." He paused. "You haven't found anything, have you?"

"Nothing conclusive."

"You *will* go to the consulate?"

"Yeah, right after I run an errand."

"An errand? Are you shitting me?"

"I promised to return something to the Dome of the Rock."

"Are you listening? I said there's no protecting you there."

"Your warning came a little late." I rushed on. "Thanks, Mitch. I'm sorry you almost got killed because of me. Tell Sarah not to worry, that I'll stay away. Goodbye for now.

"What the hell, Alex..."

I clicked my phone off. And turned off the power so I couldn't be found by some super-duper NSA satellite.

Mitch had tried to help and almost got killed. I really was toxic, wasn't I?

Chapter 56

My fingers drummed on the table, my feet tapped the cobblestones. The triple espresso wouldn't let me sit still. I paid the bill and left the café. I found a post office on Plugat Ha-Kotel near the Broad Wall. I ducked in to buy stamps and a bulky envelope. First, I addressed a large package to the Dome of the Rock, Jerusalem, Israel. Then I scrawled a note to Katie and included it in a smaller package. I mailed them both.

I passed through the Old City walls at Jaffa Gate and wandered by the site of my wrestling match with the bulldozer driver. No plaque, just a dent in the wall of the building. Life went on.

I turned on Gershon Agron, following the route I'd followed when staying at the Sheraton a few centuries ago. I leaned against a lamppost and looked across the street at the unprepossessing house of Jerusalem stone with a tile roof. No sign on the front door proclaimed American ownership of the building. Instead, the familiar bald eagle gripping olive branches in one claw and arrows in the other was displayed discreetly on a side door. To get there, I'd have to go back to the street corner. Too much traffic to jaywalk. I could be home tomorrow. No more paralyzing claustrophobia, no more Ark, no more Saudi assassins. But mission *not* accomplished.

Gripping the lamppost, I was a man on an island amidst a

sea of pedestrians. Israelis had the same get-out-of-my-way attitude as New Yorkers, and they knocked and jostled me. When a sharp elbow slammed against my ribcage, the pain made me whirl around to look for the perpetrator. Then I felt something sharp penetrate skin and muscle in the crook between my left shoulder and neck. Before my head had even turned ninety degrees, I felt consciousness slipping away. There was a spectral Rivka running ahead and I was reaching for her. Didn't make it. Oblivion.

* * *

My eyes opened into complete darkness, but the bouncing of rubber on asphalt told me I was in a moving vehicle. I could breathe but felt the moisture of my exhalations reflect back on my face. A hood had been pulled over my head. My hands were cuffed behind my back. I breathed faster. A claustrophobic reflex as if I were stuck back in the tunnel. At least then I could see by the light of the flashlight.

Cold metal bit into my wrists, and straps held my torso in place. My head was an orange being squeezed in a juicer. I took in a deep breath and puffed it out. Counting, focusing on the numbers, had worked in the tunnel. I started again at one. By the time I reached eighty, my rational self was pushing the panic back into its box.

How did Al Ghamdi know I'd got to the consulate? Could his agents listen in on my iPhone? Or had they followed me? Arrogance. Mitch was right. I was no match for pros. I was probably being taken to a safe house in Arab East Jerusalem. Even if torture awaited, pain would be better than terror. I began to sink back into that familiar, fathomless pit of claustrophobia.

What returned me to rationality was the wetness I sat in.

Whatever muscle relaxant they'd stuck me with had done its job on my bladder.

The car stopped. The straps came off my torso, and I was dragged along just as I had been a few hours before on the Temple Mount. Down a hallway, up stairs, all without a word from this latest set of manhandlers. They strapped me back into a chair. I started counting again.

* * *

The quick whisk of the hood coming off awakened me. I'd escaped by dozing off. I blinked and there before me, looming over me, was not a Saudi intelligence agent in sunglasses, but a man wearing wire-rimmed spectacles with clear lenses. He looked no different from when I'd last seen him. As if he owned no other clothes, he wore the same blue polo shirt and gray polyester jacket. His face still featured two-day-old whiskers.

Trying to hold my lids up against the light, I said, "Cohen, you motherfucker."

"I apologize. I asked some of my colleagues if they could arrange a meeting between us. I should have been more specific on how they carried out my request."

"Fuck you and everyone else in Shin Bet."

He shook his head and rubbed a hand against his whiskery chin. "I am sorry, but you caused the problem. You did not pay attention to my warning. Look what has happened to you. You came to Israel a reputable American businessman, and now you want to take a swing at me." He wagged his finger at me. "Don't. It will get us nowhere. We want the same thing."

"I doubt it." I didn't think Cohen gave a damn for the Ark.

He reached down and unlocked my handcuffs. If he hadn't said anything, I might well have taken a swing. Which, of course, is why he had said something.

He replied, "You don't want to keep peace between Israel and its Arab neighbors?"

"What's going on is peace?"

"It's not all-out war."

"Listen, I'm not talking to anyone while I'm sitting in my own piss."

"You're sitting in it. I'm smelling it. We took the liberty of picking up a change of clothes for you at Professor Golan's." He pointed to a gym bag on the floor.

"Should I say thank you?"

"There's a bathroom through that door."

The line between stubbornness and stupidity can be thin. I picked up the bag.

Thirty minutes later, I'd showered in the adjoining bathroom and was sitting on a wingback chair in clean clothes facing Cohen across a natural wood coffee table. I had ended up in a safe house, but one run by Shin Bet, not the Saudis. I hoped it was the better alternative.

Chapter 57

"I've been wondering how you knew what I was up to."

"We're the security service," Cohen said.

"It was the Saudis who told you I was coming to Jerusalem the first time and that I'd come back, wasn't it? They bugged Professor Golan's flat and told you what I was up to. Who knew Shin Bet cooperated with the Saudis?"

"An unsubstantiated accusation."

"Well, next time you talk to him say hello to Colonel Al Ghamdi for me."

"Who?"

Cohen was good.

"The Saudis were worried about anyone finding the Ark except them. They'd tried to find it themselves years ago. Professor Al Ghamdi disappeared looking for it."

"I thought you said—what was his name? Al Ghamdi?—that he was a colonel," Cohen said.

I didn't pay attention to the interruption. "So the Saudis—was it the colonel himself?—came to you because you had a common interest in making sure I was stopped. The Muslims rioted thirty years ago, and you stopped Goren and Getz from digging. Now they tell you what I'm up to and you tried to stop me. Don't you want to know the truth?"

"No, not particularly. I'll let the politicians and the rabbis fight about the truth. My job is to make certain they're around to have their fight."

"What the hell's the matter with you guys? Why does it make sense to give control of the Temple Mount to the Muslims? The First and Second Temples are under there."

Cohen leaned toward me. "You think I like it? My grandfather fought in the 1948 War. After it was over, the Jordanians kicked the Jews out of the Old City where we'd lived for three thousand years. They destroyed—brick by brick, stone by stone—twenty-one synagogues. Our armistice agreement said Jews would be able to visit the Wall to pray."

Good. I had gotten under his skin.

"But they didn't allow it," I said. "So tit for tat. Why wouldn't Israel have taken control of the Mount when they conquered the Old City in the Six-Day War?"

"Your grandfather's old friend Rabbi Goren wanted to blow up the Dome and the Mosque. He didn't get his way, and sixteen years later he started jackhammering."

"My grandfather stood for truth."

"Death can be found in truth," he said.

"Yes, I know the legend of the Golem," I said. "Speaking of death, Colonel Al Ghamdi and your other Saudi friends have been trying to kill me."

"Yes, that is unfortunate. Once we realized what they were up to after the incident with the bulldozer, we asked them to stop."

"If they said they would, they're lying. They tried again last night."

Cohen's left eyelid flickered. A tell. He hadn't known that.

"You see, Mr. Kalman, if I were to come to Silicon Valley to start a company, you would laugh. I know nothing of business. Here, you come into my city, and you start blundering around. You know nothing of the situation here. Action is no substitute for planning and analysis. You are playing a dangerous game you are not prepared for. Colonels in Saudi intelligence do not play for plastic poker chips. They play for keeps."

"All that would be fine, except for one thing."

He sighed in exasperation. "And that would be?"

"I saw the Ark of the Covenant in a cave under the Dome of the Rock."

"Please, Mr. Kalman." Cohen put his hands on both sides of his head. "I do hope you are not naïve enough to spread such rumors. If you are believed, it will lead to riots and death."

"This is no rumor. I saw it."

"Tell me where."

"No, I don't think so."

Cohen stood. "Suit yourself. Please continue to enjoy our hospitality."

"If I am a prisoner, I am entitled to see a representative of the American embassy."

On his way out, Cohen turned and said, "A prisoner? Oh, no, Mr. Kalman. You are being naïve again. You are still a guest, a distinguished guest."

When Veronica and I had entertained weekend guests in Woodside, we hadn't put them in a room with no windows. Nor did we place a guard outside the guestroom door.

Chapter 58

Pacing around my room in the Shin Bet safe house, I tried to push any suspicion out of my mind, but I found myself wondering whether Rivka was somehow implicated in this imbroglio. Cohen had to know she'd been helping me, but he hadn't mentioned her name. So I hadn't either. I'd left her—not by choice—up in the security shack by the Temple Mount with her fellow officer. Where was she now? Still there? At home? At work in the tunnel? In a room next door being questioned by Cohen?

I cursed my paranoid brain. What I wanted, what I needed, was my partner here in this room with me discussing next steps. Ought we to forget what we'd seen in the interests of Israeli-Arab peace? If we did, would we regret our betrayal of truth as my grandfather had? How could we prove anything without the photos that had been in Rivka's smashed camera? We'd need to go down to the Ark room again, but was the Ark still there? Had putting it in the corner kept it out of sight of Al Ghamdi and the Saudis? Or had they made it into the room themselves and found it?

I had nothing to write on, but I shut my eyes and imagined a chalkboard hovering in front of me. After an hour, I'd mapped out a course of action on the make-believe board. The chance of success was low, but the payoff was high.

I started with a little reconnoitering. The ventilation registers were far too narrow to crawl through. And I'd had enough crawling through narrow passages to fill up my nightmare quota for the rest of my life even if I lived to a hundred and twenty. The bathroom mirror was a sheet of polished metal—no way to make a weapon out of that, but I wasn't really looking for a weapon anyway. The guards in my temporary prison were only temporary enemies, not people I wished to harm in any permanent way. Let's not ignore the obvious. I put my hand on the doorknob. It turned. I swung open the door and was met with the white-toothed grin of a crewcut, thick-armed man in a T-shirt and jeans leaning against the opposite wall. He wouldn't need a gun to handle me, but he had one anyway.

"Sorry to bother you, but I'm hungry," I said.

Five minutes later I was sitting on the couch fueling myself with pita, hummus, and salad.

After dinner—or was it breakfast by now?—I went back into the adjoining bathroom where I'd showered and picked up the shaving cream. I laid down a nice thick layer right in front of the door. I stood on the table—standing on tables was getting to be a habit—and reached up to unscrew a bulb from the ceiling fixture. The light from the bathroom provided enough illumination for me to see what I was doing. I took off my belt and my shirt. I wrapped the shirt around my right hand and brought my belt's brass buckle up to the fixture. Here goes. I plunged its tongue into the socket's empty maw. I heard a crackle and all the lights in the room went off.

Jumping down from the table, I took three steps to the side of the door. My T-shirted friend—at least I suppose it was him—swung the door open and ran into the room. I wish I could have seen him step into the shaving cream and watch his feet shoot up over his head. Ah well, even if the lights had been on, I wouldn't have waited around for the show. I was in the dark hall now. Voices in Hebrew were calling out. I jogged with one hand on the wall until I came to another hallway. Twice I heard shoes slapping on the floor and pressed myself into a doorway as someone rushed by.

Another turn and I could see a front door with a transom above it. Through the transom shone streetlights. It wouldn't be long before someone took the tongue of my belt out of the socket where I'd left it and then threw a few switches in the fuse box. Okay, let's make a dash for freedom.

Five steps, hand on the knob, turn, pull, rattle. Shit. Close the door, undo the security chain, swing the door open again, step onto the threshold. A blinding light smacked me in the eyes, and I brought my arm up to shade them.

"Very good, Mr. Kalman. We won't underestimate your ingenuity again."

I brought my arm down. As I did, Cohen lowered the Maglite he was pointing at my face.

Chapter 59

"We found the Ark," I told Cohen again.

He leaned forward in his wingback chair. We were back in the guest room.

"I'm not certain what you found, but it was not the Ark," he said.

"How the hell do you know?"

"We followed the tunnels you dug, and we examined each room. We had to widen a last passageway with a jackhammer, but we found nothing."

"Didn't Rabbi Goren make a mistake of using a jackhammer down there?" I asked. "The noise alerted the Muslim authorities on the surface of the Temple Mount."

"We have quieter jackhammers than he did."

"You say you followed the same path I did. Show me."

Cohen took a pad of paper and a yellow mechanical pencil from the pocket of his ratty jacket and sketched a pretty reasonable map of the route Rivka and I had taken to find the Ark.

"What's this?" I pointed.

"That's another tunnel into the anteroom. It follows the path of an old cistern."

"Where does it start from?"

"From up above, but we didn't follow it to that end." He gave me a we-are-not-as-crazy-as-you look.

That explained how the Saudis, or whoever they were, had got in.

"And what did you find here?" I asked.

He put his index finger on the room where we'd found the Ark. "We found a wooden platform. It looks ancient. The archeologists will do their carbon dating to get us to the right century."

"Just a platform?" I asked.

"Yes, just a platform."

Cohen's expression revealed no tell this time. Hiding the Ark in the corner hadn't worked because they'd entered the room. But who had entered it first? The Arabs who'd chased us or these Israelis? Who had the box, the Ark? I tried not to let my shoulders slump or my face sag as his eyes scrutinized me.

"Did you know that room is under the Temple Mount?" I asked.

"Israelis"—he looked at me and started again—"Jews shouldn't be there. You could start a riot. Or a war. People could die."

"I guess an old platform isn't worth it, is it?"

"We don't quite know how you and the professor found yourself on the Temple Mount. Very dangerous for you. You're most fortunate."

So they hadn't found the trapdoor in the ceiling either.

"Where is the professor? I'd like to talk to her."

"Ah, but she doesn't want to talk to you."

"What do you mean?"

He shrugged. "Women are unpredictable. I have never understood them. Who can account for what they want?"

"Yeah, right."

"See for yourself." He handed me my phone.

I tapped Rivka's number, only to get a recorded voice spouting Hebrew.

"It's saying the number you have reached has been disconnected."

"Why?"

"She *really* does not want to talk to you."

"Or you don't want her to talk to me. What have you done with her?"

"Vanity. You cannot believe she does not wish to talk to you."

"Bullshit." Blood pounded so hard in my head that I seemed to be looking at Cohen through a crimson cloud. I jumped up and took a roundhouse swing.

But I was too slow. No toreador facing an onrushing animal could have moved faster than Cohen. He tilted to the side of the chair and gave my left arm a quick wrench upward as it passed him. He might as well have used a bayonet. I fell on my left shoulder and the stab of pain told me I'd dislocated it for the third time, the second in twenty-four hours.

Looming above me, he said, "*Krav maga*. Not gentle like judo. Sorry."

He sat back down in his chair. He didn't look sorry. He looked satisfied.

I didn't think I needed Rivka's battlefield medical skills this time. I sat up and put my left arm in back of my neck. I used my right hand to pull it down toward my right shoulder. Harder. The shoulder snapped back into its socket.

Cohen got off his chair. He crouched next to me, his face inches from mine.

"This time you will leave Israel and not come back, Mr. Kalman. No name changes, no sneaking through Eilat. You are not welcome here. You say you look for truth. Human life is more important than truth. *Shalom*."

I said nothing.

He held out his hand. I did not take it.

Chapter 60

"Daddy, you're telling me inside this package is one of the broken shards from the Ten Commandments?"

Katie sat on the bed in my room at the Harvard Faculty Club while I perched on the edge of the desk chair.

"Could be."

"And you mailed it to me because?"

I looked at the bubble envelope she was holding with no memory of the green, blue, and pink of the Israeli Arbor Day stamps in its corner, even though I must have pasted them on in the Jerusalem post office. "The first shard we got was stolen. If I held on to this one, chances were good it would happen again. Go ahead and open it."

She tilted her head. "Aren't you jet-lagged?"

"Must be," I said. "I didn't sleep on the plane." My flight from Israel had landed at JFK five hours ago, and I'd taken a JetBlue flight on up to Logan.

"But you don't seem tired. Different maybe?"

"That's the beard and haircut," I said.

She leaned closer. "You know, it's not that you're different, it's that you're back to being the same." I raised an eyebrow. "You're back to being the way you used to be. Energized, like before you sold your company. Look at the way your foot is swinging."

My right leg was slung over my knee with the foot fibrillating on its own. I grabbed my shoe to stop the shaking.

"Open it," I said.

She pulled against the flap. The glue stretched thin before snapping like a teenybopper's gum.

She started to reach into the envelope and then stopped. "I should get a pair of gloves."

"I touched it and am still here."

"Not because it's dangerous. Oh, never mind." She reached in to extract the piece of—extraterrestrial?—granite. She moved over to the desk and flicked on the desk lamp. Her head bowed over the fragment in her hand.

After a couple of minutes, I got up and tapped her on the shoulder. She whirled and put her head against my chest.

"What is it, sweetie?" I asked.

She laughed. "You sure you didn't pick this up from a street vendor?"

"That's what the professor at Hebrew University thought."

"What professor?"

"Amit Ben-David."

"You talked to Professor Ben-David? He saw this?"

"You've heard of him?"

"Of course. What did he say?"

"He saw the stolen shard, not this one. He thought it was from a street vendor, too."

"He's the authority, Dad." She put her hand on my arm.

"But I didn't buy it from a vendor. I found it on the floor of a cave under the Temple Mount near a five-by-four box covered with okapi skin."

She looked up at the ceiling. "I think my dad's gone crazy. He seems to be telling me what I'm holding in my hand is a piece of what Moses brought down from Mount Sinai."

"Could be," I told her. "Still, humor me and take a look at the writing."

She gripped my forearm. “Dad, I’m a junior in college, not an expert on this stuff.”

“Humor me anyway.”

She let go of my arm and held the fragment back under the light. “It looks like some ancestor of Hebrew. The Samaritans still living in Israel write in a Hebrew-style alphabet that hasn’t changed since 1000 BCE. This would antedate that.”

“You might not be an expert, but that’s the same thing your authority Ben-David came up with. Sweetie, would you turn the lights out?”

Katie flicked the switch. With the heavy drapes closed, the room was dark, almost as dark as a cave.

After thirty seconds, I said, “You can turn them back on.”

“What were you looking for?”

“When we were under the Temple Mount, some of the writing glowed blue.”

“This piece didn’t.”

“Right. It was the tablet in the box that glowed. We found this piece on the floor of the room, not in the box.”

”Dad, is there any way to prove where you found this?”

“We had photos but lost them.”

“Then there’s no way to prove anything. It would have been better to have left this *in situ*, where you found it. Then the archeologists could make their assessments.”

“There won’t be any assessments in a hollowed-out room under the Temple Mount.”

“I guess not.”

“Do you believe in the Torah?”

“Maybe not word for word, but there’s a lot of history there.”

“Sort of a treasure map for archeologists?”

“Yes, that, but I believe it’s divinely inspired, too,” she said.

“Why?”

“Faith.”

Faith. That's what it came down to, wasn't it?

Chapter 61

My eyes opened with a flash of déjà vu. Was I back in Rivka's apartment in Jerusalem when the midnight marauder had stopped by? No. I was in bed at the Faculty Club. Yesterday Katie and I had gone shopping in Harvard Square, and I'd bought a little stringed sack—the kind of thing forty-niners had kept their gold in—which I wore around my neck, the shard inside. So the Saudis were coming again. It hadn't taken them long. How did they know? Only Katie and I knew I had the shard.

I heard breathing and a few steps. Shit. I'd thought about buying a gun, but hadn't. I had nothing to protect myself with. Being killed in bed, in the dark, had little appeal. Like every indoor space in New England, my Faculty Club bedroom was overheated, and I was lying on top of the blankets. I rolled on to the floor.

"Aron? Aron, are you awake?"

From the other side of the bed, I reached up to the lamp on the nightstand and turned the switch. There stood Professor-Major Rivka Golan, blinking in the light.

"I frightened you," she said.

I stood up. "You're okay. They told me you didn't want to talk to me."

She walked toward me and put her arms around me. All I

had on were the bag around my throat and a pair of nylon running shorts.

"Did you believe them?" she asked, wriggling in my arms as if to get comfortable.

"No," I said.

"They took my phone. I knew they would be watching my email."

"But they let you leave?"

"Here I am."

"How did you get in here?"

"I was at Harvard last year. I'm still a member here, so I just checked in. It wasn't hard to get a key to your room."

I held her until I felt stirrings.

"You're moving away from me now?"

"I think it's the prudent thing to do."

She folded her arms. "Since we met, what have we done that's prudent? You asked me why I was helping you. I told you. You came to Jerusalem. It was *beshert*. Not just finding the Ark. You and me?"

"My wife left me. I'm fifty years old. I'm a burnt-out case."

She closed the two feet between us, put her hand behind my neck, and pulled my face down to hers. Her lips were soft. After a moment, she pulled away.

"You don't feel burnt out," she said and moved back against me.

After another kiss, a deep one this time, I said, "I haven't had sex in a long time."

"For me it's been since my husband died," she said. "Let's see if we can remember how the parts fit together."

She pushed back her scarf, and we were kissing again. Without taking my lips from hers, I scooped up the major and laid her on the bed. My knees sank into the soft mattress on either side of her hips, and I leaned down. She dug her strong fingers into my back. I kissed her neck. She purred. I undid her bra, and something the size of a stick of gum fell out.

"Don't worry about that now," she said.

She arched her back and her fingers dug into my shoulder blades. I came back up for more kissing and then reached down to take off her shoes. I pulled down her cargo pants and underwear.

"Pink lace?" I asked.

She reached over and turned off the lamp. "Shut up and get back here."

Twenty minutes later, ready to burst, I entered another tunnel. This time I did not care whether I ever came out.

* * *

The room was dark, but since the curtains were closed it could have been any time. Rivka slept with her head resting on my chest. I could feel her bare breasts pushing back and forth against my ribs with each breath.

I'd felt no change in the rhythm of her respiration when she whispered, "What are you thinking?"

"I'm thinking maybe this makes it all worth it. Maybe this is why I went looking for the Ark."

"*Dayenu.*"

"*Dayenu*? From Passover, right?"

"Yeah. On Passover, we say if God had only freed us from slavery in Egypt, *dayenu*—it would have been enough. But the funny thing is it wouldn't have been enough. What would it have meant if we'd never been given the Torah or if we'd died in the desert?"

"Okay, I get it."

"You're the same. You say *dayenu*, that this is enough, but it's not, is it?"

"Being here with you should be enough," I said to the top of her head.

"But it's not. We have more to do."

"Well, my grandfather saw the Ark, but that wasn't enough for him. That's why he found me—to bear witness, to get to the truth."

"No reason to be sorry. We're partners, right?"

I squeezed her. "Right."

Chapter 62

Staying at the Faculty Club was like staying in a friend's comfortable but shabby guestroom. The kind of friend who tossed you the keys and left it to you to make your own way. No room service, no laundry, no paper by the door when you wake up.

We went for an early morning run along the river past the college boathouses. Loping along, we moved faster than the bumper-to-bumper traffic on Memorial Drive. Even though Rivka had her own room at the Club, we'd come back to mine for a post-workout shower. We ended up together under the spout in the white cast-iron tub. I kneaded shampoo, which the Club did provide, into her thick, curly reddish-brown hair and moved her head beneath the showerhead. While the water cascaded down from her hair to shoulders, to breasts, to belly, to thighs, she soaped up her own hands and started moving them in circles around my chest. That did it. A naked embrace under the jets of water, and then I picked her up again, feeling her skin slick as a dolphin's under my fingers. Tossing her onto the bed, I dove after her. With both of us sopping, I was glad for the overheating now.

In the next forty-five minutes we never dried off. Near the end, as her body quaked, she opened her eyes to look into mine. Seconds later, done and drained, I collapsed onto her, and she wrapped me in her arms.

We might even have dozed off for a moment before we went back to the bathroom to complete our shower *interruptus*.

Now I was pulling on khakis and an Oxford shirt, while Rivka watched from the bed with nothing on except for a towel around her head. Lean and angular, fashion models looked their best on the runway, couture dresses hanging just the way the designer intended. The headscarf, work shirt, cargo pants, and boots that constituted Rivka's everyday attire did not show her off to best advantage. Her thighs were smooth, her midsection rippled, her breasts firm globes. She was put together with curves, not lines, and looked best dressed as she was.

"Some burnt-out case," she said.

"You look like an odalisque in an Ingres painting," I said with a smile. "Lolling and naked."

"I guess even a burnt-out candle can be relit."

I went over to the bed and bent down, first pecking her on the lips and then dodging the arm that meant to hold me there.

"Apparently," I said. "Let's get dressed. I'm hungry. And we need to make plans. I don't think this is a good place for that. Too many distractions."

She put her fingers to her mouth. "Aron, you can't be thinking of doing it another..."

"Get dressed, please."

Twenty minutes later we were at a café Rivka knew on Putnam Street—Petsi Pies.

When not in Israel eating falafel cannonballs, I followed Dr. Zweig's advice and ate healthfully, eschewing white foods—refined flour, sugar, potatoes, rice, dairy. So here I sat munching on a whole-grain bran muffin and fruit salad while sipping green gunpowder tea. Rivka was devouring the first of a mound of three heavily buttered scones and washing it down with a cream- and chocolate-topped cappuccino. A golden slice of sweet potato pie patiently awaited its turn.

"Is this place kosher?" I asked.

"It doesn't have a rabbi's *hekshe*r, but I'm careful about what I eat."

"As with everything."

"As with most things," she said.

Based on recent examination by hand and eye, I could testify that whatever diet she followed agreed with her. Maybe she could write a bestseller—*The Archeologist's Diet: The Happy Side Effects of Digging for Ancient Treasure*. Only a few faint stretch marks at her waist gave any clue at all to the fact she'd given birth to Ori.

"So Cohen told me you didn't want to talk to me anymore," I said.

She looked around the room. The orange-walled restaurant, on the first floor of a double-decker house, was crowded with dark wood tables and trendy metal chairs but not with people. The one other patron, a woman Katie's age, sat twenty feet away, tapping on a laptop, every few seconds pushing a corn-rowed blonde braid out of the way. The slender, pony-tailed, goateed, tattooed guy behind the counter was scribbling the day's offerings on one of the five chalkboards above the counter.

"They questioned me for a day," Rivka said. "Bathroom breaks only."

"No food?"

"A few energy bars."

"Well, you're making up for it now. Are you going to lose your job?"

She started on the next scone. "I don't think so. They took my passport, though. They'll wonder where I am. They'll expect me back for reserve duty on Thursday."

"In a week?"

"Yeah. I need to go."

"Or you'll really be in trouble."

"It's my duty."

"Okay. So how did you make your way back here?"

"I'm not afraid to steal a good idea."

I stroked my beard. "You keep your American passport up to date?"

"Yeah."

"You used it to cross from Eilat into Jordan?"

"Good guess. And flew to London on Royal Jordanian."

"Probably not the airline of choice for IDF officers."

"Not much of a risk."

"How did you know where I'd be?"

"Lucky guess."

"Really?"

"Okay, I called the front desk from New York."

"So now you're Becky Goldschmidt again?"

"In the eyes of American immigration and my mother."

"What did the Shin Bet want to know from you?" I asked.

"Mostly about the Ark."

"They assumed it was the Ark?"

"I think so. They called it the 'aron.' That's Biblical Hebrew for Ark."

"Like my name?"

"It sounds the same in English, but it's spelled differently in Hebrew. Scholars argue whether the words are related."

She folded her arms across her chest and leaned toward me.

"What is it?" I asked.

"They wanted me to tell them what we'd seen."

"And you did?"

She was breathing hard and didn't answer right away. I waited.

"Yeah. Hope that was okay? I know we're supposed to be partners, but you weren't around, and I figured better that Israel got the Ark than the Arabs."

So that's how Cohen knew where to look. "The right

decision. If I'd been a little more rational, I would have told them, too." I paused. "But they didn't know where it'd gone?"

"I don't think so," she said. She leaned back and smeared a mound of marmalade onto the third scone.

"So the Arabs we heard in the tunnel got it?"

"If they did, we'll never see it again." She shook her head. "But I can't believe you did all that digging only to end up with the Ark gone again." She brought her head up, tilted it, half-closed her eyes, and asked, "Are you convinced yet that it was the Ark?"

"I'm a skeptic," I said, "but I guess it's possible. The first question to answer is 'Why didn't the ancient Israelites put the Ark and the Commandments back in the Holy of Holies once the Second Temple was built?'"

"You have a theory?" she asked.

"I've been reading. In the Bible, in Second Kings, what the Babylonians looted is called out, almost as an inventory list. Pails, scrapers, ladles."

"Right. Everything that was bronze, gold, or silver, and even Solomon's two forty-five-foot columns."

"But no mention of the Ark, the most precious item of all."

"So?" Rivka could change her persona the way some women changed shoes. I'd seen her shift from archeologist to military officer back on the Temple Mount. In less than an hour, she'd morphed from a passionate lover inspiring lust in the middle-aged to a dispassionate professor employing the Socratic Method.

"They didn't get their hands on it because the Ark had been hidden in a cave under the Holy of Holies where we found it," I replied.

"So why didn't the Jews retrieve it when they rebuilt the Temple?"

"My guess is by the time they returned from the Babylonian Captivity anyone who'd known the hiding place was dead."

She nodded. I was teacher's pet. "Who would have known?" was her next question.

"They would have wanted to keep the secret of where it was hidden to a small group. I count nine possibilities. First are the four people we found down there. They had to close the trapdoor from below on their own."

"Who else would have known?"

"The chief priest. His name was, what, Seraiah? Something like that?"

"Yes." She dug into the pie. Mouth filled with sweet potatoes and crust, she said, "You *have* been reading your Bible."

"So Seraiah and a few helpers arranged to hide the Ark."

"They sure came up with a good hiding place," she said.

"Right. The Babylonians didn't find it. Nebuchadnezzar had Seraiah, his deputy, and three men called guardians of the threshold all put to death. Then thanks to Rabbis Goren and Getz and my grandfather, we found it."

Rivka's fork descended, speared the last bite of sweet potato pie, and hovered in front of her mouth. "Maybe we found it, but we don't have it," she said. I shook my head. The fork finished its mission, and Rivka chewed.

Chapter 63

Folding her hands across a midsection whose flatness belied its capaciousness, Rivka sighed.

"Saying we saw the Ark won't mean much. Ark sightings in Africa and the Middle East are like UFO sightings in Nevada and New Mexico."

"Yeah?"

"Some people say Menelik, the son of Solomon and the Queen of Sheba, brought it back to Ethiopia, where it still sits in a church."

"Really?"

"Is it really there? No, it's not. A couple of years ago an archeologist named Tudor Parfitt wrote a book that traces the Ark to southern Africa. He says a replica still exists."

"A replica?"

"Carbon-dating shows it's about eight hundred years old. So it's not the original Ark, and his theory doesn't take into account what happened to the tablets anyway."

"Our theory takes into account the tablets," I said. Reaching around my neck, I slipped off the leather strap and laid it on the table.

Rivka loosened its strings and pulled out the shard.

After a quick look, she grinned. "You picked this up in the

Ark chamber, I guess. But how did you get this by Cohen and the Shin Bet guys?"

"I mailed it to Katie from the Old City."

Her grin grew wider.

"We know where we found it and what it might be," I said. "Can't prove anything, though. As Katie told me, archeological practice dictates leaving objects like this *in situ*."

"In which case it would have disappeared forever." She leaned over the table, put her hand under my chin, and kissed me. As she sat down, I saw the other patron looking at us, open-mouthed.

Rivka took a quick survey of the room. Her back was to the aghast laptop user, and the tattooed youth behind the counter must have gone to the kitchen. She held the hem of her jacket down with her left hand and snaked her right under it and up toward her chest. After a moment of jostling, her hand emerged, holding a memory stick. She laid it on the table.

"Is this what I think it is?"

"Oh, yes. All the photos we took in the Ark room."

"Wait. That's what fell out of your bra?" I asked. "Why didn't you tell me?"

"I winked on the Temple Mount to let you know it would all be okay.

"I thought you were saying we'd gotten away from the Arabs."

"That, too. Besides, you didn't tell me about the shard," she countered.

"I was preoccupied."

"Me, too."

"You had the memory stick there the whole time they were questioning..."

"No Israeli man would dare touch an observant woman there."

"Especially not a major in the IDF. And you made it through airport security with it, too?"

"Sure. It's mostly plastic." She picked it up and returned the one-inch-long device to its hiding place. It was my turn to lean over the table and deliver a kiss.

"Between us we have a shard that might have come from the original Ten Commandments and photos of what might be the Ark of the Covenant."

"We're getting close to *emet*."

"What would happen if we went to a newspaper with this? I know some reporters at the *Times*. Or you could write a serious paper for *The Cambridge Archaeological Journal*."

"During Hanukkah, we're supposed to put menorahs in the windows of our houses to publicize the miracle. Are you trying to do something like that here?"

"Maybe. I think that's what my grandfather wanted."

"Even if it started a war?"

"He must not have thought it would." I stood up. "Let's go for a subway ride."

* * *

A few minutes shy of an hour had elapsed by the time Rivka and I had recounted what we'd found and how we'd lost it.

Rivka, Rabbi Zweiback, and I all raised the cups of hot liquid to our lips in the study of the house in Brookline.

When I'd introduced Rivka to the new Bialystoker Rebbe, he'd given a little bow, but they had not touched. He might have been my cousin-in-law, she might have been my lover, but I could feel they had something in common with each other that they did not with me. Jewish observance filled their bones right along with the marrow. In a modern age where personal autonomy was considered a virtue, their lives were ruled by a belief in the Almighty and a connection to ancestors and scholars who'd lived long ago.

The Rabbi replaced the cup in his saucer. "You have this piece of the tablets that *Moshe Rabbeinu* shattered?"

Rivka translated, "Moses, our teacher."

I reached around my neck and laid the pouch on the table.

"Would you open it, please?" he asked.

I took out the shard.

He looked at the proto-Hebrew characters.

I picked it up and held it out to him.

"No," he said. "It is not for me to touch the holy words of *ha-Shem*." He turned to Rivka. "You say this rock is not of this world?"

"A colleague of mine in Jerusalem examined one of the other fragments. He thought it might have come from an achondrite, a meteor."

"We have photos, too," Rivka said. "Would you like to see them?" Was she going to reach into her bra again in front of the rebbe?

"Of course. Very much."

"Does your PC have an internet connection?" she asked, gesturing toward his desk.

"Yes," the rebbe said. "Let me disconnect my phone first." An iPhone identical to mine was plugged into the computer's USB port. This rebbe was no prisoner of the past.

A minute later, as her hands flew across the rebbe's keyboard, Rivka said to me, "I did a little uploading in the business center during the layover at Heathrow."

Smart, very smart.

She moved away, and the rabbi sat down. I went around the chair and leaned over to look at the 21-inch monitor along with him. She'd gone to a site on Flickr and chosen slideshow mode. One after the other, photos of the Ark room slid across the screen. When a picture of me stuck in the tunnel flashed up, it was as if a hand squeezed my gut.

"Stop," the rabbi said.

We were looking at a photo of one of the tablets. The proto-Hebrew lettering was glowing blue.

"The aura around the letters is from the flash?"

"No."

The rabbi bowed his head and started chanting a *shehechiyanu*, and Rivka joined in.

"I am blessed to have seen this, to have a piece of the tablets before me. Tell me again, please, Alex. Your grandfather, all he asked was for you to find the truth of what he saw?"

"Yes, but he must have meant more than just seeing the Ark."

"Why do you say that?"

"Because he saw the Ark himself."

"Yes, so by definition that was not sufficient. You're asking me what else you need to do."

"Should we advertise the miracle, like on Hanukkah?" I asked. He raised his eyebrows. "Professor Golan's analogy."

"If you can show that what you found was the Ark and that this is a fragment of the tablets Moses brought down from Mount Sinai, it would prove the Torah is what we have always believed, the words of *ha-Shem*. Perhaps that would lead more people to listen to the Torah's calls for *shalom*, for wholeness, for peace."

"The American and Israeli governments are afraid of exactly the opposite, that discovery of the Ark could lead to violence," Rivka said. "Judging from what's happened so far, it looks as though they're right."

"In the Talmud, Shimon ben Gamliel says the world is sustained by three things," said the rebbe. "Two of them are *emet* and *shalom*."

I folded my arms. "But what if there's a conflict between truth and peace?"

"That's where the third comes into play. *Din.*"

"Which means judgment," Rivka said.

The rabbi smiled at her. Then the young rebbe gave his beard three or four long pulls. He reminded me of a kid at Seniors' Day back at Palo Alto High School when all the twelfth-graders dressed as eighty-year-olds.

"Your grandfather gave you the task because he believed in your judgment."

"Why should he? He didn't know me."

The rabbi held his hands palm up toward me. "I don't know if he followed you from afar or if he decided when he met you, but I do know he had faith in you."

I snorted. "Then God help us."

"Amen," Rivka said.

Chapter 64

"Of course, Dad, you know Professor Golan," my daughter said, employing the good manners inculcated by her mother.

Rivka had said she wanted to see Katie and arranged via email for us to have dinner together. We'd agreed to meet at six, here outside the Kirkland House Dining Room.

After leaving Rabbi Zweiback's, Rivka had headed over to Houghton, Harvard's rare books library. While Rivka looked for answers to our dilemma in the library stacks, I'd sat in front of a laptop screen trying to quantify the chances of success of different approaches. The summer before business school I'd put together a matrix based on trainer patterns to find undervalued bets at New York race tracks. I made more money pushing ten and twenty dollar bills through the betting windows than I did the next summer working at Apple. I'd spent this afternoon playing with an Excel spreadsheet, deciding what to do next, where to place my wagers this time.

"Oh, yes. As I told you, Professor Golan was a huge help in Jerusalem." I felt a little guilty for not confiding in Katie, but there hadn't been time and the entrance to the Kirkland House Dining Room didn't seem like the place to start. "Where's Elliott?" I asked.

Holding up her phone, Katie said, "He texted he'll be a few minutes late and to go ahead."

Standing in line in that dining hall—smelling the food, observing the students, overhearing conversations—worked on my memory like Proust's madeleine. The Salisbury steaks we'd called mystery meat had been replaced by stir-fried tofu with hoisin sauce, but thirty years after I graduated, the melody was the same even if the notes were different. As we took our trays and went to find seats, we passed students at long tables huddled in earnest discussions on subjects academic, athletic, and political.

When we sat down, Katie introduced us to the others at the table. The students were polite enough, but two minutes later their heads had moved even closer together to discuss the content of an editorial in the school paper, *The Crimson*.

I turned my attention back to my own dining companions.

"Tomorrow night Elliott and I will be going to Shabbat services at Hillel," Katie was saying to Rivka. "Would you like to come?"

"Yes, thank you. Perhaps your father would come, too?"

"Why not?" I said.

Katie jerked in surprise and asked, "Really, Dad?"

"Why not?" I said again.

Two minutes later Rivka and Katie were debating the pros and cons of whether the Hyksos people mentioned in hieroglyphic inscriptions were in fact the Israelites Moses had led out of Egypt.

I fingered the pouch I wore around my neck. An obscure terrorist had shot a man in Sarajevo a century ago, and the result was world war. Would finding the Ark be this century's assassination of Archduke Ferdinand?

Then Katie was saying, "Can I, Dad?"

"Sorry, sorry, my mind was wandering. Can you what?"

"Dig under the Wall in Jerusalem this summer with Professor Golan?"

"Did the professor invite you?"

"She said they would be taking on a few interns."

Rivka looked at me. I wondered about the propriety of having a woman I was sleeping with hire my daughter.

Before I could answer, Katie looked over my shoulder and said, "Elliott."

As he strode up, he started to lean over Katie as if to peck her on the cheek. I could almost see him recall his entrance, shirt over head, when I'd first met him. He must have remembered the same incident and pulled up before delivering the kiss.

We shook. "Nice to see you again, Elliott." His handshake was still firm.

Katie introduced him to Rivka and then asked, "What took you?"

"Sorry, I was watching CNN. Lots of stuff going on in the Middle East. Abu Hazem, a long-missing terrorist, was assassinated in his house in Damascus."

"We found Abu Hazem?" Rivka asked. She turned to me. "He was Arafat's hatchet man. He assassinated dozens of moderate Palestinian Arabs in the 1980s."

"A team broke into his house in Damascus and slit his throat," Elliott said. "The Israeli government claims to have had nothing to do with it."

"What else?" Katie asked.

"Rumors of a bioterrorism incident in Saudi Arabia."

"What about it?"

"Well, reporters aren't allowed into Mecca, but they think someone's spread around some anthrax there. Probably some branch of al-Qaeda."

"Anthrax?" Rivka asked.

"Yeah."

She looked at me. "We've got to go."

Chapter 65

"What?" I asked.

We sat on the cold stone steps of Widener Library watching students crisscross Harvard Yard on their way to study at the libraries, experiment in the labs, or eat dinner in the resident houses.

"Remember what happened when the Philistines captured the Ark?" Rivka asked.

I had been studying my Bible. "Sure. It's all in the Book of Samuel. The Philistine idol was knocked over, their fields were overrun by mice, they got hemorrhoids, and the people in the cities where the Ark was taken were afflicted by boils."

"Most modern scholars think the boils were caused by anthrax."

"Oh, c'mon," I said. "You're making a leap here."

She moved her face close and grabbed my wrist. Warm steam leaked between her lips as she hissed, "Why not?"

"So you're saying the Saudis have the Ark, and God is punishing them with boils?"

"Yes, that's exactly what I am saying."

"Elliott said al-Qaeda was suspected."

"And how does *ha-Shem* work in the twenty-first century?" She let go of my wrist and moved her hand in a karate chop. "Do you think *ha-Shem* splits the sea in half like in the Bible?"

"You think God intervenes in the twenty-first century. I don't."

"In fact, we really agree. *Ha-Shem* works through people. Why were you sent to Israel? I said it was *beshert*. That's a way of saying it was the Divine's doing."

"The Department of Homeland Security has been afraid of an attack like this in the United States since 9/11. Al-Qaeda targets Saudi Arabia, too. It just happened there first."

"The Philistines took the Holy Ark. The inhabitants of the cities where it was taken were struck by boils. Now the Ark is missing again. We think Saudi agents were in the Ark Room right after us. Mecca is struck by boils. It doesn't take a genius to figure out where the Ark must be."

"Let's go check on what's happening."

Back in my room at the Faculty Club, we fired up the laptop and skipped among news sites—nytimes.com, cnn.com, haaretz.com, and times.co.uk. The news was sketchy. All foreign correspondents were stationed in the Saudi capital, Riyadh. Mecca, where the anthrax had broken out, was the hometown of Mohammed and the site of the al-Kaaba, the Cube. Millions of pilgrims visited each year, but the city was out of bounds for non-Muslims.

Rivka clicked on a video report from Christiane Amanpour, who reported from Riyadh against a background of huge cylindrical, ultra-modern buildings.

> *There are rumors of a cloud of black dust settling over Mecca two days ago. In a city regularly visited by desert sand storms, it caused little notice. Now, however, it appears the black dust might well have been spread over the city by bioterrorists. Government sources here in Riyadh point to al-Qaeda, but there has been no statement from the terrorist organization. I have also*

heard reports that riots have broken out among the millions of pilgrims on the hadj. The king is meeting....

"Ew," Rivka said in response to the picture on the screen that I'd clicked to. Even the strict controls of Saudi Arabia could not squelch news in the Internet Age. The *New York Times* site displayed a photo tweeted from Mecca of a young girl of eight or so holding her arm out, showing three suppurating ulcers with red rims and black centers.

CNN, headquartered in Atlanta, had posted a video interview of an expert from the Center for Disease Control, also in Atlanta. "Cutaneous anthrax," Dr. Loren Vincent was saying, "is the most common variety of the disease. It shows up as sores on the skin but is almost never spread from person to person. The good news is this form of anthrax responds well to antibiotics. The United States has large stores of Ciprofloxacin ready to go."

"Will we be sending any of it to Saudi Arabia?" Wolf Blitzer asked him.

"We're getting half a million doses ready for shipment just in case."

"Doctor, do you have any insights into how an anthrax outbreak like this could happen?"

"I'm not sure. Perhaps, if *B. anthracis* spores were dispersed from an airplane, people whose skin or clothes were contaminated with spores would come down with cutaneous anthrax. We haven't heard anything about the inhalational variety of the disease, which probably means the spores were too large to pass into the lower airways."

Rivka tapped the laptop's volume down button a couple of times and then went to the nightstand and opened the drawer.

"Don't hotel rooms have Bibles anymore?" she asked.

I walked over to my overnight bag and pulled out the one I'd bought—at retail—in Jerusalem. I handed it over.

She found the passage she was looking for and started reading it aloud:

> *Then the Lord said to Moses and Aaron, "Take a double handful of soot from a furnace, and in the presence of Pharaoh let Moses scatter it toward the sky. It will then turn into fine dust over the whole land of Egypt and cause festering boils on man and beast throughout the land." So they took soot from a furnace and stood in the presence of Pharaoh. Moses scattered it toward the sky, and it caused festering boils on man and beast. The magicians could not stand in Moses' presence, for there were boils on the magicians no less than on the rest of the Egyptians.*

"Okay, okay," I said. "What's happened in Saudi Arabia sounds like a Biblical plague."

"In Hebrew it's called *shkin*."

"I said *like* a Biblical plague, not an actual one."

"I heard you."

"Okay, let's assume God is bringing a plague down on Saudi Arabia. I know you said the Koran treats the Ark as holy, but if it's bringing a plague down on them, won't the Saudis destroy it?"

"They wouldn't dare," Rivka said. "Many Muslim scholars think it's up to the Mahdi, their messiah, to find the *Tabut E Sakina*. Destroying it might stop the Mahdi from coming."

She knew her stuff.

"Okay. So they'll hold on to it," I said. "Brought out at the right moment..."

"Like after Israel falls."

"Yeah, then it could strengthen the Saudis' claim to be the defender of Islam."

"So what now?" she asked.

"If the Saudis have what's really the Ark, they should give it up. Hmm. Let's play it your way."

"What do you mean?"

"Let's assume the Saudis are suffering God's displeasure."

She tilted her head. "Do you think so?"

"I think it was al-Qaeda. What better way to undermine the Saudi royal family than to show it cannot protect pilgrims during the *hadj*? But it doesn't matter what I believe."

"No?"

"No. What matters is what the Saudis believe."

"So what do you have in mind?"

Chapter 66

"This is not a good time, Alex," Mitch Samuelson told me.

"Yeah. You've got a crisis on your hands in Saudi. That's what I'm calling about. I think I can help."

"Why, you have a supply of Ciprofloxacin?" He sounded tired. That bullet in his shoulder must have diminished his once considerable stamina. In college he'd stayed up seventy-two straight hours to finish that senior thesis on the Rough Riders.

"Not exactly. You told me the secretary was going to have the Saudi ambassador bawled out on my behalf."

"That's done," Mitch said.

Rivka had one bud of the headset in her ear so she could listen. Partners.

"Yeah. I want to meet the ambassador. ASAP."

"Oh, right in the middle of this crisis? He's going crazy."

"Set up an appointment for tonight. Use my name. I'll bet he wants to see me."

Rivka hit me in the biceps. I held up my hand. I wasn't about to forget her. Her face was six inches from mine. Beads of sweat were collecting on her forehead. Damn overheated East Coast rooms. She still smelled good, though.

"Who do you want at this showdown?"

"I don't want an entourage. Just you and me and a professor of archeology."

"What?"

"Mitch. Listen to me. You gotta trust me on this one. Life and death." I looked down at my watch. "We'll catch the eight-thirty shuttle. We should be at the State Department around ten."

"No, not at the State Department. I'm in the Situation Room at the White House waiting for the president to show up. I'll come out. Have the guard at the East Gate call for me. Alex?"

"Yes, Mitch."

"I sure as hell hope you know what you're doing."

"Me, too."

Chapter 67

Rivka went to her room to collect a few things. As for me, I went to the bathroom, washed my face, and threw on a navy blazer. I was going to a meeting with an ambassador.

I ducked out of my room, turned left, and opened the door to the stairs that would take me up to the third floor and Rivka's. As the door swung shut, I heard knocking and Rivka's voice from around the corner, back by my room.

She must have taken the elevator. I reopened the door and heard her calling from around the corner, "Alex, we need to get going to be in time so we aren't late for our meeting with Professor *Sakana*."

Why was she calling me Alex and not Aron? And *Sakana*—what did that mean again? Shit. On the door to her office. "Danger." I peeked around the corner. Rivka stood facing the door to my hotel room. To her right stood a charcoal-suited man—holding a gun. An identically dressed man was positioned behind her. I couldn't tell if he had a gun out, too, but chances were pretty good he did.

That crimson mist fell over my eyes again. I took a deep breath. Gonna rush them, save Rivka. Another deep breath and I eased my raised right foot back on to the carpeted floor. The rational part of my mind asserted itself just in time. I'd be a target fifteen feet before reaching them. I was no martial arts expert, and even Chuck Norris was no match for a man with a gun. What about sneaking down the stairway to get help? No, they'd get away with Rivka before the police arrived. Rational or not, I was not going to let them leave with her even if it did mean rushing them.

Rivka knocked on my room door again and called out to remind me again of our supposed rendezvous with the aptly named Professor Sakana.

Next to my arm was a fire alarm. Two feet from it was a red cylindrical fire extinguisher, the kind that hangs in the hallways of every hotel in the country. Shit. In removing the extinguisher from the metal bands that held it in place, I'd clinked it against the wall. I froze. No, didn't hear footsteps. I took out the safety pin and hoisted it up into firing position. I extended my right index finger from under the extinguisher and yanked the lever of the alarm.

A pulsating siren sounded. I ran around the corner screaming, "Fire, fire, fire!"

Big and bearded, the man behind Rivka turned toward me. At fifteen feet away, I squeezed the trigger on the extinguisher and a jet of white foam hit him smack in the face. He dropped his gun with a scream and brought his hands up to his eyes. I turned the hose toward the man on Rivka's right whose finger was on the trigger. The explosion of a gunshot. Clang. The vibration against the cylinder combined with the leaking slimy foam made the cylinder start to slip out of my hands. Ten feet away, I tried to hold on. A shot. Another clang. The mist was back. Not waiting for a third shot, I screamed, "Fuck you," and hurled the cylinder at the man's head. This clang, of steel against scalp and skull, was answered by a growl from deep in my gut.

The man trying to wipe the foam from his eyes cried out, "Baroom." As if in response to the summons, a third man strode around the corner at the far end of the hall. His smile revealed a missing eyetooth. He started walking toward me, still smiling at the prospect of finishing what he'd tried once on Ben Yehuda and again in Rivka's flat. He raised his gun and pointed it toward me. Mistake. I was not the primary threat. Rivka came out of the doorway. Her arm went up and then came down like the blade of a guillotine. The impact of her hand against the man's wrist produced a crunch audible even over the blaring alarm. A blow from her elbow slammed a cheekbone back into his face. The man—was his name Baroom?—teetered and then collapsed as if imitating a slow-motion video of a building demolition.

"*Krav maga*," I gasped.

She nodded.

The first man had wiped enough of the foam from his eyes to spot his fallen gun. He reached for it, but my heel landed on his wrist with the crack of a dry wishbone on Thanksgiving. God help me, I found the sound of his screams, which mingled with the fire alarm, savagely satisfying. He curled into a fetal position. Before I could kick him in the side, Rivka pulled me away.

"Let's call it even on saving lives," Rivka yelled.

"Partners don't keep score," I yelled back.

"I do think we had a little more than our share of luck."

She kicked the cylinder with her foot and stopped it with her toe after it turned 180 degrees. Two deep steel-gray dents scarred the red paint. We looked around. No one in the hallway —it was dinner time. But police and firefighters would be on the way. The one conscious man, who whimpered still with his broken wrist, had enough foam on his face to pose as a model in a Barbasol ad. Rivka grabbed him by the lapels and screamed at him in Arabic. I presume she asked him who he was. He said nothing. She ripped open his jacket and there on the inside was a label. I recognized it. Darwish the tailor must still be in business.

"Shall we wait for the police?" she called.

That crimson mist must have lifted since I almost smiled at the idea of the university police, accustomed to no more of an emergency than escorting inebriated undergraduates back to their dorms, handling these guys. "No way. If we do that, we'll never get to D.C. in time." My mouth was two inches from her ear.

"In time to meet with their boss?" She tossed her head toward the sprawled bodies.

"This was their last chance to stop us."

"Last?"

"Hope so."

We followed behind a couple of other guests in the stairwell coming down from the floors above. Rivka and I walked past the front desk and outside into a crowd of tweedy academics and elderly widows who'd been eating in the dining room. We spotted a Town Car with tinted windows parked across Quincy Street, its tailpipe blowing out steamy exhaust. Was it standing by to whisk Rivka and me away? Not waiting to find out, we headed in the other direction, around the old Freshman Union on to Massachusetts Avenue.

Halfway down the stairs to the Harvard Square subway stop, Rivka stopped and pushed me against the wall. "Using a fire extinguisher as a bullet-proof vest? What were you thinking back there?"

"Thinking? I wasn't."

"Again, you weren't. I told you before. Run *away* from danger."

"Let's go catch our train," I said. Did the crimson mist only appear when someone I cared about was threatened? Rivka, though, was a soldier. She defended her country. But maybe we weren't any different. For her, defending Israel from those who wanted to drive the Jews into the sea came down to protecting family.

The dirty brass tokens we'd used on the T thirty years ago were long gone. So was the fifty-cent fare. I slipped my Visa into a machine, and we used the two cards it spit out to open the automatic gates. We ran holding hands and made it into a train whose doors closed on Rivka's foot. She yanked it through the rubber flanges, and we found seats. It took us twenty-five minutes to get to the airport.

Chapter 68

"You want to get out now?" the cabbie asked.

He'd pulled up to Seventeenth and Pennsylvania in our nation's capital.

"Yeah. We'll walk from here."

We really had no choice. After 9/11, five-foot concrete cylinders blocked off auto traffic in front of the White House. We walked to the West Gate. Behind its iron bars ran a roadway between the White House and the Old Executive Office Building. We pushed a button on the gate. A uniformed and armed guard left his little hut and approached us.

"Mr. Samuelson is in the Situation Room and is expecting us," I told him.

I looked down at my watch. 10:07.

We stood at the gate staring across the lawn at the Executive Mansion, lit and sparkling in the crisp air of an early March night. Once there had been no gates here. During World War II, cars could park on the roadway as if it were an ordinary city street. A time of a different type of threat. V-2 rockets maybe, but not suicide bombers. Uniformed armies, not shadowy cells.

I was brought back to the here and now by the wriggling of my iPhone in my pants pocket. Wrestling it out, I checked the screen.

"Hi, Sweetie."

"Daddy, I've been trying to reach you," Katie said. "You left in a hurry, and then there was a mess at the Faculty Club. Are you okay?"

"A mess?"

"Frannie went over there for the *Crimson*. Three men were beaten up. They think someone pulled the fire alarm to cover up what was going on. You're okay, aren't you? Professor Golan, too?"

"She's fine. Me, too. What did Frannie find out?" Frannie was her roommate and news editor of the school paper.

"Not as much as she wanted. The Harvard cops cordoned off the area, and the FBI is there. Frannie thinks something big is going down. The three men went to the Mount Auburn Hospital in an ambulance. One's in the ICU. I'm so glad you weren't there. Why did you have to leave in such a hurry?"

From a side door in the White House, Mitch emerged and started scrunching down the driveway toward us.

"We're fine, and my appointment is coming."

"At 10:10?"

"It was the best time. I love you. Gotta go."

"Love you, too, Daddy." Her voice sounded uncertain, but I chalked that up to strange circumstances rather than loss of affection.

The gate creaked open. Rather than inviting us in, Mitch stepped out.

"Mitch Samuelson, this is Professor Rivka Golan."

They shook.

"This way," he said.

We followed Mitch west on Pennsylvania back to the corner of Seventeenth. "We wait here," he said.

"A little cloak-and-dagger-ish, isn't it, Mitch?"

"You have no idea," he said.

So setting up the meeting had been no picnic. We watched

traffic go by. About three minutes later a black stretch Cadillac limo pulled up. The dark windows afforded no view inside, but the diplomatic license plate offered a clue as to its contents.

A man in livery jumped out of the passenger side and pulled open a door for us. As he leaned forward in a bow, his jacket fell away, and I could see holster straps running over his shoulder.

"*Salaam aleikum*," Mitch said.

"*Aleikum salaam*," the man said in response.

Mitch ducked into the seat first, then Rivka and me. The three of us were on a bench seat facing two men. Both wore keffiyehs of some expensive shimmering white fabric together with yellow-trimmed brown robes. The back of the limo was big enough that I had to stand up to reach over and shake their hands as Mitch made introductions. The motion of the car pulling away plopped me back on to the car seat.

Mitch introduced us to the Saudi ambassador, whose face was clean-shaven and unlined. A technocrat who'd succeeded a prince, he looked to be in his late thirties, but I'd read he was ten years older than that.

The ambassador in turn gestured to the man next to him.

"I would like to introduce you to my associate Colonel Al Ghamdi."

A few seconds later I found myself shaking the hand of the man who—it was odds-on—had tasked his minions to kill me with a rifle, bulldozer, and handgun. I expected him to say something like "We meet again, Mr. Kalman," but I'd watched too many old movies at the Stanford Theatre. He'd been loquacious enough on the plane, but now he said nothing.

"I was sorry to hear about your brother," I told him.

"He is resting comfortably in Paradise now."

"After recent events in Damascus?"

The good colonel squeezed my hand harder, but that was enough to tell me he'd avenged his brother. Desert code. Arafat and his cohorts hadn't wanted the Ark found by anyone, not even a Saudi professor. The Israeli government had told the truth when it denied assassinating Abu Hazem.

Al Ghamdi's face was covered by the keffiyeh, a neatly groomed beard, and that pair of sunglasses—sunglasses at a hundred minutes before midnight in the backseat of a limo with tinted windows. When Mitch introduced Rivka, the two Arabs looked at the scarf on Rivka's head and did not offer their hands. Huh. They knew better how to handle an observant Jewish woman than I had. The colonel's mirrored lenses stayed focused on Rivka.

"So here we are," the ambassador said, spreading out his hands. "Ever since I was at Georgetown for graduate school, I've wanted to play a part in an American spy movie."

"It's your show," Mitch said to me.

"Mr. Ambassador, Colonel," I said. "I understand there's been an outbreak of anthrax in Mecca."

The ambassador leaned forward and looked from Mitch to me to Rivka. "I hope I'm not here to listen to blackmail," he said. "His Highness the King would be so gravely disappointed to learn that your two countries had instigated an incident of bioterrorism in the Kingdom."

"Mr. Kalman is a prominent American business executive," Mitch told the ambassador. "I have known him for over thirty years and vouch for him."

"And his associate is a member of the army of the Zionist entity?"

Ah well, you'd have to figure they'd do their homework.

Rivka was savvy enough to let me answer. "She is a distinguished professor of archeology at Hebrew University. Like most of her compatriots, she's in the Reserves as well."

The colonel did not turn his head from her as he said his first words, "Assigned to an intelligence unit," he said with the same British accent I'd heard before.

I turned to look at Rivka. She was looking at our two hosts. Hmm. They knew more about her military responsibilities than I did, too.

"May I start again?" I asked.

They nodded.

"Professor Golan is an archeologist responsible for digging under the Wall in Jerusalem. She and her team have made many important discoveries. I have recently joined their team. Let me move to the bottom line. We believe we found the Ark of the Covenant, the *Tabut E Sakina*."

"I do hope that you are mistaken," the ambassador said. "In the fragile environment of the Middle East, such a discovery by the Zionist entity—excuse me, we are off the record here—by Israel could have untoward consequences."

"But it would have been okay if the colonel's brother had found it?" I asked.

The colonel remained stock-still. The ambassador shook his head before replying. "The *Tabut E Sakina* disappeared two thousand six hundred years ago. Any announcement of its discovery by Israel could only be interpreted as an excuse to seize control of the Temple Mount. Wars have started over less."

Rivka spoke for the first time. "I think my government is concerned that such a discovery could be destabilizing as well. But the fact remains, we have found it and have proof."

"Proof?" the Ambassador asked.

"Yes. We have a fragment of what we believe to be the Ten Commandments, along with over fifty photographs of the Ark and the room it was hidden in. The fragment and the photographs are in secure places. Perhaps the Colonel could have Mr. Baroom and his other associates stop trying to get their hands on them."

The shard was four feet from the ambassador in the pouch

around my neck. Probably should have left it somewhere safe, but where the hell would that have been?

The colonel's eyes narrowed. Was it because Baroom was acting on his own? Or because he had failed in his assignment? I'll bet it didn't matter under the laws of the desert.

"Mr. Kalman," the Ambassador said, "the Kingdom would do nothing to harm an American citizen such as yourself."

Wasn't it Ambrose Bierce who defined diplomacy as the patriotic art of lying for one's country?

"That is reassuring to hear," I told the ambassador. "Of course, Professor Golan is an American citizen as well."

He waved his hand dismissively toward me. "Let us go back to your alleged proof. A piece of stone, photographs. A stone could be etched. Thanks to Photoshop, photographs don't prove anything." He leaned forward toward Rivka. "Where is the Ark itself? Why don't you produce it?"

"I think you know the answer to that, Mr. Ambassador," she said.

"And what do you mean by that?"

"Do you know the story of the Ark told in the Book of Samuel in the Hebrew Bible?"

The ambassador shook his head.

"When the Philistines seized the Ark, inhabitants of the cities where it was taken came down with boils."

"Boils?"

"Yes. Modern scholars believe this refers to anthrax."

"So what does this have to do with us?"

"Your king is known as the Keeper of Holy Places."

"Yes?"

"I know you would want to do whatever you could to end the anthrax in Mecca where millions of Muslims come for the *hadj*."

"You seem to be saying that the Zionist entity has let loose bioterrorism and is trying to blackmail the Kingdom."

I picked up the ball. "No. What we are saying is that should the Ark be in the Kingdom, misfortune may befall it."

"You are saying that we have the Ark?"

"We are saying *if* you have the Ark."

"Come now. It is the twenty-first century. You are saying the Jewish God is causing anthrax in the Kingdom."

Rivka spoke softly. "There is only one God. We are saying if you have the Ark, that God—Allah to you, *ha-Shem* to me—is punishing you."

"Hah," the Ambassador said, tossing back his head. "Be serious. Mitch, I am disappointed to think your government would countenance this kind of approach."

"You may not agree with the approach Professor Golan and Mr. Kalman have taken," Mitch said. "Nevertheless, if something untoward should happen to either of them, the Secretary has reaffirmed he would hold you and the Kingdom responsible."

"Accidents happen," the colonel responded.

"The secretary expects you to make certain no accidents happen to these two."

The ambassador reached for a microphone and said something in Arabic to the driver.

Five minutes later, we'd been dropped off back at the corner of Pennsylvania and Seventeenth.

"I appreciate your words to the ambassador about untoward accidents," I said to Mitch as the three of us walked back toward the West Gate. "It seemed to carry weight coming from you."

Mitch shook his head. "Alex, a biblical plague? Be serious."

Rivka said, "Alex thinks it was al-Qaeda. I'm the one who sees the hand of God in this."

"And what matters is which the Saudis believe," I added.

He started muttering as if to himself. "What am I going to say to the secretary? Don't pay attention to our embassy in

Riyadh, to what Saudi intelligence has told us. It's not bioterrorism, it's God's work. He's going to want to know what this meeting was about. God, if the whole story gets back to him, I'm mincemeat."

"Sorry, Mitch. You'll come up with something before you see him next."

We stopped in front of the gate.

The guard swung it open. He walked through and looked back over his shoulder. "Come up with something before I see him? Yeah, that gives me about two minutes." We watched until he was back inside the West Wing.

The gate banged shut.

Chapter 69

Rivka was singing. So were Katie and Elliott. The song was *Oseh Shalom*, something about peace, but the words were Hebrew, and my attempts to follow along were halting and garbled.

After the services, a group of Katie and Elliott's friends surrounded us. I focused on the hands I was shaking. Fingers tapered and stumpy, nails bitten and painted, palms calloused and soft. With each shake came both a "nice to meet you" and a "*shabbat shalom.*"

As we munched on cookies, the students wanted to know what Rivka thought of events in Saudi Arabia. A banner headline in the *Washington Post* we'd picked up at the airport that morning screamed "Bioterrorism Targets Muslim Pilgrimage" with a subhead that read "Mecca Hit by Riots, Quarantine."

"Come on," urged a ponytailed blonde wearing a yarmulke. "Do you think it was al-Qaeda?"

"I'm a professor of archeology," Rivka said. "Any expertise I have on Middle Eastern events ends about fifteen hundred years ago."

"But Israel couldn't have been behind it?"

Charlotte Ann Page, known for her top-level contacts on both sides of the Middle East conflict, had written in her *New*

York Times column that senior Saudi officials were accusing Israel. Made sense. The Saudis were the keepers of Islam's holiest places. Far easier to blame the "Zionist entity" than a security breakdown against al-Qaeda or the hand of Allah. It didn't help that a source in the Quai d'Orsay, the French foreign ministry, had pointed at Israel as well.

"I'm just speaking as a citizen here, but no," she said.

"But if the Saudis believe it, it could mean war."

"Let us continue to pray for *shalom*."

We'd stayed the previous night at a hotel in Virginia a few miles from Reagan Airport and flown back up to Boston on an early flight. We'd spent the day e-shopping, surfing news sites, and running along the river until it was time to meet up with Katie and Elliott for services at Hillel.

"That wasn't so bad, was it, Daddy?" Katie asked when we were outside the Hillel building.

"No. It was terrific. Thanks for inviting us. It looks like you've found your community."

She reached up on tiptoes and gave me a hug and kiss. And to my surprise she performed the same ritual with Rivka. We said our goodnights, and Rivka and I headed back to the Faculty Club while Elliott and Katie went in the other direction toward Kirkland House.

"Did you really think the service was terrific?" Rivka asked me.

"Yeah. Katie did seem like she belonged. The power of praying seemed magnified by numbers."

"That's why we Jews say you should have at least ten people for a service. But what about you? What did you think?"

"Are you proselytizing?"

"No." She laughed and put her arm around my waist. "Well, maybe a little."

"Do you really think there's a God out there, one who will intervene in human affairs?"

"Are you asking if I believe that *ha-Shem* is behind what's happening in Saudi?"

"My phone," I said and reached into my pocket. Saved by the buzz. "It's Mitch. Hey, Mitch."

"Professor Golan said she had pictures of the Ark," Mitch said. "Was that a bluff?"

"No."

"Can I have copies?"

"They're on the Web."

"Shit. For anyone to access?"

"No, no. They're password protected." I looked over at Rivka, who nodded. I gave Mitch the URL. "The password is templemount, one word."

"Templemount, huh?"

"What about the piece of the tablets?"

"There are some photos of the tablets, too."

"And the actual piece? Is it safe?"

"For now." I fingered the pouch through my shirt.

"I'll let you know if I need that, too. Thanks. G'bye."

* * *

Observant Jews don't work on Shabbat. In Talmudic times building a fire counted as work. As brought forward into modern times, that injunction meant light switches weren't turned on either. In the neighborhoods on the Lower East Side of New York where Italians, Irish, Jews, and others were mixed in a fruit salad of national origins, the della Maggiores or Leahys would come by and turn the light switches and stoves on and off for the Levys or the Rosenthals. They were known as *shabbos goys*, Sabbath gentiles. I served the same function for Rivka. We went up to her room. I turned on the lights and TV set.

CNN was showing smuggled videos of rioting in Mecca.

Pilgrims clad in the brightly colored cloth of West Africa, the robes of Arabia, and the jackets and trousers of the West were scrambling over bodies lying on the ground. There were no secrets in the world of the Internet.

"Why would God have done this?" I asked her. "They're religious pilgrims. They've done nothing wrong."

The clipped tones of newscaster Anderson Cooper interrupted. "Pressure is growing on Israel's Arab neighbors to take reprisals against the Jewish state. It's after eight in the morning in Cairo, and crowds have already begun to gather outside the U.S. and Israeli embassies there."

It was ten-thirty at night in Cambridge, and I clicked off the TV and turned the radio to WBUR, the NPR station. "...the Iranian president has promised that Israel, which he called 'the outlaw Zionist regime,' will regret its use of bioterrorism in the city of the Prophet. Tanks are rolling through downtown Tehran and being cheered by crowds..." I flicked off that switch.

Rivka sat on the floor hugging her knees up to her chest, tears running down her cheeks.

I sat down next to her.

"Do you blame me for this?" she asked.

"Blame you? Why not me? Far better lies and hypocrisy than what we just saw on TV."

"You followed your destiny."

We were lost. I put my arms around Rivka and held her. She shook with tears. I pulled away and brushed my lips against hers. Then I looked at her and kissed the tears on her cheek, tasting salt. I was kissing her again, not for comfort anymore. My mouth ground against hers and our teeth clicked. It was as if each of us wanted to swallow or be swallowed by the other.

I yanked her blouse upward and then her bra over her breasts. I pulled her skirt up and put my hand on the panties we'd just bought that morning. She was wet and I put my mouth to hers again.

I pulled away to ask, "Is this okay? On Shabbat?"

"It can be a special mitzvah to make love on the Sabbath."

She pulled me back down to her. With my lips on hers, my hand rested on the thin cotton that stretched over the sharpness of her hip bone. In the middle of the kiss, I scrunched the fabric between my fingers and ripped the panties off.

She guided me into her right there on the floor. Her hips rose to meet each thrust. Our mouths stayed together and, as we climaxed, the groan that came from deep inside her collided with my own.

Even with death looming, we reaffirmed life.

Chapter 70

I awoke next morning still on the rug, but I was covered by a blanket and my head rested on a pillow. Rivka's eyes were open and looking at me from six inches away.

"You been up for long?" I asked.

She shrugged.

I pulled her over, and she rested her head on my chest. We'd reached an oasis in time.

About forty minutes later I asked, "You want to see what's on CNN?"

"Huh? I'm sorry. I must have dozed off."

"Shall we check on what's happening?"

"No, no. Enough. It's Shabbat."

"Shall we go for a run then?" I asked.

"Good idea. I want to take a shower before we go."

"Really? After the run for me."

"I'll take another one then, too," she said.

"Okay. I'm going to go downstairs to pick up the papers, the *Globe* and *Times*." Rivka raised her eyebrows. "I'll just look at the sports pages until Shabbat is over."

"Okay. And we'll get breakfast after the run?"

I pulled on an old T-shirt whose front proclaimed "Sibyl Predicts Success," running shorts, and Nikes.

Rivka said, "If my mother is waiting in the hall, I'm in

trouble—sneaking back to my room in the same clothes I wore last night."

"I won't tell."

"After you pick up the papers, come back to my room."

"Do you sing in the shower?"

"I could."

Sure—why not check out the sports while listening to a serenade accompanied by the sound of the lucky water droplets pattering against her skin?

We went out to the elevator, and she headed up to her room, and I went down to the lobby. I picked up the papers at the front desk and folded them over to avoid seeing the headlines.

I took the stairs back up and opened the door to her floor. My head was down, checking out the *Globe*'s wire service account of the Giants' 10-3 spring training loss in Scottsdale. I turned the corner and bumped into a man, and dropped the other paper.

Polite—to a fault—he bent down to pick up my *Times*.

I knew this man. I'd sprayed foam into his eyes the night before last and then stomped on his wrist.

I didn't think. He was twenty-five feet from the entrance to Rivka's room. I brought my knee up as hard as I could. It hit the bottom of his chin with a crunch, whether from bones or teeth or both, I didn't know. Didn't care. The blood lust had risen.

He went down and I went down with him. His eyes were closed, but I didn't care. I put my hands on his neck and squeezed. Five fingers were trying to pry my hands away. I felt the tendons of his neck straining underneath his skin and squeezed even harder. He hit my head with his cast. "Shit, what is it with you guys?" I gasped. The second blow with the cast wasn't nearly as hard as the first. His face, suffused with blood, was turning purple.

I heard footsteps behind me. I started to turn, but I didn't see who was coming. My sightline was blocked by a moving black shoe. When it hit its target, my head, I ended up on my back, next to the panting Foam Man, woozy but not unconscious. The man who'd just knocked me off his colleague leaned down to me. He was also wearing a charcoal suit. He tried to say something. Was it "friends?" He didn't get a chance to explain. A human torpedo had already been launched. Rivka came in flying, parallel to the floor. The crunch the instep of her bare right foot made against the temple of my assailant was even louder than the one between my knee and the colonel's jaw. Now a second Saudi was moaning on the floor. That blessed *krav maga* again.

She peered down at me.

"You okay?" she asked.

"They were watching your room."

"I thought they were going to leave us alone."

"We'd better get out of here."

Another man came from around the far corner. The overhead lights gleamed in his mirrored lenses. The colonel stopped a safe ten feet from us, swiveling the barrel of the gun he held in his fist between Rivka, now standing, and me, still supine.

"Get up," he said to me in his British accent. I did. "Now both of you, back up." He waved the gun to emphasize his demand.

"This is how you obey the secretary's request?" I said to him.

"Yes, that is what we are attempting to do. We cannot allow anything to happen to you. It would ruin everything."

He said something in Arabic and then said to us again in his plummy British accent, "Back up."

The first man, the one with the cast, the one I'd almost strangled to death, tried to dust off my T-shirt as if he were a one-armed valet. Then he and the colonel started dragging their unconscious colleague.

As they reached the corner, the colonel looked up. I could see Rivka's reflection shimmering on the lenses of his glasses. "No need to come looking for us," he said.

Chapter 71

"What the hell was that about?" Rivka asked. "Why would they have us at gunpoint and then just leave?"

"They said they were trying to protect us."

We were back in her room.

The three Saudis had melted away.

I dropped the newspapers on the floor and went over to give her a hug.

"We need to figure our next move," I heard her muffled voice say.

"I need to figure out what to do with the shard."

"I should leave Monday."

"The day after tomorrow?"

"I told you my annual reserve duty starts Thursday."

I hadn't forgotten, but what did that mean for us, for her and me? Those few words turned her into an apparition, about to float out of sight. Was I destined to revert to the listlessness of life before Rabbi Zweiback's call? She squeezed against me. Her breasts poked the piece of the tablet against my sternum. No, this was real: *she* was real. I rested my head on her shoulder and squeezed back. I stared at the carpet without seeing anything. Then my eyes focused. On the newspaper. The *Globe* had unfolded to expose its front page. There was the headline over two columns—"Secret Talks Between Israel, Saudi Reported." It took a second to sink in.

"Holy shit," I said.

Rivka's face emerged from the burrow of my chest. "What?"

I pointed at the paper.

"I thought we weren't going to look at the news till after Shabbat," she said.

"You'll want to make an exception," I told her. She swooped down to pick up the papers and started reading, "According to a senior Turkish official, representatives of the Israeli and Saudi governments met today in Ankara to discuss an outline for a comprehensive Mideast agreement."

We looked at each other. The day after our escapade in D.C.? How long had this been cooking?

"Let's go to my room and check the Internet," I said.

"We can try the TV first."

I picked up the remote, but before I pushed the power, my iPhone began to jerk in the pocket of my running shorts. As I pulled it out, the phone's spasms sent shivers up my forearm.

"Who is it?" Rivka asked. I held the device up to her. Across the LCD screen was splayed the name Mitch Samuelson.

I cranked up the volume and held the iPhone a couple of inches from my ear. A couple of inches from Rivka's, too. I pushed the talk button. "Hey, Mitch?"

"Have you heard the news?"

"About the talks in Ankara?"

"Yeah."

"Just saw it in the *Globe*."

"This is going to be the real thing. Tomorrow the president is going to issue an invitation to the prime minister, the king, and the head of the PLA for talks here in D.C. They're going to accept."

"Don't most successful summits have the key issues decided beforehand?"

"You always were a good student of history," Mitch said.

"You mean... Wow. Great news."

"I called to say thanks."

"Thanks? For what?"

"Just thanks." He hung up.

"Turn on the TV," Rivka said.

We heard the familiar voice emanate from the plasma screen even before we saw her. She was finishing her report. "The Saudi government attributes the disappearance of the plague that had besieged pilgrims at Mecca to the fast and effective work of its public health department. Christiane Amanpour, CNN, Riyadh."

"The anthrax is gone?" Rivka asked. "That means the Saudis did have the Ark. They must have returned it to Israel."

"Or their public health department did fast and effective work."

The room phone rang. I reached to pick it up. Rivka didn't stop me.

"Hello?"

"So nice to hear your voice again, Alex. Or should I say Aron?"

"Cohen?"

Chapter 72

Cohen was leaning forward. It might be in the 40s outside, but he still wore a polo shirt under the same gray jacket. He, Rivka, and I were sitting on three leather armchairs in the Faculty Club Lounge. Next to my chair squatted a wooden contraption with long slats for holding daily newspapers. The pages of three different *Times*—New York, London, and Financial—along with those of the *Journal*, *Globe*, *Post*, and *Le Monde* swayed as the crackling logs in the fireplace belched hot air in their direction. Here there were no screens for reading the news, only ink and paper. If we'd been wearing tweeds and smoking pipes, it could have been 1950.

"We went down to the room," he was saying. "Four mummies, a platform, but no Ark." He took a sip of coffee. Two of his fingers fit through the looped handle of the white porcelain cup.

Rivka repeated his last words. "No Ark."

"You heard me. There was no Ark when we got there."

"But Colonel Al Ghamdi and his men must have taken it. And now they've given it back to you," I said.

"A plague if they kept it," Rivka said. "But if they destroyed it, their messiah might never come."

"Interesting theory," Cohen said. "Interesting, but dangerous."

"We have another theory to try out on you," I said.

"Please," Cohen said.

I paused and looked over at Rivka, and she started the story. "The Arab side was divided on searching for the Ark, just like us Israelis. Rabbis Goren and Getz and the Orthodox wanted to find it, but the government said no. The Palestinian Arabs didn't want to find it, but at least one Saudi archeologist did."

"A bullet settled that disagreement," I said.

"Right," she said. "Arafat or one of his people found out that Professor Al Ghamdi was under the Mount looking for the Ark. They sent Abu Hazem to get rid of him. The Saudis didn't know what had happened till we found his body."

"Why didn't the assassin get rid of Professor Al Ghamdi's body?" Cohen asked.

"My guess is the professor lived long enough to shut the door behind him," Rivka replied.

"That door might have been thousands of years old," I said, "but we couldn't get through without a key, and I'll bet Hazem couldn't either. When the professor didn't show up, Hazem knew he was dead and figured the body would be sealed up forever."

"An ingenious theory," Cohen said, as he replaced his cup in the saucer.

We sat in silence for minute, and then Rivka said, "In the end it *was* Al Ghamdi who found the Ark and got it back to Saudi Arabia."

"Speaking of the colonel," I said, "from the moment I visited our State Department, he was keeping an eye on me—or maybe I should say an ear—and keeping you in the loop." Cohen sat expressionless. "This Abu Hazem hadn't been seen in fifteen years. I wonder who knew where he could be found. Who—what country's intelligence service—could have passed on the location of his hideout to Colonel Al Ghamdi?"

"I have no idea," Cohen said. "Foreign intelligence is the Mossad's business, not mine. I must say, though, that you're starting to think like an Israeli." He raised his daintily held cup toward me.

"Enough bullshitting. Let's cut to the chase," I said. "You have the Ark but are not admitting it. Fine, but why fly all this way, then? The Faculty Club coffee's not that good."

"To convey the appreciation of the Israeli government. You read the papers. There could be peace."

"Appreciation can be conveyed by telephone. What if we think the world should know of the Ark?" I asked.

"What evidence do you have?" Cohen asked. He folded his arms. "Let me tell you there is no record of your ever having been to Israel."

"Come on, now. I flew there on El Al. You put me on an El Al flight yourself."

"El Al has no record of your flying to or from Israel."

I rose from my seat. "What the hell? What about Royal Jordanian, the Sheraton?"

He shook his head. "Sorry, no records."

I felt Rivka's hand on my forearm. "We have a shard," she said.

"We spoke to Professor Ben-Amit," I said.

"Who thinks the shard was inscribed with a laser."

"And our photos?" I asked.

"Pfft. Proof? In the age of Photoshop?" Same thing the Saudi ambassador had said.

"What about the incident with the bulldozer?"

"How could you be the unidentified hero? You weren't even in Israel when it happened."

The leather cushion sighed as I sat back down. "The real reason you came was to warn us that if we try to publicize anything, we'll be made out to be kooks?"

"The world has lived without the Ark for over two

thousand five hundred years. It can live without it for a few more."

"But some day?"

"Perhaps."

His cup rattled as he put it down a last time. Without a handshake, with nothing more than a slight jerk of his chin, he walked out of the Faculty Club into the world outside.

"You made the biggest archeological discovery of all time," I told her.

Rivka shrugged. "There are more important things," she said and took my hand.

* * *

I was staring out the windows into the early March gloaming. My trips to Israel had never happened. I'd never been stuck in the tunnel. I'd never seen the Ark. Part of my life had—poof—vanished. But it wasn't all fantasy, was it? Rivka sat next to me in the Faculty Club lounge, reading the *New York Times'* take on the news from the Middle East.

My phone started wriggling against my thigh. I looked down at the screen.

"It's Veronica," I said.

"You should take it. I need to go to the bathroom anyway."

"You can stay."

As I pushed the talk button, Rivka escaped from the arms of her leather chair and walked out with a wave.

"Hello, Veronica," I said.

"There's no sense beating around the bush," she replied. "I'm getting married."

"To the same guy as before?"

"Yes."

"That's what you want?"

"Yes. I'm sure."

"Then that's great. I wish you the very best."

"And Alex, um, what happened between us in your room at the Faculty Club, um..."

"I don't remember you in my room." If tickets and receipts could vanish, why not a conversation? Looking back, it seemed like a surreal dream anyway.

"Thank you."

"So we'd better hurry and get divorced," I said. "I'll find a lawyer Monday."

"Here's something I do want you to remember," she said. "I was the one who called the whole thing off. Knowing you, though, you'll start feeling guilty like you drove me to it or something. Don't go that way. We had a good run and reached the end. We still have Katie. Goodbye."

Before I could say congratulations or thank you or best wishes or anything else, she hung up.

Another chapter of my past life finished, buried, gone.

Chapter 73

Sitting in the Samuel Adams Bar at Logan Airport on Monday afternoon, Rivka, Katie, and I watched the president's press conference.

The Saudi king and Israeli prime minister meeting at the White House? The president tried to tamp down euphoria by abstaining from lofty rhetoric and warning that the road to peace would be twisty and long. The stock market paid no attention to his warning, soaring nine percent, while commodity traders pushed down oil prices by twelve dollars and change. It was the Islamic Jihad who confirmed the wisdom of the president's cautious stance by airmailing a few dozen rockets from the Gaza Strip to the Israeli city of Ashkelon.

Rivka was on her way to JFK and from there to Ben Gurion and her stint of reserve duty that began on Thursday. Maybe, halfway across the Atlantic, she'd pass the dignitaries who were flying in the other direction.

We sat at a table for three, me sipping my Sam's White Ale, Rivka a Cointreau, and Katie a Coke. "Can you believe it, Dad?" Katie asked. "Me, right there on the site of the Temple? I am so excited and grateful, Professor."

She wouldn't really be right on the site of the Temple, but next door—close enough. Katie and Elliott had agreed to spend the summer with Rivka digging under the Wall.

"If we're going to be working together, you should call me Rivka."

After a discussion of the various underground projects in Jerusalem with her boss-to-be, Katie excused herself to go to the bathroom.

Rivka leaned across the table and murmured, "What we told Cohen was right. In the end the Saudis must have believed what we told them—that they were being punished by *ha-Shem*, by their Allah."

"No wonder they opted for peace. Who wants to oppose a country backed by the Almighty?" I took a long pull on my beer. "Just like the Philistines, they had to give it back. So Israel really *must* have it, no matter what Cohen says."

"Only nine people knew where the Ark was hidden when the First Temple fell. I doubt any more know now."

"And they won't talk."

"Maybe some day."

My phone beeped and started quivering on the table where it sat between our glasses.

"Who's it from?" Rivka asked.

I peered down at the screen, tilting it back and forth to try to capture some light. I'd soon have to surrender to the unceasing march of time and buy a pair of reading glasses. "I guess Rabbi Zweiback does know how to use that iPhone of his. His text says, 'One may distort truth to preserve peace.' R. Nachman of Breslov.'" I raised my eyebrows.

"A famous Hasidic rabbi from a couple of centuries ago," she said. "I think he's right."

I stared down at my beer. "I hope so."

"Your grandfather was right, too. It was the search for *emet* that gave us the chance for peace. Do you think he foresaw what would happen?"

"Foresaw what?" Katie asked as she retook her seat. I raised my head up from my beer to answer her. A streak of motion took my eyes to the mirrored wall behind the bar. As if watching a showdown on an old TV Western, I watched a man in the concourse outside the bar reach down to his hip and come up holding a revolver. He held the gun in his left hand and had a plaster cast on his right. Baroom. Rivka's *krav maga* four days before had left the side of his face from forehead to jaw vivid purple. He wasn't giving up yet after all. He'd failed so far but would succeed in the end.

I pushed hard against the café table and saw the surprise in Katie's blue eyes as she tumbled backward in her chair. Rivka asked no questions and rolled next to us just a moment before a bullet thumped against the table top that now protected us. *Krav maga* wasn't going to help now. On the floor, I twisted and looked around the table's edge. The man was entering the bar and raising his gun again to take care of unfinished business. I covered Katie with my body.

Take me, God, but not Katie, not Rivka.

I heard a shout in what sounded like Arabic and looked up to see our assailant turn around. The concussive explosion of two guns fired at once struck my eardrums. The lips of the man in the entrance made a round O, and Baroom lifted his cast-encased arm to try and plug the hole that had appeared in his neck. He dropped the gun and crumpled to his knees.

People were screaming and running.

Katie was wriggling from side to side, trying to get out from under me.

I got up. People were scurrying away from the bleeding man. Me, I had learned nothing and walked ten paces to stand over him.

The man on the ground stared up at Rivka, who'd followed me. He moved his fingers away from his neck and a crimson spurt splattered my right shoe. "Zionist bitch." As he said the words, a bubble of spittle and blood formed on his lips. Then he tipped over head first onto the floor as if readying for prayer. I kicked him in the side and he toppled over. Not my daughter, you fucker.

Al Ghamdi had sent him to kill in Rivka's apartment, in the Faculty Club, and now here at Logan. He'd been the phantom attacker on Ben Yehuda and probably the sniper who'd missed me and hit Mitch. Now Rivka and I watched him drown in the red sea of his own blood.

Rivka tugged my sleeve. Twenty feet away down the concourse another man was down.

We rushed over. There on the floor with blood flowing through his fingers was a bearded man wearing mirrored lenses.

He gritted his teeth and said, "He ignored an order from the king. The fool did not want peace with the Zionists."

"No talking," I said. Rivka took off her head scarf and squeezed it against the growing red inkblot spreading across his belly.

Colonel Al Ghamdi almost smiled. "He did not like being brought to his knees by a woman."

"Hold on," she said.

"*Salaam aleikum*," he said.

"*Aleikum salaam*," Rivka and I replied together.

Three Massport police ran up, guns drawn. The cops pushed us aside, and one took the mirrored glasses off Al Ghamdi. His black eyes were open, but saw nothing.

A jittery voice boomed over the loudspeakers asking all persons in the terminal to exit.

As the tide of people swept us toward the exit, Katie screamed in my ear, "What just happened?"

"The first man tried to shoot us and the second one shot him."

"Why? Who was the second one?"

"A guardian angel," I said.

Chapter 74

Rivka tried to book a flight back to Israel the next day but got nowhere. Only when she told the El Al agent she had reserve duty did a seat appear. As we approached the security checkpoint on Tuesday afternoon, Katie said, "Oh, Daddy. I've got to use the ladies' room."

Just after her bio break the day before, all hell had broken loose. I nodded.

Katie extended her hand. "Professor, uh, Rivka, I'll see you this summer." They shook in a professional, collegial manner. "Dad, come find me after you've said goodbye."

We watched her walk away. Rivka turned toward me. "Your daughter says she never knows what's going on, but this time she does."

"What do you mean?"

"Never mind about that. Focus on coming back to me," she said. "Two weeks from tomorrow I'll get off duty."

"I'll be waiting for you." The plan was for me to leave for Riyadh tomorrow for Al Ghamdi's funeral. From there I'd make my way to Amman and then back to Jerusalem. Where I would wait.

She placed a brass key in my hand. "You can let yourself into the flat."

I gave her a peck on the cheek and started back to station myself outside the women's bathroom.

Two steps and I heard her call, "Aron."

I turned around. "Rivka."

She was in my arms and I was kissing her. I don't know for how long. Our lips melted together.

When we finally broke apart, I told her, "I love you."

"That's what I wanted to hear," she said.

We kissed again.

As we broke apart, a gray-haired woman in her sixties, wearing what looked like a Dior jacket, patted my shoulder as she walked by and said, "Oh, God, that was so romantic."

Rivka smiled back at her as she wriggled out of my grasp. She extracted her passport—the blue and gold American one—from the pocket of her cargo pants, showed it to the guard, and walked toward the security area's conveyor belts. Without turning around, she stuck her hand over her head and waved. She knew I was watching. And I was, as she shucked her shoes to pass through the metal detector. And I kept on watching until she was out of sight.

I retraced my steps to find Katie outside the ladies' room looking down at the front page of the morning's *Globe*, with its photograph of the Israeli prime minister and Saudi king flanking the American president in the Oval Office.

"Hard to believe, isn't it?" I asked.

She looked up and rooted around in her purse before coming out with a tissue. After wiping it across my mouth, she waved it once in front of my face. No, I couldn't miss the red smudge.

"Uh," I started.

"It's all good, Dad. I love Mom. I love you. I prayed for you both to be happy. She's happy. You're happy too, aren't you?"

What had happened since the call to my grandfather's

bedside? A chance for peace in the Middle East. A chance for peace in my personal life. Hope.

"You know, I think I am."

—The End—

Acknowledgments

Don't we all imagine the writing process to work like this: the solitary writer churns out his or her prose in a garret, a tortured soul with a bottle of whiskey at the ready to keep the cerebral gears turning?

That cliché doesn't apply to my writing process, not by a long shot. Hundreds of people helped me get this book to you, and I am happy to share the credit (or the blame?) with them.

Temple Mount's moment of conception occurred on a trip to Israel led by Yoshi Zweiback and Jacqueline Hantgan. When my son and I passed a distinctive patch in the tunnel under Jerusalem's Western Wall, we learned that Rabbis Shlomo Goren and Yehuda Getz had been digging there some three decades before in a quest to find the long-lost Ark of the Covenant. Seconds later, something like this novel began gestating in my brain.

To do the actual writing of *Temple Mount*, I commuted to "my office"—a corner table at a busy café a few blocks from my house. I am in debt to the staff at Quattro for keeping me supplied with an endless stream of green tea—not whiskey—and making sure the music didn't get too loud. Dr. McGuire Gibson, Professor of Mesopotamian Archaeology at the University of Chicago's Oriental Institute, answered my queries on the tools used for stone lettering over three millennia ago and the methods archeologists employ to estimate the age of the lettering from that time. Dr. D.P. Lyle, himself a talented novelist, gave the manuscript a medical checkup. Several passages benefited from the engineering ingenuity of Craig and Tommy Seidel. Early readers Loren Saxe, Dena Raffel, Wes

Raffel, Josh Getzler, and Larry Vincent provided their usual no-pulled-punches criticisms and much-appreciated encouragement.

One hundred ninety-three friends, fans, and family members came together via Kickstarter to provide the wherewithal to publish and publicize the book you are holding in your hands or viewing on your screen. I am so grateful to them. Thirty of those co-publishers took the time to pore over an earlier version of the book and make suggestions that made it more readable and enjoyable. Dr. Paul Hochfeld deserves special mention for coming up with over 3,000 edits and comments; my initial inclination toward premeditated murder has ripened into genuine appreciation. The gimlet eye of copy editor Jennifer McIntyre, of Jennifer McIntyre Writing and Editing, smoothed out any remaining rough edges in the manuscript. Designer *extraordinaire* John Donaghue and my sister Dena get the kudos for *Temple Mount*'s original and striking cover.

Of course, my wife and four children deserve profound gratitude for encouraging and supporting the curmudgeon-author in their midst.

Few authors write just to get words on the page. We write to tell readers our story. If you weren't out there, *Temple Mount* would not have been written. My love of writing would be for naught. Thank you.

Keith Raffel
Palo Alto, California

If you enjoyed this book by Keith Raffel, please leave a review or rating online! You might also want to check out his other novels:

Dot Dead

"A murder mystery worthy of a Steve Jobs keynote presentation."

—*New York Times*

Smasher

"Raffel blends computer world wheeling and dealing with the academic world's lust for glory and fame in his compelling second mystery."

—*Publishers Weekly*

Drop By Drop

"No one puts the crosshairs on Washington, terrorism, and intrigue better than Keith Raffel."

—Andrew Gross

A Fine and Dangerous Season

"A rare historical novel—exciting and utterly believable—with Jack Kennedy as you've never seen him. Raffel is a master storyteller."

—Gayle Lynds

About the Author

Before turning to writing full-time, Keith Raffel watched over the CIA, supported himself at the racetrack, founded a software company, taught Harvard freshmen, ran for Congress, and sold DNA sequencing to medical researchers. He became a published author in 2006 with *Dot Dead*, which the *New York Times* called "a murder mystery worthy of a Steve Jobs keynote presentation." These days he can usually be found tapping his laptop's keys and power-drinking green tea at a café around the corner from his home in California's Silicon Valley.